Pilgrim

Pilgrim

Louise Hall

MERCIER PRESS
Cork
www.mercierpress.ie

ISBN: 978 1 78117 616 0

10 9 8 7 6 5 4 3 2 1

A CIP record for this title is available from the British Library

Printed and bound in the EU.

CONTENTS

Prologue 9

1981

1. The Franciscan 13
2. Sarah 23

1982

3. Jen 33
4. Charlie 46
5. Suzanne 58
6. Iva 79
7. Jen 90
8. Charlie 97
9. Suzanne 104
10. Charlie 113
11. Jen 124
12. Iva 137

13. Jen 146

14. Jen 157

15. Suzanne 173

16. Charlie 181

17. Jen 196

18. Charlie 202

19. Iva 209

20. Charlie 214

21. Suzanne 227

22. Jen 240

1992

23. Charlie 255

24. The Franciscan 269

Author's Note 280

Acknowledgements 285

For you, Dad

PROLOGUE

On 24 June 1981 six children from a poor Catholic farming village in the communist country of Yugoslavia claimed to have seen a vision of the Blessed Virgin on a small mountain called Podbrdo. The children said that a beautiful woman appeared to them on the hill, holding the baby Jesus in her arms. They said that the woman they saw was young. She had black hair, blue eyes and wore a greyish-blue dress with a long white veil. A crown of twelve gold stars sat comfortably on her head. However, they became frightened and ran away.

The following day they returned to the hillside and the children, who were aged between ten and sixteen, saw her again. This time, they said, they spoke to her, asking why she had appeared. Her reply was simple: 'I have come to tell the world that God exists.'

1981

1

YUGOSLAVIA

THE FRANCISCAN

The foreigners come in droves, laden down with heavy backpacks and full suitcases that have been rooted in and pulled apart by the milicija at the airports of Mostar, Dubrovnik or Split. When they arrive in the village they flock to the hillside of Podbrdo, their bare feet scraping off the loose stones. In the evenings, the pilgrims camp on the outskirts of the village beside the forest, two-person tents lit only by small torches. At night, I hear the strumming of guitars alongside the chirping of crickets, the hint of laughter and singing. When it stops I know the milicija have come and moved them on from their makeshift campsite. The language barrier does not matter; the milicija get their message across. In their eyes there is much suspicion. Their voices are stern as they shoo away people like they are unwanted dogs. After the foreigners gather their belongings, they walk along the dark, dusty road, unable to see a footstep in front. But the lights inside the church of St James stay on, so they move in that direction. They move towards me.

Some will pause and sit outside the church for a moment. They will kneel beside the local woman whose lips move in prayer. At the gable end of the church there is a trickle of water that falls from a rusted pipe. In the humidity of the night they will queue here and wait patiently for their turn. Then they will move around to the back of the church and sleep in the fields as the locusts swarm above their heads.

In the morning time I see their faces more clearly. They are men and women who come from the continent and further afield. Young men with uncut hair, whose shoulders are heavy from the load in their lives. Women of all ages, some holding the hands of their children. There are those who are giddy with excitement; others subdued with awe. Their skin is warm and sallow, or pale like porcelain and they all pull at their clothes to allow some relief from the hot air. They are all unique in their own wonderful way, yet one thing they have in common: eyes that are wide with curiosity.

'Why such a large church for such a small village?' they ask.

'Where are the children who see the Gospa?'

'When will she appear?'

'What message does she bring?'

They ask the questions with urgency but I do not answer. 'Go inside to the church. To Holy Mass,' I tell them, pointing to the oak double doors at the entrance. Inside, the monstrance sits patiently in the tabernacle until the hour of adoration arrives. On the altar are clear vases filled with fresh flowers and the scent softens the clammy air. 'That is where the Gospa's son is, and He is waiting for you.'

I have a responsibility now to many: the locals, the pilgrims, but most of all the children. Given my humble beginnings in life, I never expected to be involved in something like this. Lord knows I took a strange, looping path to get here.

***

My parents were simple people who lived on and farmed the hills in a neighbouring village. Although we had very little, Tata taught us the way of the land and sang songs of old as we toiled throughout the day. At night, Mama would wash the dust and grit from our clothes, telling bedtime stories as she cleaned. When we looked into the tapestry of the rolling hills, which seemed to stretch forever along the skyline, we saw a huge part of ourselves in them. They belonged to us and we revelled in the beauty of their majesty every moment of every day. Each morning, I would watch my father rise before the sun and step barefoot out through the frail wooden door of our small house. After just three steps, he would fall to his knees and stretch his arms wide as he reached out to the mountains. And he would stay there for some time, allowing the air to fill his lungs and the earth to seep into his skin. From his right pocket dangled a pair of wooden rosary beads that Mama had made for him. When he lowered his arms, he would take the beads from his pocket and for the next half hour he would lose himself in prayer. Towards the end, when he was just finishing the final mystery, Mama would come up behind him and place her weather-beaten hand on his shoulder.

'Come, Josip,' she would say, 'let us sit and eat so you have nourishment to start the day.'

And Tata would smile at her and say, 'My darling Vesna, it is from you and the children, from the sky and the mountains, and God himself, that I find nourishment.'

I was the youngest of five and unlike most of my brothers, who preferred to learn the ways of the land, I enjoyed going to school. Each morning after Mama had fed us, she took me by the hand and we walked between the hills for more than five kilometres before reaching the classroom of a small school. There were days when the air was so humid we could barely catch a breath as we walked. At other times the rain poured from the heavens, drenching our skin and saturating our clothes. Yet we persevered. We walked in the bitter cold, when the mountains were covered in a blanket of fresh snow, and in the spring, when the first shoots were dotted on the hills. In the afternoon I walked home by myself, my belly empty but my mind brimming with information.

Just like my father was fulfilled with the sky, the mountains, his family and God, I became satisfied with knowledge and books. But soon the knowledge I received in that small school in the neighbouring village did not seem enough; there was an emptiness inside me that longed to be filled. That was how I found myself drawn closer to Tata. He seemed to possess a rare, effortless peace in his life. We had so little and at times life was very hard, but Tata would always urge us to be grateful for what we had, reminding us that there was always someone else worse off. I began to rise with him each morning and go outside, where we would kneel and face the mountains to pray. At first, I was just going through the motions, whispering the prayers I had been taught to recite from a young age. But soon these words began to hold true meaning. They consumed my thoughts and took hold of my soul. It was as though someone had clicked their fingers and suddenly I was at one with God. Now I could see why my father was so happy, why he wanted for so little. He put all his trust in God, and God was always by his side. I knew then that I wanted to dedicate my life to prayer.

The only thing I had to do was tell Mama.

'But you could be anything you want,' Mama said. 'You could travel to Zagreb and train to be a doctor. Your teacher tells me how interested you are to learn about the sciences.'

I understood her concerns. Although I would be educated well in the seminary, becoming a priest would automatically make me an enemy of the communists. Mama often saw our local curate being pulled aside and questioned by men of the regime. She pointed out how the curate's uncle was one of the many Franciscan priests whom the communists murdered at the monastery in Široki Brijeg. We all knew of how the communist soldiers had stormed their church one afternoon in February 1945. They lined the Franciscans up and shouted at them, saying there was no God, no Church. They ordered them to remove their habits but the priests refused and began to pray. They would not denounce their faith and, for this, the communist soldiers took thirty of them outside, slaughtered them and then burned their bodies with gasoline. But even as they had stood facing their executioners in their final moments, the Franciscans prayed and asked God to forgive their attackers. This image of these martyrs is one that is ingrained in the hearts and minds of many of our people.

'I will place my trust in God, Mama,' I told her as she took a handkerchief from Tata and dabbed her wet eyes.

As I spoke, I looked over to Tata for reassurance. His smile was wide, making the lines on his weathered face smooth. I knew I already had his blessing. I got it the first morning I came out of the house and knelt down beside him in prayer. Soon after, I began my vocation.

***

I was a young man on leaving the seminary, full of zest and eager to progress. Initially, I moved from parish to parish, between Zagreb and Sarajevo, working with the people of my country, who had so much faith that I was sure it kept them alive in the harshest of times. During that time I furthered my studies and concentrated on psychology, as I was always eager to try to figure out the complexities of the human mind. When I got the opportunity to go to America, I accepted, and spent many years stationed at a parish in the borough of Brooklyn. I worked with the addicts who slept beneath the statues in our church when the streets became too rough for them, and with the poor women who knocked at the side door of the sacristy with crying babies in their arms, their tiny forms wrapped in a cocoon of blankets to protect them from the bitter cold.

Then, earlier this summer, I began to hear stories of what was happening back in my home country. The communists were calling it a revolution. The locals were calling it a sign from God. I wrote to my father, pleading with him to send me on any information he could gather. He got my brother, Tomislav, to pen the letter. Tomislav was only one year older than me and had been born a cripple with twisted legs and no hand at the end of his left arm. His mind was as sharp as a knife, however, and all his strength lay in his right hand. Growing up he hadn't been able to make the long trek across the mountains to attend school, so every night, just after Mama's stories and just before prayers, I sat with him on top of our father's winter coat and taught him to spell and read. So when Tata heard of my request, he paced around the room and dictated a response that Tomislav fervently transcribed:

My dearest son Petar,

The stories you hear are true. There have been some strange things happening in the municipality of Čitluk these past few weeks. It started just after mid-summer, on the Feast Day of St John the Baptist, and it has been happening every day since. The stories come from the hamlet of Bijakovići, in the village that is nestled between the hills. News travels faster than the wildfires that burn the mountains in the month of August. Each day we wake to some new information.

There are six children and they say that they have seen the Gospa and that she has spoken to them. My bones have become too weak to walk far, but Mama travelled to the village to see for herself. She went to the hillside where the children gathered one evening and watched as they glided up the mountain of Podbrdo. She said it was like their feet did not touch the soil, like they were carried by an invisible force. The locals followed behind, and even though Mama found the terrain uneven and the climb tough, she said she needed to see for herself if these claims were true.

And these children, Petar, some of them are not much older than you were when you left for the seminary. Mama knows of their parents, farming folk like us. They are worried about their children's claims and at times wonder why they would choose to bring this on their kinsmen. But the children tell them not to worry. That is what the Gospa tells them. She has chosen this village, these people. They must not be afraid.

Mama told me how they behave. When they reach the top of Podbrdo, one minute the children are murmuring prayers, and the next they fall to their knees in unison, their eyes transfixed on one solitary, invisible spot before them. Their lips move, she said, but no sound escapes their mouths. It is like they are out of time and out of place. They are lost in an ecstasy unknown to us. And those who gather around the children stay quiet. Yet they see nothing. Every one of them wants to see something, but it is not there. Not before their eyes anyway.

And now the milicija have arrived on the streets. There is a curfew in the village and the children have been told not to go to the hillside. They are forbidden and must stay in their homes. It is said that the authorities have sent them in to stop this 'revolution' from the local people. 'What revolution?'

Mama has heard someone say. 'These people are simply praying.' But the milicija mock the locals. They spit at their feet and keep their hands on the guns that are strapped to their belts.

Mama has spoken to a cousin who says that the children are frightened. They yearn to go to Podbrdo to see the Gospa, yet they are kept hidden. Armed milicija roam the streets, waiting for something to happen, but they are blind to the reality of it all.

We have heard that cars came for the children. Each one was taken from their homes and driven to Mostar where they were put in separate rooms. The communists interrogated them for over five hours, without their parents by their side. A psychologist travelled from Sarajevo to assess the children. Mama heard from the cousin that the psychologist, herself an atheist, left Mostar with some comments to the chief in charge. She told him, 'There is nothing wrong with these children. They are telling the truth about what they saw. It is the people who brought them here who need to be assessed!'

There is a difference in the air around the mountains, Petar. I cannot explain the change with words.

These children have been chosen. Why? I do not know.

And though you can see the joy in their eyes, I am told, their bodies also tremble with fear at times. The local bishop is not happy. He does not give them his support and so they are left with no guidance for now.

Pray for them, my dear son, that they might find that guidance in their lives. And soon.

Your loving father,

Josip

Shortly after receiving the letter, I made the decision to fly home to visit my family. It was early morning when the plane flew over the mountains I was reared in and skidded onto the runway of Zagreb Airport. The arrivals hall was so hot and packed with people that I felt faint as I queued for passport control. When I got to the top of the queue, I was pulled aside and my only bag was searched. From it, they took my Bible and began to tear at the pages as though I had something hidden inside. It seemed they were not happy to find nothing on my person that could get me into trouble. I was brought into a room and left sitting there with no water for what seemed like hours. Eventually they told me I was free to go but that they were keeping my passport for the time being. It seemed that my visit to my family would be a long one.

***

When my provincial superior heard of my predicament, he had no choice but to reassign me. This is why I am now stationed in the village that Tata wrote about. Every day more people arrive. These pilgrims. They leave the comfort of their own homes in their own countries and somehow find their way to this tiny village. They have many questions. Not all of them can be answered. After all, we are all still students in this newfound school.

I will not lie. I too had my doubts when I first arrived. After all, why would the mother of God appear to six children from a poor farming village hidden behind the Iron Curtain in the country of Yugoslavia? Has she nothing better to do?

But then the children came to the church one night, crying and banging on the doors.

'Father, Father, please let us in. They are chasing us.'

I could not ignore the pleas of these children, who were being chased by the milicija. I released the heavy bolts on the door and ushered them inside.

'Come,' I said, as I led them through the church. 'You will be safe here. I will not let them harm you.'

We stayed in the darkness of the sacristy for many hours that night. No sound escaped our mouths as the milicija pounded on the church doors and demanded to be let in. After some time, they gave up banging and shouting and all was quiet. It was then that I spoke with the children properly for the first time. No pilgrims, no locals, no other priests. I lit a candle so I could see their faces as they spoke and I listened to them as, one by one, they shared their story.

When they left later that night, I slept little. A million thoughts whirled around in my mind and, just as the children were frightened, I felt my own fears gather. Yet one thing was solid and unfaltering. These children were telling the truth. For through their eyes I had been able to peer into the gateway of their souls. In them I saw no lies. They had indeed seen the Gospa. She had spoken to them.

2

DUBLIN

SARAH

'I think she's gone.'

I hear the deep drone of a man's voice between the shards of pelting rain hitting tarmac. Though my eyes are half-closed, I can see that the sky is a deep navy and littered with stars that shoot across the canvas, changing sizes as they move. The moon is full and clean and it spins like a brilliant white disc that's stuck at the highest point in the night sky. And I'm warm inside, so very warm. The pool of murky water that has spilled out from the drains on the roadside soaks through my skirt and sucks at my skin.

'I think she's gone,' he repeats.

I want to tell him that I'm not gone, that I'm still here, but my lips won't move.

'Keep working on her,' someone else says. 'I'll not lose another one this week.'

They work in haste, their brows sweating and arms pumping. Big men with thick, dark hair, who are swamped beneath puffed fluorescent coats. The lines beneath their eyes are etched deep into their weathered skin. If I look close enough I can see all the pain and suffering they have witnessed over the years swimming around in the pools of their eyes. Their minds yearn for respite and their bodies long to pause, and yet they continue to work, continue to sweat, continue to pump.

And all I can do is lie here watching the moon watching me.

They'll never get to Charlie in time. I'll be carried away before he even gets the news. I left without my handbag or purse so they'll not know who I am or where I live. I could be a serial killer or a mad woman, and yet, here they are, trying to stop the flow of crimson blood that oozes out from God knows where. Still they are trying to hold on to the sliver of life that lingers within my body. While one is keeping pressure on my head, the other is pumping down on my chest, cracking my already broken ribcage.

On the footpath, dark shadows stand in silence. Some place their right hands over their mouths. Others toy with gold necklaces that dangle close to their chests. They try but are unable to suppress the horror of what they are witnessing: the flashing lights and the stillness of my body that lies motionless on the now quiet main road.

As I lie here, I start to wonder if I'm ready to leave. Or indeed whether the world is ready for me to go. I think about this morning and how I woke with the feeling that everything would be all right. Things would get better with Charlie and we could be as we once were: carefree and happy, with our entire lives laid out before our feet. We would sit down tonight, I told him. We wouldn't let things fester for any longer. And I had other news to share with him. Something that would bring change. Positive change.

I can hear people talking. They are saying there's a car overturned behind the wall of the Esso petrol station up the road.

'There's a man trapped inside,' someone says.

'He's unconscious,' says another.

I hope they get to him soon and that someone tells him it will be okay. Even if they aren't sure whether or not he can hear them.

'It's not how long you live, Sarah,' my ma used to say, 'it's what you do during your life that counts.'

And yet I've never done anything worth mentioning. Nothing that anyone else hasn't done, anyway. I married Charlie and had Jen. They have been my greatest achievements. There's nothing else.

Charlie. I hope this doesn't break him. I know Jen, for all her youth, will be strong, but Charlie is delicate inside. His heart is tender and can crush like crêpe paper.

'Don't read it out to me, Sarah. Read it in your head for crying out loud,' he'd say if I tried to read out the headlines in the *Herald*. 'I don't want to hear about it.' Whether it was a child killed in a farming accident down the country, a horse tortured to death in the fields beside the dilapidated concrete flats, or the teenage victims burnt alive inside a Valentine's night disco because the emergency exit doors had been bolted too tight, Charlie said that he couldn't cope with the images. They messed with his head.

It's as well that he's not here now.

For a moment, I think I can feel my body once more, but then realise it's only because I'm closer to the stars. They've lifted me onto a stretcher. My legs are warped at a strange angle and my head is prevented from falling to the side by a thick neck brace. They've stopped pulling at my half-closed lids and shining the small torch inside.

'Move back, please,' one of the men says, as they shuffle towards the back of the ambulance.

'But I know her,' a woman's voice cries from the footpath. 'That's Charlie Carthy's wife. She only lives down the road. Not five minutes from here. Just down past the Littler shop and at the end of the cul-de-sac, I think.'

She's pointing down past the row of lush evergreens whose leaves are hanging low from the weight of the rain that had been falling most of the day.

'Do you have a telephone number, love?' the man at the top of the stretcher asks. 'For her husband.'

The woman taps her long nails against her temple.

'She might not make it, missus,' he pleads.

'I don't even know if they have a telephone,' she says. 'I don't know her that well. Only from seeing her down at the Saturday market with her little girl buying wool and needles.'

I think about the new pattern that's sitting in my handbag. Jen hasn't seemed too interested in learning so far, but I take her along all the same, hoping she might find a hobby or some sort of escapism to pass the long summer days, instead of spending them up in the woods with no one for company but young Francis Nelligan. Though they're good friends all the same; they look out for one another. But she won't see as much of him when she starts the girls' secondary school in September. I hope she makes new friends. She hasn't found that too easy in the past.

'Is it down on the Close?' some man pipes up from behind just as they're placing me inside the ambulance. 'Yes, that's Charlie Carthy's wife. Jaysus, this will kill the poor man. He's already going through a rough time, I hear.'

Two gardaí, who wear soaked uniforms with loose ties and dark peaked caps, move closer to the man.

'We would appreciate you showing us the house,' the younger one says. 'We'll do the rest ourselves.'

'Beauvalley is the hospital on call tonight,' the paramedic says, about to close the back doors of the ambulance. 'We'll be bringing her straight to A&E there.'

The guards nod and take a step back.

They'll have to bang hard on the door of our house, I think, because Jen will either be asleep or have her headphones on in her bedroom upstairs. And Charlie, if he has made it home, will be sleeping on the couch with the television on full blast. He always does this after we've had a row. He'll sleep downstairs on the couch, and the next morning, when I come down, he'll kiss me gently on the cheek and whisper that he is sorry.

I think back to this morning. I had played music in the house for the first time in what felt like an age. I kissed Charlie's head and made him tea. He smiled, bemused. But the atmosphere changed as the day went on. First, I found all the letters from the bank. How he thought he could keep them buried was beyond me – the envelopes with big red stamps and letters detailing months and months of arrears. But I still wanted to help. We were in this together. He needed to know I was there for him. And I had other news, too. News that would lift his spirits and remove the damp from his soul. It was only when he told me that he was going to give Pat O'Mahony a dig out in The Beauvalley House this evening instead of staying in to talk with me – as he'd promised he would – that I snapped. I was sure I heard my own heart crack as he said it.

'Since when have you been friends with that miserable so-and-so?' I said. After telling him the things I had heard about Pat O'Mahony and his pub, I asked him to stay away from it, but he told me not to speak to him like he was a child. That he would be home later and we could talk then. I showed him the letters I had found, the ones with the red ink stamped on them. And I asked him how long he thought he could keep them a secret from me. Then I told him to leave, if that's what he wanted. And he did.

When Charlie left I cried like I hadn't cried in years. But I couldn't let things go. I couldn't settle. There was an urgency pounding in my chest as the evening wore on into a dark, wet night.

I needed to see him. I had to tell him the news. Our news. The thought of him not coming back till all hours and us not sorting things out had me driven demented as I paced the kitchen floor.

'Never go to sleep on an argument,' my ma often said.

So I left the house just before eleven o'clock and went to find him. Up to the top of the cul-de-sac where I took the small wall like I was taking a hurdle. On down the slip road that was hidden behind the Littler and out onto the main road. I just kept on running, knowing that when I found him all would be well. I didn't care that the roads were flooded and my eyes were blurred from the rain.

That's why I failed to see the car.

If Jen comes to the door as well when the gardaí knock, then she might catch Charlie when he stumbles and she'll be able to grab the keys and lock the house after them as they rush to the hospital. They won't have to go in the car with the gardaí; they can just take the shortcut into the church grounds at the back of the house and through the gap in the prefabs at the primary school. The wall is not fully built yet, only four feet high, so Charlie can give Jen a leg over and then climb up himself into the hospital grounds. That way, they'll get there quicker than if they drive on the main road.

And I know that I'll hold on. Not just until they arrive, but for some weeks after. I'll pull and grab and grasp and hold on to any bit of life left lingering beneath my skin. I promise that I will.

Promises are made to be broken, Sarah.

Not now, Ma.

I try hard to focus as we burst through double doors and bypass the waiting area of the emergency room. The fluorescent lights overhead dazzle. Heads turn as the trolley wheels scrape along the floor. There are too many people packed into this small room. A footballer with a broken leg wears his blue-and-white-striped club shirt proudly as he sits on a chair and waits to be seen. Elderly people lie on steel trolleys, hoping that someone will eventually notice them. A drunk sways as he leans against the wall and touches the bandage that is wrapped around his bloodied head, wondering what on earth happened to him. The trolley I am on glides past them and into a closed-off room. People's eyes move with me before likely returning to stare in the direction of the nurses' station as they wait for their names to be called.

A doctor with thick eyebrows and a stained white coat stares down at me in this new room. He is trying to figure things out. Others appear and look over his shoulder, down at my too-still form. One of the paramedics speaks to him. 'Female, mid-thirties,' he says. 'Hit and run accident on the Beauvalley Road. A stolen car is what the witnesses reckon. Tore through a red light like a mad man, ploughing through her as she crossed the main road. She has two broken legs and a dislocated hip. Severe trauma to the head with multiple bleeds. There's a lot of swelling. Left lung is collapsed. We've been working on her at the side of the road for the past twenty minutes. She's coming and going. We didn't think she'd make it here, to be honest, but she's hanging on for something.'

'Has the family been informed?' the doctor asks.

In my mind's eye, I see Charlie racing through the hospital doors, his hair all tousled and his T-shirt wet from the rain. Jen grips his left hand, her body shaking. The bottom of her pyjamas are soiled with mud. A pretty nurse with wide eyes and tied-up hair avoids their questions as she leads them into another room.

The lights overhead are getting brighter with each passing second. The desire to be closer to them is overwhelming. But I hold myself back. I won't go just yet. It's not my time. I'll fight. For Charlie. For Jen. For us.

Memories flood my mind. The first time I saw Charlie standing awkwardly in the corner of the dance hall. The moment I grabbed his arm and pulled him onto the floor. The apprehension of the first night we shared a bed after we wed. The wonder of holding our first-born in our arms. The first fight, the first tears, the first time we realised it was all part of the motions. Helpless laughter as we shared a cheap bottle of wine. Joy as we flicked through piles of developed negatives from a camera we bought ourselves one Christmas; the pain of cruel words we threw at one another and the relief at knowing they could never be true. They move like a motion picture before my eyes.

Someone says it again.

'I think she's gone.'

But I'm still holding on.

'Keep working. We mightn't lose her yet.'

It's there if they listen hard enough, pulsating slowly beneath the flesh. Not one heartbeat but two.

And I'm smiling inside. They don't understand how I'm still here when I should be gone.

But I do.

I think of Charlie and Jen. I see them, entwined in a fearful embrace. Their bodies moulded together, their pain lessened because of their unity.

'I'm not gone,' I whisper to them. 'Never gone.'

1982

3

DUBLIN

JEN

I hear the pebbles tap against the bedroom window and pull the curtains back to see Francis sitting on the kerb. I'm already dressed, as I slept in my clothes last night. It saves time in the morning and it also keeps me warm. Downstairs, I close the front door gently and motion for Francis to stand up. We say nothing as we walk down the quiet street, right up until we get close to the back wall of the new hospital. Then we cup our hands around our mouths and shout out owl sounds towards the nearby trees.

Behind the boundary wall of the hospital lies a woodland. The tall trees are planted so close to one another that their branches create a grand canopy. Deeper into the woods a stream gushes from somewhere unseen, bouncing off rocks and slithering through reeds. You could sit there for hours with a net in your hand and you'd never see a fish. Not even a pinkeen – the ones that only live for a day. But the reason I often sit there has nothing to do with catching things; instead, it's about doing nothing but feeling everything.

Me and Francis kind of feel like we own the woodland. It has become our turf. And though we know that it really belongs to the trees – the ones that have stood strong for so many years – we also know that they don't mind us being here. The outcasts. After all, some company is better than none at all.

I don't know why no one except for Francis Nelligan and me comes into the woods any more. Some mornings, though, we do see an old homeless man with fingerless gloves curled up on a brown couch that someone dumped among the trees. The springs stick out between his legs and he shudders beneath the two coats he has on, even though the weather is mild. When we cough, he wakes and begins fixing himself and smoothing out his grubby clothes, as though he is embarrassed that we should find him in this state.

Francis is always looking out for the old man. He usually leaves his house before me in the morning and meets the milkman on his rounds, just as the sun rises over the Dublin Mountains. 'I'd give you a job any day,' the milkman always says to Francis, before patting his shoulder and handing him a bottle of milk. 'The early bird catches the worm.' Though he is tempted, Francis resists the urge to rip off the lid. He waits first, to see if the old man is in the woods. If he is, Francis stands there with one hand tucked deep into the pockets of his corduroy trousers, the ones that stop short above his bony ankles, and the other hand holding the cold milk bottle. He wears the waist of his trousers high above his hips and tucks his grey T-shirt inside, which makes his legs looks unusually long and the top part of his body too short. He tries to hide his tufts of ginger hair beneath the woollen hat that he wears. It has a bobble on top with threads so loose that they are sure to give way any day. When the old man sits up on the brown fabric couch, Francis hands him the pint bottle of milk and watches him gulp it down. The old man never stays for long. He just licks the milk from his moustache, tips his flat cap in our direction and heads on his way. To where, I don't know.

***

Above the stream that we now sit beside, a thick rope hangs from one of the branches of an old oak. I know the tree is old because it leans over like a hunchback that is too tired, beaten and worn to stand straight. Some days, if I'm really quiet, I swear I can hear it sigh. All the same, the tree holds on to the fat, frayed rope as if it's waiting for someone to come along and jump onto the knot that sits at the end. Maybe it misses its former popularity: the pull and tug of kids, the rows about whose turn is next. Maybe it misses looking over the quiet ones who would sit and watch as their friends swung over the stream as much as it misses the daredevil kids who would shout, 'Higher! Higher! Push me higher!' Maybe it even misses the deep cuts and purple bruises, the fractured arms and legs. Ma always told me that you only miss things when they are gone and you can't get them back. She used to say that life isn't like a tape in a VCR. You can't rewind to your favourite bits.

As we sit here in the woodland, I listen to the rush of the stream, but I know that Francis is listening out for any sounds from the woodland animals. He prefers the sound of the creatures to the flow of the stream: the grey mice that scurry through the fallen tree bark; the red squirrels that hop from branch to branch, their black eyes bulging when they hear the crunch of a foot on the soft ground; and the birds, whom he imagines having conversations with one another as they chirp through the air. Sometimes we make weak daisy chains from small flowers and Francis leaves them beside the trunk of the large oak as a gift for the animals.

'Did you hear that?' he asks, excited.

I shake my head.

'Thought I heard a cuckoo's call,' he says.

Francis is named after Saint Francis of Assisi, he tells everyone. His ma had the name picked even before he rushed into the world, two months early. He only got to see her for three minutes, he says, before they whipped him out of her arms. But he says he can remember her raven hair and gold loopy earrings, and the way she sang travelling songs to him while he was still in her womb. The midwives wrapped him up tight in a cotton blanket and placed him in an incubator. And with all the cooing and fussing over the tiny baby with the mop of ginger hair named after the patron saint of animals, they never noticed Mary Nelligan thrashing around on the bed. She died before they even realised what was happening.

When Old Man Nelligan stumbled out of the early house across the road from the hospital, he took one look at his lifeless wife and muttered, 'It's one of stronger stock I should've married.' He didn't ask about the child, nor did he even so much as glance at his newborn son when they took him from the incubator and held him out to his father. And Francis swears that to this day his da rarely looks him in the eye.

I never ask Francis how he can remember all this, when he was only in the world a wet minute and should have been concentrating on taking his first few breaths. He tells it so well that I don't want to point out that it might not be true. I've heard them in the schoolyard, calling him a *half-blood gypsy* and a *tinker's child,* but he's proud of his roots. He says he remembers living with his mother's family near this woodland for a time. He took his first steps there, he says, and rode bareback on a piebald Shetland pony called Tipper. He helped the older children push prams that were heavy from carrying buckets of water and watched the men come home in the evening hauling wheelbarrows full of scrap. He also remembers how, one morning, he heard the roar of heavy engines and caught the smell of diesel and how everyone jumped out of their beds and ran outside only to be met by strange men who wore hard hats and yellow vests. One of the men held out a pile of papers. They had to leave, he told them. They were there to clear the land so the new hospital could be built.

Francis doesn't like this part of his story. He doesn't understand why his family brought him to Old Man Nelligan's house a few days later. He doesn't know why they left him there with a plastic bag holding the only things he owned: a hand-knitted jumper that was faded grey, two pairs of trousers that were one size too big, a vest, some underwear, a pair of green wellington boots and a picture of him with Tipper standing in front of an open fire, its black smoke stretching far into the sky. And though he remembers the water in their eyes and the whispers and the way they paced around and put their hands up to their heads, they had left him. This was his da, they told him; he was going to take good care of him.

Francis tells me he will be reunited with them one day. That he knows his family will come. He tells me this over and over. And today, like every other day, I listen like I've never heard it before.

'Where will you go?' I ask, as he stands up and searches for conkers beneath a pile of leaves.

'Wherever the road takes us,' he says. 'When they come for me, I'll be ready. I have my bag packed and hidden under the bed. I won't keep them long. I'll just put it on my back and be on the road.'

And I smile and nod because we all need to believe in our dreams. Francis most of all.

Old Man Nelligan doesn't talk much, but when he wants something, he calls his only son by the name 'Francie'.

'My name's not *Francie*. It's Francis. That's what my ma named me,' Francis mutters under his breath. 'The same as the one who loves the animals.' He knows he should keep his mouth shut, that it's not worth the pain. But he says it anyway. An act of defiance before he feels the clatter of his father's knuckles.

'That'll teach you to back-chat me, ya little knacker.'

On the days when he's angry, Old Man Nelligan goes at Francis, chasing him all around their house and into the garden. When he can't catch him, he walks to the shed and watches as Francis stops, his eyes full of fear.

'Leave them, Da.'

It could be a stray dog already troubled by parasites, or a sparrow with a broken wing that needs time to heal. Somehow these creatures in need always find their way to Francis, who minds them like they are special stones. He makes beds from straw and cut grass, and leaves out saucers overflowing with milk. At dinnertime, when Old Man Nelligan isn't looking, Francis spits chewed food into a piece of tissue and shoves it into the torn pocket of his trousers. Later on, he feeds it to the animals. Most of the time, his da pretends not to know they are in there, hidden behind rusted paint tins and stiff brushes – right up to the point where they become useful.

'Leave them alone, Da,' Francis will plead once again, just as his father reaches for the bolt on the shed door.

Francis knows it's no good, so he walks over to his da and his last thought before reaching Old Man Nelligan is of his ma with the raven hair and gold loopy earrings, who sang travelling songs to him when he was still in the womb.

But there are times when Francis isn't at home, like the time he took in that heavily pregnant cat. The cat's keening went on all that night. The following morning Francis poked his head inside the shed before the sun came up and saw that she had given birth to a litter of six. He skipped to school that morning and, for once, he didn't mind so much when the other kids taunted him. Instead, he spent the day thinking of names and possible homes for the kittens. When he arrived home that afternoon, he could hear the sound of running water upstairs. Francis didn't call out to tell his da he was home. Old Man Nelligan didn't like noise, unless he was making it himself, and Francis often worried that he would say things too loudly and so said nothing at all, hoping he might avoid a slap. As Francis crept up the bare stairs, he cursed his ankles every time they cracked. He would have been better off never waking up at all that morning, Francis later told me, as what he saw when he pushed open the bathroom door made his insides hurt.

Old Man Nelligan was kneeling on the floor, his fat belly spilling over the edge of the bath. With his thick arms he pressed a black bin bag down under the water, taking no notice of the tiny claws that tore through the lining of the bag and the pink noses that struggled for air. And though he knew Francis was standing behind him with his hands covering his mouth and legs weak with shock, Old Man Nelligan pressed and pushed until the claws stopped their desperate scratching.

The care workers have been to his house more than once. But they stopped calling. The last time they were there, Francis told me, his da ran them out of the house and chased them down the road, waving a rusty axe above his head. And so it's here to this woodland that me and Francis Nelligan go when life beats down so hard that we feel we are suffocating in our own skin.

'Will ya bring me back a stick of rock?' he asks as we share a sliced pan he robbed from Mrs Baldwin's doorstep.

'I will if there are any, Francis,' I say, noticing how the bruise over his left eye has gone from purple to yellow, and the cut that needed a stitch but never got one has finally stopped weeping and is starting to scab over.

'And a postcard too?' he asks.

'I will. But I might be home before it arrives to you. It takes a week for a postcard to come from Galway, and I'm going much further than that.'

Francis' nose scrunches up and his eyes close a bit. 'What are ya going to do there?'

'I'm not really sure,' I say.

'Will ya have to do lots of praying?'

'I suppose I will,' I say.

His eyes move down to his runners, the ones with the soles hanging off. And he rubs his hands together, then scratches at the back of his ear. 'Can you ask for something when you're over there, you know, in your prayers?'

I nod, even though he's not looking at me. I know he is going to miss me, just like I will miss him. It's only for a week, I tell him. I'll be back before he knows it. Part of me doesn't want to go. But at the same time, I know that I have to.

'Will you pray for me da?' Francis asks, before his voice cracks and his shoulders fall. 'Tell them he's broken. And that he needs to be fixed.'

***

When I wake the next morning, Da is squatting low on his hunkers beside my bed.

In his hands he holds Ma's mohair cardigan, the one she had worked on for months before the accident. The colour is gold and it has a round neck with wide sleeves that hang almost like bat wings when the arms are outstretched. He lifts the cardigan to his nose and mouth and sucks at the wool like he is gasping for a last breath of air.

I wonder how he keeps his balance when his lids are heavy, eyes red and face torn. He hadn't been home when I got back from the woods yesterday evening, and the stink off him means he spent most of the night at the pub again.

'Da,' I say, 'let's get ready. We don't want to be late for the airport.'

As he squats there, inhaling the scent of Ma's cardigan – the one I wrap my feet in at night – I see the same twisted pain eat him up as the night he told me. It hasn't even been a year since he said those words: 'She's gone, Jen. She's gone.'

But, really, it wasn't my da who stood before me that day, croaky and unshaven with his shirt buttoned up wrong and hair a mess. He'd changed over the months since the accident. My da had always been tall and strong and confident. His shoulders didn't hunch and his smile was always there. Even when he fought with Ma over this, that and nothing, he'd always come into my room, knowing there was nothing playing on my cassette recorder even though I had the headphones on. ''Night champ,' he'd say with a wink before closing my bedroom door. The next morning I'd hear his footsteps, slow and soft, as he crept into the kitchen. He'd walk over to Ma, who was standing stubbornly by the kettle, and I'd hear him whisper to her, 'You know I love you, Sarah; more than life itself. Whatever I've done, I'm sorry.' They never stayed angry for long; things always went back to normal the next day.

Until there was no next day.

But on that day when he told me she was gone, it was a much older man who stood in front of me, a stranger whose shoulders were heavy with an invisible weight. His blue eyes had turned grey and his face was smothered with creases and lines.

'She's gone, Jen,' he repeated before collapsing onto the step of the hall staircase. 'Sarah's gone.'

I wanted to get down on the step beside him, to shake him by the shoulders and beg him to tell me it wasn't true. That he'd made the whole thing up. That Ma was still in the hospital, that she was actually sitting up in the bed and eating her favourite apple crumble, and that she was asking for me, her only daughter, her only child.

But I didn't.

Instead I just stepped around his shaking body and raced upstairs to my room, slamming the door behind me before I collapsed onto my bed. For a while I stayed still with my head buried under the pillow, even though it meant I struggled to breathe. I could hear Da, one floor down, sobbing like a five-year-old child and saying the same word over and over again: 'No, no, no, no, no.'

It didn't hit me like it had hit him. Not then.

Months later, when I began to talk about it more with Francis, he said it was 'shock'. I'd heard adults say it was 'a delayed reaction'. Francis said the same thing happened to him after his terrapins died, that he kept thinking they were paddling away in their tank. I hadn't the heart to tell him that his smelly terrapins could never compare to my ma, because I knew his heart was in the right place.

Da doesn't talk much to Francis. I heard him call Old Man Nelligan all sorts of bad names to Ma when she was alive. But he never tells me to stay away from Francis. Not like the other parents tell their kids. But then again, Da doesn't do things the way the other parents do. Not lately. Not now.

He is still holding Ma's gold mohair cardigan up to his nose. He breathes in deeply before saying, 'I wonder how long her scent will stay on it for.'

I know that scent so well: the smell of toast from breakfast in the morning mixed with the flower-scented softener she used on the clothes, even though it wasn't cheap to buy; the woody musk from the perfume Da bought her for her birthday; and the cream she made from crushed lavender that she rubbed into her hands at night to stop her skin from cracking.

'Come on, Da,' I say again, hoping that the tears won't start. 'We'll be late for the airport.'

He takes Ma's cardigan from his face, not caring to wipe away the bits of wool that stick to his skin and clothes. His grip is so tight, the need to hold on to anything that contains a little piece of her, that his fingers begin to pale. He clears his throat and swallows hard before placing it back at the foot of my bed.

We get ready in near-silence, the creaking of the floorboards beneath the carpet the only sound that travels through the house. When I pull the net curtains back, the sun's rays break through the glass but do nothing to lift the greyness that masks Da's face.

'I just don't know how in God's name I ended up getting roped into this,' he says.

'Aunt Suzanne put our names forward when there was a cancellation, Da, remember? She says it will be good for us.'

'I wish they'd all just leave me alone,' he says.

And I know by 'they' he is talking about Aunt Suzanne, Granny and Granda, Mrs O'Driscoll on the left of our house, Mrs Baldwin on the right, my teacher and my principal. Even the milkman, who sometimes sees my da sitting on the kerb, eyes bloodshot and head hung low, and asks if he needs help with anything. Da wants them all to leave him alone. To disappear. To go away.

I don't. I want them here. Someone is better than no one, after all, and Da hasn't exactly been around much the past few months.

I take his hand and try to hold it steady. 'It'll be good, Da,' I say. 'It'll be good for you and me.'

'It's not a holiday, Jen,' he says. 'It's a bloody pilgrimage. There'll be nothing but rosary beads and Holy Joes. And it's a communist country, for crying out loud. In the middle of nowhere. I've never even heard of the airport we're flying into and I can't pronounce the name of the village we're staying in.'

'Neither can I,' I say. 'But Aunt Suzanne says it was meant to be – what with the cancellation, I mean.'

I want to tell him more of what Aunt Suzanne has said. 'Oh Jen, you'll love it,' she told me when she took me grocery shopping after she discovered that we had been living on cereal and sour milk for a week. 'It's a little piece of Heaven on Earth.' Her eyes danced as she spoke. 'If I could just put it in a bottle and bring it home and give it to your da, and if he could experience what I experienced,' she said, 'then maybe, just maybe, he could start living again.'

But I can't say things like this to Da any more. Not after Ma's accident. Not after her death. No one is allowed mention God or Heaven around him. But they do anyway, ignoring him when he huffs and puffs and throws his eyes upwards.

Outside, I hear the beeping of a horn.

'Mr Baldwin is waiting,' I say.

Da reluctantly stands and rubs his hand over his unshaven chin.

At the foot of the stairs sits our battered suitcase, the one I packed last night. 'You go ahead,' Da says as we walk down the stairs. 'Tell him I'll be out in a minute. I just want to lock up and throw the key under the mat.'

Outside, Mr Baldwin sits in the driver's seat, yawning. As I walk towards the car, I can picture my da standing in the hallway, his left hand on the banister holding him steady and his right hand grasping a naggin of whiskey. He'll drink it neat and barely wince when it scrapes down his throat. Overhead, the birds have only just sung their first song. The curtains are still pulled tight in the windows of the cul-de-sac. There is no sound of buses or cars travelling up the Beauvalley Road, nor is there the sound of bicycle bells or the clanking of chains. People are still asleep. Everything is still and at peace. Except for my da, who stumbles out of our house and slams the door behind him. I look into his eyes, the ones that have lost their shine, and I search them to see if there is something that can be saved.

'Right,' he slurs as he gets into the passenger seat, 'let's get this over with.'

'For the love of God, Charlie Carthy, have ya no cop on at all,' Mr Baldwin says as he rolls down the window of the car to let the smell of sweat and stale alcohol out.

On the drive, Mr Baldwin is quiet. I know he's annoyed at Da because he can't stop tutting and shaking his head. When we are almost at Dublin Airport, he fixes his mirror and looks at me in the back seat.

'Where is it you are going to again, Jen?'

I tell him all I know. The same as I told Francis Nelligan.

'Well, let's hope you find a miracle over there,' he says as he watches Da's eyes close and his head slump forward. 'God knows, you're going to need it.'

4

DUBLIN

CHARLIE

We're catching the early flight from Dublin in a few hours. As I sit here at the foot of Jen's bed, clutching Sarah's mohair cardigan like some sort of security blanket, I think about how at least I'm getting out of this place for a while. I won't have to put up with the disappointed looks from that young fella behind the bar at The Beauvalley House. And he only a whippersnapper working the weekday shifts while he sails through an arts degree in Trinity College. Looks at me, he does, like one of his lecturers might look at a student who's failed every module throughout the year. Disappointment. Bewilderment. Sheer and utter disgust at the lack of effort. It doesn't help when Jen comes bursting through the doors of the pub, casting her eyes around the room until they fix on the snug in the corner. She stands there with drenched hair and wearing last week's clothes, looking at me with her mother's disappointed eyes. And there I am, one man occupying an area made for six. No one ever comes near me. I'm left there like a leper to pick at my own scabs. Only Jen will talk to me, plead with me.

'Da,' she'll say, 'the electricity is gone again.'

Deep inside, I know that it's not just the electricity. It's the fridge with the rancid cheese and sour milk; the grimy bathroom with the overflowing wash basket that will never be seen to; the bunker in the back yard that houses three pieces of coal which are too wet to burn; the heavy drapes that are pulled closed for too many hours during the day; and the emptiness that lingers in every room every morning of every damn day.

It hasn't always been like this.

Looking back, I can remember with such clarity the joy I felt joining my da in his workshop in the city centre. There is something about the feel of a hand-bound leather book that compares to nothing else. All your senses stand to attention from the moment you allow your hand to caress the front cover, and as you smooth each page, there's a current that travels through the fingertips and up the arms. The rustle of paper tickles your ears and distinct tones can be felt on your tongue even without licking a page. And when the smell of clean leather reaches the nose, it's impossible not to inhale it like a craved-for drug.

Handmade leather bookbinding takes time and precision. It's an art that cannot be rushed. 'What's the hurry, Charlie boy?' my old man used to say as he leant over the workbench where he sewed the tapes that ran across the back and sealed the signatures. 'Good things come to those who wait, my son.'

I spent much of my youth in his workshop, which was on Mary Street, in the upper floor of a building that had been on the council's list for demolition for years. Through the grime of the chipped window frame you could see the skyline of the north city centre, where chimney tops puffed out black smoke and tall buildings competed with one another as they reached for the sky. Beneath him was Murphy's Butchers, who swore they sold the freshest spring lamb, even though everyone knew it was mutton.

On Saturdays, my old man brought me into town with the promise that I could have a wander around Hector Grey's toyshop at lunchtime. Halfway down Henry Street, just before we turned the corner where the small church with the big stained-glass windows stood, the air would change. Even before you turned that corner, and before the butcher's sign with the 'U' and the 'Y' missing came into view, the stench rose up as though it was being siphoned out of the drains. When we got close, I'd let go of my old man's hand, take a deep breath in and try to hold it until we reached his workshop.

Sometimes, Mr Murphy caught him at the end of the stairs to talk about rent increases or council rates. The smell of raw meat, fresh from the slaughterhouse, clung to his bloodstained apron and settled on the hairs of his sweaty skin. Even the flies followed him out to the staircase. They buzzed around his earlobes and ignored the fat hand that swatted at them.

There was a time when I held my breath for too long. Mr Murphy was giving out about a gurrier who had robbed a piece of liver sitting on the countertop.

'And I know it was one of those young fellas from Henrietta Street,' he said, wagging his pus-filled finger in my old man's face. 'They're forever sniffin' around here with the arse hanging out of their trousers, gettin' up to no good. A clatter across the legs is all they need. And if I get my hands on them, they'll be gettin' that and more, the little–'

I picked at the glue behind the peeling wallpaper on the staircase as I kept my lips tight. Everything about him was rotten, from the breath that poured out of his putrid mouth to the tufts of hair that grew within his nose. I remember thinking that the teeth that had fallen from his rancid gums must have been relieved to be gone.

'And I hear there's a new butcher's opening up on Moore Street beside the street traders,' he shouted at my old man, like it was his fault. 'As if they haven't got enough going on up there. It's a monopoly if ever I've seen one. There's not a hope of getting a pitch anywhere up there unless you're blood.'

Still, I held my breath and I wondered how my old man could stay there for so long and not flinch at the pungent smell that surrounded Mr Murphy. Then the light grew dim, my legs went from underneath my ten-year-old body and I tumbled down the rickety staircase. 'Books are all I can smell, son,' he told me later when he carried me up the stairs and fetched me a glass of water. 'I've been working so long with them. Leather and parchment. Nothing else.'

That was the way I remembered my old man: the smell of clean leather off his skin, off his hair, even when he wasn't working in his shop. Every Saturday I worked a full shift. He taught me the art of bookbinding and said it wasn't everyone who had the gift. When he took me through the process, it was as though he was revealing the world's best-kept secret. And I was the chosen one. I watched as he folded each signature and smoothed it out with an ivory-coloured bone folder. He measured up the spine of the book with a piece of graph paper and then punctured the holes he had marked out and he would sometimes let me hold it down as he placed it in the spine of the book. There were many uses for little hands, he always said, and this included when it came to threading the needle for the sewing of the signatures. It was a slow process but a rewarding one. Every week I improved. At the end of the day he would stand straight, roll his shoulders back and say, 'Good lad, Charlie. You have the knack for it, that's for sure.'

***

Going to work for Da seemed the right thing to do after I left school. Everyone was looking for a trade and I had started my apprenticeship from an early age. He had a way with the customers but I preferred to do my work hidden in the back of the shop. Ma didn't think it was healthy for a young fella to be holed up in a business that never seemed to move with the times. 'Who has time for old books any more?' she would say. 'It's a trade in plumbing or a job with the council he should be looking into. Let the lad stretch his wings a bit.' Da wouldn't bite back; he could see that I enjoyed it. I think he was happy knowing that he had someone to carry on the business for him after he was gone.

The thing about losing your father is, no matter how long you have them in your life for, it is never enough. I remember shaking his hand one Friday night after work and I thought that he held on to it a little longer than normal. His mouth was open but it was as though he couldn't get the words out. And I think he could've stayed there all night, standing in the middle of the street below our workshop with nothing but the city and his son around him.

'Are you all right, Da?' I asked.

'Grand, son,' he said, 'just grand.'

Ma said that when he got home, he had a sort of melancholy that she had never seen in him before. He poured himself two whiskeys, climbed the stairs at a slow pace, fell into bed and never woke up.

'Oh, what will I do now?' Ma cried for days on end.

Sure it didn't make a blind bit of difference what she did or didn't do. Two months later she was dead herself. Seemed her heart couldn't cope with the grief.

Though it wasn't the same without him, I went into work every day. Then, a few years after I inherited the business, and on the anniversary of my old man's death, the council finally decided to demolish the old building on Mary Street. In the registered letter, they gave me two weeks to clear out. Mr Murphy below didn't seem too bothered. The new butcher's shop on Moore Street had already robbed his best customers. It seemed they had access to tender, succulent lamb and fly-free meat. He was going to retire, he told me, and spend his golden years fishing on the Shannon. He always had a fancy for fish, he said. And if she was lucky, he would let Mrs Murphy come with him.

I didn't have the same savvy as my old man when it came to business. I didn't realise that the location of his workshop was a prime spot for customers, many of whom had other business in the city. In a way, I was a bit relieved to get out from under the smog of the city centre and the din of the crowds. Over a few days I moved the contents of the workshop into the concrete shed in our back garden in Beauvalley: jars of stiff brushes with short bristles and wooden handles; large tubs of honey-coloured beeswax moulded into solid shapes; white muslin cloths cut into long strips and placed in neat piles; spools of strong thread and needles with various eye sizes; a wooden sewing frame that my old man made with fine craftsmanship; reams of typewriter paper in various shades of white; a box of tools that would be the envy of any carpenter; and a long, solid workbench that had every shred of my old man's soul carved into it.

It wasn't all work and no play, of course. I was madly in love by that time, and love is always a great distraction to reality. Especially when reality doesn't completely go your way. Sarah and I just went with the tide back then. We didn't think too much about the future. A day at a time was enough for us and we were happy to live in the moment and not look too far ahead. Dating had been fun. Marriage was exciting. And then parenthood came along and the fun and games really began. In between all this, I just got on with work. I just went with them. The changes, I mean.

Sarah must have found it strange having me home all day, but if she minded she never said. And I didn't miss the trawl of running for packed buses and pushing through crowds. The winters had been the worst: getting up in the dark, coming home in the dark. We developed a routine when I started working from the shed. Once the haze of the early morning sky lifted, Sarah would stand over the gas cooker, waiting for the whistle from the tarnished kettle. Beside it, the teapot would already have the lid off and the leaves would be sitting in a pile at the bottom. I liked it strong and she knew this, so after she poured the boiling water in, she would leave it to sit for a while.

'You go on down to the shed,' she'd say. 'I'll bring it down to you.'

If you climbed over our back wall, you were in the church and primary school grounds. The silence of the day was only broken by the sound of children rushing out to the yard at *sos beag* and lunchtime. At this time I would stop and listen to them: skipping ropes whipping off the ground, the children shouting rhymes as they jumped; a football being kicked with power against the nearest wall; and the pounding of feet as they played hopscotch on faded chalk. When a whistle blew at the end of the breaks, feet shuffled into line. And once they returned to their classrooms, I went back to cutting and folding paper.

Every day, shortly after half past two, Jen pounded through the house, dropping her schoolbag at the foot of the stairs in the hallway.

'Hi, Ma,' she'd say to Sarah as she raced through the kitchen and out the back door.

I still picture Sarah standing there with her left hand in a sink of suds and the wrist of her right hand rubbing at her brow, trying to catch the stray hair that had fallen into her face.

'Well hello to you too!' she'd respond before going back to washing the chipped plates.

Outside, the shed door was already open. For the first few seconds, Jen would stand in the frame of the door, blocking the afternoon sun. She would tug at the elastic of the wine-coloured tie that sat too tight around the stiff collar of her white shirt, pull it over her head and open the top button of her shirt. Only then would a smile creep across her flushed face. I would stop what I was doing, stand up from my bench and wonder how it was that my baby had grown up so quick.

'I'm home,' she'd pant. 'What do you want me to do?'

I would walk to the door and take an over-sized shirt down from a hook at the back of the door and throw it in her direction. 'First things first, let's get you covered. We don't want to get your uniform destroyed now, do we? Once you've that on, go over and get the saucepan off your ma and you can make me more paste.'

It didn't matter that her stomach felt empty or that she had homework to do, Jen would still begin to measure out the wheat flour into a small bowl. After she had poured two cups of water into the saucepan, she would spoon the white wheat flour in slowly and mix it as she went.

'Now beat it hard until it smooths to a paste,' I instructed, and then watched as she gripped the eggbeater and put all her strength into whisking.

When we were happy that it was of the right consistency, Jen would go back into the kitchen and place the saucepan over the gas hob.

'Make sure you don't burn the bottom of that saucepan,' Sarah would warn, and I knew Jen wished there was a gas hob back in the shed so she wouldn't have to listen to her ma giving out.

This was the hour that broke the monotony of the day, the sight of my only daughter helping me with my labour. Little did I know that a few years later she would have left primary school, made the leap into secondary school and watched her mother's coffin sway into a six-foot hole in the ground.

Every day for the past few months, she's still done the same thing. She comes in from school, drops her bag by the end of the stairs and races through the now empty kitchen, not bothering to close the swinging door behind her. Then she stands in the door frame of the shed – her head edging closer to the top each time – and calls my name.

On the days when I am able to lift my head off my old man's workbench, I stare at her through glazed eyes. My foot slips, making the empty bottles topple and hit against the legs of the workbench. And she exhales heavily through her nose to show me she isn't happy. That is always enough.

It's not in me to explain myself. I don't see the point in words any more. I've had so many empty ones said to me over the months since Sarah's death that I have trained my ears not to listen.

It doesn't help that, on top of Sarah's death, the customers for my bookbinding have dwindled away – though, to be fair, that process began as soon as I moved out of the city centre. I still go down to the shed every morning, as if by being there some work will magically appear. Sure if it did, I'd make a mess of it anyway; if it's one thing bookbinding needs, it's a steady hand. I thought by keeping to my routine, I would keep functioning. Keep surviving. Keep fooling everyone along the way. But I've come to realise that that's not the case. Dust has settled on top of the old books with the fragile parchment. Tools remain unused in their boxes. Everything has become damp. Some days I slip into a dream-like state and see my wife in the garden, her skirt lifting high as she twirls.

We first met at a Saturday night dance on Parnell Street. I could have watched her all night, twirling and spinning in the centre of the dance hall, her green eyes closed to slits and her long, chestnut hair draped well below her shoulders. She danced like the music belonged to her alone. And then it was as though she snapped out of her trance. She turned and scanned the dance hall until her eyes fixed on me. There I was, standing in the corner with my hands stuffed into my pockets, staring at this wondrous sight and asking how in hell she had let her eyes fall on me. There was no point in trying to protest. Sarah glided along the dance floor, her arms outstretched and fingers pointing in my direction.

'Come on,' she said to me, 'I love this song.'

It could have been that she was caught up in the music. It could have been that anyone would do. It could have been just one night and one night only. I'd never danced a step in my life up until then. And she didn't laugh at my awkward footwork. She didn't mock me like I saw her friends mock others as they tried to imitate the latest moves. I moved with her guidance and she didn't flinch when I pulled her closer to me as the music slowed down.

'You've got nice shoulders,' she said.

And so I kissed her gently.

When we began courting, every song was 'our song'. She dragged me along to dance lessons in the city, where a petite lady of Italian descent taught us how to waltz and tango and jive and twist. A few years ago, when I told Sarah my dancing days were over, she took Jen to dance lessons with the same lady in the city centre. When they got home, they lowered the needle onto the record and I watched as they tried to move like John Travolta in a scene from *Saturday Night Fever*.

But the records are gone now and the radio too. I cracked every one of those vinyls over my right knee one morning recently and threw the radio out with the rubbish. I didn't need reminding of those nights when we were just starting out. All our hopes and dreams, as simple as they may have been, laid out before us. We talked of a house by the sea with bedrooms full of kids. We talked of travelling to faraway places where the food would upset our stomachs but we wouldn't mind. We talked about the different careers our children would have once we put them through university. We talked of growing plants and growing old and minding our grandchildren for our kids. But the one thing we never talked about, the one thing we could never foresee, was a life where we weren't together.

And when I'm doing these things that I do now, drinking myself into oblivion, I watch Jen watching me. Even when my eyes are closed, I see her. But I can't help myself. I can't make it stop. All I want is for things to go back to normal.

***

'Come on, Da,' she says now as I sit at the end of her bed. 'We'll be late for the airport.'

Already I can smell the desperation. Cripples looking for the cure; fanatics looking for their own personal apparition; Bible bashers and the moral brigade telling you what's right and what's wrong. A circus full of misfits and freaks. I should have started a row, I realise, back when the idea for the trip was first floated. That might have got me out of this. Only, through the haze and the fog, I had seen a little glow in the eyes of my daughter. An immediate belief in something she knows little about.

'How can you have faith in something that you cannot see?' I asked Suzanne when she came back from the place. She had done nothing but rave about it to Sarah when she came home, talking about it like it was some sort of magical kingdom in Disneyland. And I was conscious of Jen standing at the corner of the table while her aunt spoke and sipped Lyons tea between sentences.

'Ah, Charlie Carthy,' she mused when I rolled my eyes. 'Always the sceptic. You don't have to see things to believe in them. True faith is believing even if you don't fully understand everything.'

'Diving head first into something you don't fully understand can be a dangerous thing,' I told her.

She just laughed. 'Everyone is searching for it,' she said. 'I've found it.'

The passenger side tyre of Mr Baldwin's car has a slow puncture, I remember, as we drive out of the cul-de-sac. I'm praying for a blowout on the way to the airport so we won't make our flight. I can smell myself inside the small Ford car. He doesn't try to be discreet when he rolls down the window and gasps at the morning air like there'll be none left in a few minutes. The bar won't be open in the airport, but they'll have to serve me on the plane. There's a lump on the back of my skull, which I can feel when I lie back against the headrest. It's fresh and hard but I can't remember how it got there. Jen sits forward in the back of the car, her body squeezed between the front seats with her backpack resting near the gear stick.

I'll close my eyes I think. That way there won't be any questions. But Mr Baldwin asks them anyway. Just as I'm slipping into that old familiar state when consciousness is reduced, I hear him talking about miracles, and I'm wondering if he too – like Suzanne and Jen, and everyone else that's going on about this place – has gone completely and utterly mad.

5

DUBLIN

SUZANNE

It's Jen I worry about the most. Sure isn't Charlie Carthy big and bold enough to take care of himself. Saying that, though, God there are times when I could murder him. Times when I want to shake the life out of him. But sure what good would that do? Hasn't there been enough lives lost and destroyed this past while? I've had four cups of tea already and haven't yet heard the bells of the Angelus on the radio. The pair of them would have left at the crack of dawn and I mightn't even hear a word until they get home in a week's time. That's if Charlie even got on the plane in the first place. The man has my heart broke. Sure, hasn't he everyone's heart broke.

I used to complain to Sarah about my tiny little bedsit in Whitegardens and how I'd love more space. Nowadays it's my refuge – especially after a day up in Charlie's. And Sarah used to have the house so nice, but that man has it destroyed. It's like his pain has seeped into the walls, into the furniture, into the air. There's hardly a trace of Sarah left in the house, except for Jen. She gives off that little glimmer of light, that tiny ray of hope. But sure your man is too clouded in darkness to be bothered to notice.

I'll have one more cup of tea and maybe cycle past the house. Just to make sure they've gone.

'It might be small, this little bedsit of yours,' Sarah used to say, 'but it has a great location. And sure why would you want a big garden to be tending to when you've enough to be doing from one end of the week till the next? You've so much on your doorstep. Or close enough, anyway.'

Sarah was right. There is a seaside village not an hour's cycle from here where the white sails of pleasure boats can be seen battling the current as they struggle through the estuary in the hope of gliding into the sea. In the evening time the sun burns tangerine and casts a vibrant glow along the horizon, turning the sand a rich gold and illuminating the jagged edges of the rocks. A misshapen island rests in the distance, its only inhabitants a colony of gannets that don't take kindly to visitors who travel the fifteen-minute boat journey from Howth Head. They'll often swoop down low and peck at pale necks as they guard the large eggs scattered nearby.

Most Saturdays before Jen was born, Sarah and I parked our High Nellies against the stone wall that stretched along the coastline there and listened to the sound of the waves as they fizzled and rushed to the rhythm of the moving tide. Then we cycled up to the promenade, weaving in and out of fellow day-trippers. Along this strip there was always a man with a white badger streak in the centre of his coal-black hair who sold newspapers. He placed stones on top of the newspapers to stop the pages fluttering in the light wind and he sat on a grey plastic crate with his nose stuck in a battered book. People stopped and glanced at the headlines before throwing coins in the galvanised bucket that sat by his feet. Then he'd pull roughly at the newspaper at the top of the pile, making the pages tear and the stones scatter as he handed it to the customer. Every time he sold a paper, the man would look up and study the position of the sun to see how many hours were left in that day. Then he went back to reading the book with the yellow pages, the one that held his interest the most among all the other stories beside him.

'What are you thinking, Sarah?' I remember asking her one time as she looked out to sea.

'I'm thinking that it's the most beautiful sight in the whole world and I never want it to leave my mind.'

Even now, as I sit here in my bedsit thinking about Charlie and Jen, I can't get that image of my sister on the promenade out of my head.

After her accident, Sarah spent weeks lying in the same hospital bed. Her head was swollen to twice its size and she had tubes coming out of one place and going into others. Machines beeped and flashed, inspiring hope one minute and fear the next. One day they were switching them off; the next they were giving it another twenty-four hours. During that time it was the image of that seaside village in north County Dublin – the one with the sign that read *Mullach Íde,* the one that she said she'd love to live in, if they ever came to afford it – that I hoped she kept in her mind's eye.

Even though she was still, I never stopped talking to her. 'We can all go out there, Sarah,' I'd say as my elbows rested on the safety rail of the steel bed. 'When you get well and get out of here. We can make a day of it and picnic on the beach. Jen and I will make sandwiches so you won't need to go to any trouble. And I promise I won't complain when I'm chewing on sand. Charlie could borrow Mr Baldwin's car for the day and we could tie the bikes onto the roof. You know how Jen loves the sea air, Sarah. I know where she gets it from, anyway. I can see both of you crouched down beside a rock pool, studying the hermit crabs who hijack the small shells. You'd both stay there for hours if you were let.'

I often paused, checking to see if her eyelids fluttered or a finger moved.

'Keep talking to her,' the nurse said when she came in to press buttons and refill or empty bags. 'Hearing a loved one's voice and reminiscing about times gone by can help greatly.'

In her words lay a glimmer of hope that temporarily extinguished the despair. Nothing was impossible. There was always a chance. People had woken up from comas after many years, I told myself, after which rehabilitation and therapy had allowed them to go back to their lives.

'You can feel the sun on your face again, Sarah, and let the salty sea air sting your lips,' I told her. 'We can race into the water, you, me and Jen, and allow the waves to chase us back to shore. We can get ice cream from the circular hut with the red and white striped roof that sits halfway up the promenade, and we can try to lick the melting ice cream as it drips down the wafer cone. And when we are too exhausted to do any more, Charlie can drive us home in Mr Baldwin's car. We would sleep well that night, I'd bet, and know that we could do it all again. Whenever we please. Whatever day.'

I talked until I could talk no more. Day and night. Week after week. Even when they had switched off the final switch, pulled the last tube from her mouth – still I talked. My words turned into murmurs and barely audible whispers. Then they became quiet thoughts. After they lowered her coffin into the ground and Charlie wept into his daughter's hair, I still spoke to Sarah like she was standing beside me. In the dark of night I called her name. And when a floorboard creaked or a shadow moved, I told myself that she was there. Listening to me reminisce. Listening to my stories.

Our stories.

I talked to her about the brisk September morn in 1979 when I stood among the overgrown weeds in her front garden and threw pebbles up at the bedroom window. After some time, the net curtains twitched and Charlie stuck his head out of the window.

'Are you off your head, woman?' he shouted. 'It's three o'clock in the morning for crying out loud.'

'Is she ready?' I called back.

'Ready for what?'

'Ready to see the Pope, you big eejit. What else?'

'But it's three o'clock in the morning,' Charlie said. 'Surely even His Holiness needs his beauty sleep.'

Lights began to flicker in the neighbouring houses.

'If we don't leave now then we won't have a chance of getting close to the front. People have been camping out in tents in the park the past two nights and they're expecting thousands more from the four provinces.'

I was trying to whisper, but it sounded more like a hiss.

'Your sister has lost the plot altogether, Sarah,' I heard him say as he ducked his head back inside.

Minutes later, Sarah came to the front door all dressed. In her hand she held a cup of hot tea. Under her arm she had a pile of ham sandwiches made with batch loaf and covered in tinfoil. 'I've been ready for ages,' she said. 'Pay no attention to Mr Grouchy up there. He's annoyed because I had to turn on the light to find my shoes.'

We left Sarah's house and cycled for miles with only the dim streetlights to guide our way against the pitch-black sky. Our laughter and the sound of our bicycle chains were loud against the silence of the night. Sarah slowed down when she noticed me lagging behind. An impromptu decision taken as a child to slide down the banisters of the staircase had left me with a creaky hip that still played up in the damp. That, coupled with the fact that my left leg was shorter than the right, meant I had an uneasy gait.

We seemed to cycle forever, but it was still half-dark when we arrived at the Phoenix Park in the early morning. Our eyes widened as we took in the sea of people that lay scattered across the green.

Later that day, when he came to the outside altar, we joined in with the roar of the crowd. I knew that Sarah didn't have the same interest in religion as I did but she always said that she enjoyed seeing the thrill I got from it.

'He's like a rock star to you, isn't he?' She smiled.

'Don't be silly,' I said. I didn't want her to see my cheeks blush, so I turned around and pretended to search for someone in the crowd.

Growing up, we had been as close as sisters could be. Charlie often joked that if he hadn't swept Sarah off her feet, both of us would have been destined to live together as two old spinsters in my bedsit, drinking copious amounts of tea while stray cats wove in and out of our stockinged legs.

Truth was, that was never going to be Sarah's destiny. There seemed to be a certain spot in the world for Sarah, one that she slotted into comfortably, like the final piece in a jigsaw. On the other hand, things never seemed to really happen for me. No one ever seemed to take notice. Not that I went out of my way to make someone notice me. It would have been nice, I thought, if I didn't have to make the effort. Like Sarah. She never had to make the effort; people made the effort for her.

At least I had Sarah. She understood me in a way that I didn't understand myself. Sarah could see how our parents doted on her more than me. How they made me feel invisible. 'Sarah's getting the lead part in the school play this year,' Ma would say to anyone who'd listen. 'Everyone says she's the image of a young Vivien Leigh and that she's destined for the stage, and maybe even film.' As people *oohhed* and *aahhed*, Sarah would look over to where I sat and say, 'Suzanne got an A in her maths. Nobody gets As in their maths in my class. Not even the teacher's pet.' She would wink at me then, just as those gathered turned their heads in my direction. Their gaze would be brief, but brief was good. I basked in the glow for the time I had it, right up until all the faces turned back to focus their energy on the porcelain doll who looked like the Hollywood movie star.

Da was even worse. Every time we went out to play, he would stoop down and wag his finger close to my nose. 'You watch over your sister, do you hear? I don't want any sort of shenanigans while you're out. And don't talk to strangers, do you hear me?' he'd repeat. Then he would ruffle Sarah's hair and whisper something under his breath. I like to think it was 'love you both', but I only ever heard the first two words.

We never spoke about it: how our own parents favoured one child over the next. Sarah was the same to me inside the house as she was outside the house. When I was around her I felt included. She went out of her way to make me feel like that. Deep down, I knew that Ma and Da probably weren't even aware of how they mistreated me. But Sarah made me feel loved, even when the others didn't. As I grew up I decided that I would never try to figure them out and that I would find my way, my path, eventually. It would come to me out of the blue, most likely when I least expected it. And so I waited. And waited.

I would have been lying if I said that there weren't times when I envied Sarah and what she had with Charlie, but I was so happy for them when Jen was born. They had been trying for so long for a baby. There wasn't much hope of me ever getting married at that point, so being an aunt to

Jen was the next best thing. I knew they both wanted more children but Sarah had trouble conceiving again. 'Give it time,' I told her. But time wasn't on her side.

***

The four seasons of each year tumbled in and glided out. Any secretarial work I had gotten in the past dried up like puddles on a road. 'Recession' was a word that was drummed incessantly into people's ears and fear could be seen in the eyes of every man and woman in the country. Redundancies destroyed families who were up to their necks in high-rate mortgage payments. Ferries were laden down with men and women who waved to their loved ones standing on the shore, not knowing what lay ahead or when they would see them again. For once, I felt like I had something in common with other people – these reluctant exiles. For them it was new. For me, I had felt this loss all my life.

My knees were worn out from kneeling at the foot of the statue of St Joseph in our church during this time. I lit more candles and rattled off more novenas than was normal. I was storming the heavens, begging for someone to send me a job.

Soon after, a shop of various bric-a-brac opened in Whitegardens, not fifteen minute's cycle from my bedsit. It was set up by a local man called Louis, who wore cowboy hats and colourful braces to hold his trousers up. The day I passed by the shop, Louis was standing inside the front window, trying to arrange some sort of attractive display that consisted of a Child of Prague statue with a missing arm and bottle of 4711 perfume that looked the colour of a urine sample. He took the cowboy hat off and scratched the top of his head.

'Can I give you a hand?' I mouthed from outside and he didn't hesitate to nod.

When I was inside the shop, he locked the front door and Sellotaped a 'closed' sign to the glass.

'First things first,' he said as he moved towards the back of the shop and led me into a room that was separated from the front of the shop by rainbow-coloured hanging beads. 'A nice cup of tea.'

We went through two teapots and one full packet of Mikados before the window display got seen to. Louis seemed at ease with me, as I was with him. We talked like long-lost friends. 'The golden years just aren't all they're cracked up to be,' he said about his supposed retirement. 'The days are too monotonous when you're not used to being in the house.'

He had worked as a civil servant since he was old enough to apply for the job.

'Times were different when I was a young fella,' Louis told me. 'When women got married, they had to leave their jobs in the civil service and could never go back. They had a man to look after them and so their job was freed up for someone else. Positions came up every now and again when women tied the knot and pledged a lifetime of servitude to the kitchen sink.' He winked at the last sentence and then began to laugh. It was throaty. Then it turned chesty and caused him to splutter uncontrollably for several minutes. It was uncomfortable to watch and I was unsure whether or not it was appropriate to start banging on his back. So I sat there smiling at him until eventually he got things under control.

'It was only when I started to clear out the attic of my house and the shed at the back of the garden that I realised how much junk we had collected over the years,' he said. 'But you know what they say?'

I shook my head.

'You know! "Someone's junk is someone else's treasure." So I decided to set up a type of jumble shop, where people could bring their unwanted stuff and I could sell it for small change. Whatever I make after rent and electricity, I'll give to charity.'

I remember looking around the shop and rooting through the contents that were stuffed into black bin liners. Books with pages missing; lamp shades discoloured from bright bulbs; cassettes with tangled magnetic tape; a completed Rubik's Cube; a thousand-piece jigsaw with less than one hundred pieces in the box; a doll with two eyes torn out of the moon-shaped face; and a frayed skipping rope with no handles.

'What do you think?' Louis asked. I could see the hope in his eyes.

'It's a start, I suppose,' I said as I looked at the cobwebs gathered in each corner of the shop.

'Maybe it just needs a woman's touch,' he said, smiling.

'Is that aimed at me?' I asked.

He nodded. 'It is. I can't pay much until we get it off the ground, but if you have a window open in your day, I'd be ever so grateful if you came in and gave me a hand.'

He didn't need to say any more than that. This suited me down to the ground, at least until something more solid came around. It was the idleness that killed most people who were out of work. If it didn't drive them out to the pub, it drove them into themselves. Which was worse, I wasn't sure.

Louis and I spent weeks getting the shop in shape. When I was happy that it was in a cleaner state – that is, devoid of cobwebs, dead bugs and mouse droppings – I set about trying to get some decent stock for us to sell. We designed and printed out a bundle of flyers. 'Unwanted Clothes and Household Items Required for Jumble Sale in New Charity Shop,' it read. Once ready, I took Jen with me and for an afternoon we cycled out to the suburbs of Sutton and Howth and stuffed the flyers into the letterboxes of the biggest houses we could find. A week later, we piled into Louis' clapped-out Lada as he drove us back to the houses, where we collected the bags they had left for us on their doorsteps. When we got back to the shop later that evening, we realised that we had struck gold.

'These ones still have the tags on them!' Jen screamed as she held out a pair of cashmere jumpers with fake diamonds sewn into the front. In other bags, we found delicate china cups without any chips; board games that had never been opened; hand paintings of boats bobbing in the harbour; chunky costume jewellery; leotards and leg warmers; leather school shoes outgrown by kids but with no scuffs at the toes; fur coats – faux or real we didn't know; limited edition vinyl records; and delicate evening gowns which had barely been worn. Some mornings we would arrive to the shop and find furniture sitting outside. A nest of mahogany tables or a velvet Queen Anne chair. In a matter of weeks, we had a display of gems for knock-down prices. Sarah painted the sign that hung above the window and used gold lettering in neat cursive writing for the name we decided on for the shop.

'The Humble Jumble,' Sarah said when she stood back to admire her artwork. 'It's catchy, alright.'

Louis worked in the shop from morning till night, five days a week and a half-day on a Saturday. I knew that things weren't good for him at home, even though he never talked too much about it. His wife rang the shop a few times and Louis would spend time trying to calm her down as she cried on the phone. I never asked what was wrong. It would have been rude. I heard the name Philip mentioned once or twice during the conversations. The name was said like it was a heavy load. And Louis always looked somewhat deflated when he got off the phone. Like he had aged another few years.

At first I stopped by every second day, just after ten o'clock Mass. I'd make the tea, sweep the floor, rearrange the shelves and chat to the customers who sorted through the wire hangers. Though most people couldn't afford to buy much, it gave them comfort that the wares they were looking at were always going to be more affordable with us than in any other shop.

Every week in the dole office I got the same nonchalant look from the girl with the permed hair and thin lips who sat behind the same window, chewing gum loudly. She didn't even have to say it. It was written all over her smug face. There were no jobs. Not this week. Not next week. Not for the foreseeable future.

'You would have been better off getting a trade,' Ma often said to me. 'Couldn't you do an apprenticeship in the hairdresser's like Edna Mooney's daughter?'

'An apprenticeship, Ma? At my age? It's all young ones fresh out of secondary school, not thirty-somethings like me. And all they seem to do is sweep up cuts of hair and shampoo the blue rinse out of old grannies' perms.'

'It's only a suggestion,' Ma muttered back and I'd watch her cheeks cave in as she sucked on another Silk Cut Red. 'If you had got yourself a fella like our Sarah, then you wouldn't be in such a dangerous position.'

'Dangerous, Ma? What's that supposed to mean?'

Ma ran her hands through the singed fringe of her hair. 'I'm just saying, it's survival of the fittest out there, that's all. And it would be a hell of a lot better if you had a mate to hunt for you rather than being left for fodder. It doesn't have to be the love of your life, for crying out loud. Anyone would do at this stage. It would take a lot of worry off your father's mind – and mine, for that matter.'

***

Within weeks, I was working in The Humble Jumble full-time. Louis paid me when he could, and though he never said it, I knew it was coming out of his own pocket when he did. I would have worked there for free anyway. It beat calling into Ma and Da everyday and listening to non-productive suggestions and repetitive criticisms, not only about me but about each other too. More than once I had walked in on them during a heated conversation, only for them to shift uncomfortably in their chairs and glare at me as though I was the one causing the friction. The Humble Jumble was an escape and Louis was a trusted friend. One who never asked questions, just gave a knowing smile.

'Have you seen this?' he asked during tea break one day.

We were sitting in the back of the shop and I was spooning through the sugar bowl to make sure there were no more mice droppings to be found. In his hands Louis held the daily broadsheet, his fingertips already black from the ink.

'What is it?' I asked as I tried to stretch my neck across to see the page.

'It's an article about some events that have been happening over in Yugoslavia,' Louis said.

His eyes moved about the page rapidly as though he was still reading the piece.

'Oh yeah?'

'Yeah. Here, have a read for yourself,' he said as he handed the newspaper over.

The strainer in my cup caught the leaves as Louis tilted the pot and poured some more tea.

'Tell me what you make of that now,' he said.

'I will when I have a chance to read it, Louis!'

The print was small and tucked into a thin strip in the bottom right-hand corner of the page.

'Children in Communist Country Claim to See the Blessed Virgin', the heading read.

A group of children from a poor farming village in Yugoslavia have sent their once quiet community into a hive of activity as they continue to make claims that the Blessed Virgin has appeared and spoken to them. Local media reports say that they claim to have seen the Mother of God on a remote hillside in their village and that she comes to them with a 'message for the world'.

The local bishop has refuted the claims and even though people are flocking to the area, he has called for calm amidst the mass hysteria.

'Matters like this need to be investigated thoroughly before a decision can be made about the authenticity of the alleged apparitions,' he has been reported as saying.

The communist authorities have dismissed the claims as ridiculous and nonsensical. They are calling it a 'poor attempt at a social revolution by a minority of Catholics in the area'.

'Do you think it's true?' I asked Louis when I finished reading.

'We've no way of knowing, I suppose,' he said, shrugging his shoulders.

'It's probably all a big hoax,' I said. 'Some sort of ploy to get people to travel over there.'

'I don't know about that,' Louis said, shaking his head. 'It's a different world over there in Eastern Europe. There's a lot going on that we don't know about. Repression of the people and all sorts. Public displays of religion are banned over there, you know, so I find it hard to believe that children would want to bring so much trouble on their community if there wasn't some truth in what they are saying.'

'Well, knowing kids, they'll be found out eventually,' I said. 'There is only so much you can get away with before the lies unravel.'

The newspaper article ignited a spark inside Louis. I put his interest in it down to it being a welcome distraction from whatever was going on at home. At least, I thought, it had put a bit of lively pink back into the grey that dominated his sagging cheeks.

A few days went by and we didn't talk about it again, until Louis came charging into The Humble Jumble one Saturday with a tape fixed firmly under his arm. 'Quick,' he said as he shut the door behind him. 'We're closing early today. There's something I want you to see. Get that VCR from the top shelf and plug it into the TV out the back. You're going to love this.'

'It's not even gone half past eleven,' I said.

He wasn't listening to me.

'I'll put the kettle on and you set up the VCR,' he said as he rushed through to the back of the shop, letting the beads swing high in the air before clashing back together again. 'I'm no good with wires.'

It took me a good half hour to get the TV and VCR set up and when I reached out to take the cassette from Louis, he pulled back slightly as if guarding some precious jewel. He looked me straight in the eyes and paused before he spoke next.

'This is the only copy, I'm told. So we have to be really careful with it,' he warned. 'I said I would have it back by this evening.'

'Ah, for goodness sake, Louis. Is it a blue movie you've got under your arm or what?' I teased. 'Will you give it here for the love of God and stop being ridiculous.'

We listened as the tape rewound in the silver machine, both of us saying nothing. Finally it clicked and I pressed the play button.

'Ssshhh,' Louis said when the tracking lines appeared on the screen. I couldn't stop myself from rolling my eyes.

Blurred images slowly came into focus. It was amateur footage; that much was clear, as the picture shook for the first few minutes. There was a small room with pale walls. Some natural light streamed in from a tight window. The video camera panned around the room, showing little but the backs of people's heads. They spoke in murmurs and shifted nervously from one foot to the next. A door that led into the room creaked open and the camera turned to a Franciscan priest who wore a long brown robe with a deep hood. He moved closer and on noticing the video camera motioned with his hands for it to be turned off. It was at this point that the image switched rapidly to the floor, showing nothing but sandals and a pair of dusty feet.

The video camera stayed pointing to the ground as someone, maybe the priest, began to speak in a foreign tongue.

'What's he saying?' I asked.

'Ssshhh,' Louis said back. 'Watch.'

He turned up the volume on the TV at the same time as the door creaked open once more. Almost too rapidly, the video camera was lifted up and the image went out of focus. When the hand became steady, the picture grew clear again. People were walking through the door and into the small room. They walked in a line of varying heights. They weren't adults, but children. The youngest was maybe ten, the eldest maybe sixteen. Two boys and four girls. The youngest boy looked frightened, and even though he tried to keep his eyes cast down, he couldn't. One of the girls had fair hair, full and layered throughout. Another had her hair cut short as if to match her boyish figure. When they moved to the top of the room, their shoulders seemed to relax a little and they smiled at the priest who put out his hands to them.

'Is it them?' I whispered. 'Are they the children from Yugoslavia?'

'That's them, alright. All six of them.'

Prayers were said. The priest said the first half of the prayers, while the people in the room said the second half. The children were standing beside one another and, though they bowed their heads, I could see they were distracted at times. Every so often the video camera zoomed towards one of their faces, which were sallow-skinned and line free. The younger boy had cheeks that were pinched and he sniffed every so often before wiping his nose with his sleeve. One of the girls with dark hair and full lips reached inside her pocket and handed him a handkerchief. She rubbed his shoulder before returning back to her prayers.

In the tightly packed room, people waited. The looming sense of anticipation was almost tangible, even through the television screen. I could see the priest move back from the children to lean against the white wall. On his brow, beads of sweat glistened. The weight of his robes must have been unbearable in the heat of the room. A crucifix hung on the wall in front of the children. This was the direction they looked in as they continued mouthing their prayers. Then, in a brief moment, their lips stopped moving. All six of them fell to their knees. The children's heads were raised and their eyes were focused on a solitary spot before them.

The room hushed. Nobody moved. Even the priest kept his head lowered and did not raise it after the children dropped to the floor.

It lasted less than ten minutes. Each child spoke, but no words were audible.

When they came out of it, their heads flopped forward. One of the girls began to cry. Another rubbed her hands over her face. The people in the room pushed forward and the priest tried to hold them back. In the small stampede, someone knocked against the video camera and the picture was cut off.

Louis stood up and ejected the cassette from the VCR.

'Now do you think it's all a hoax?' he asked.

I wasn't sure how to answer. It was hard to tell what was going on. All I knew was that something had happened in that room. And only the children could see what it was.

That evening, I decided to call in to Ma and Da on the way home from the shop, wanting to tell them about the tape. In my head, I was thinking that maybe it would at least steer the conversation in a new direction. But I could hear the roaring before I put my key into the lock of the front door. Their shadows showed arms flailing in the air. Sarah's name dominated their words. Both of them spoke of her with passion, like all of humanity depended on her for its survival. They threw in comments about Charlie's business and minor mentions of Jen, but it was Sarah who was their central focus. Nothing I would say could deflect their attention from her. So I turned from the house I was reared in and made my way back to my dingy bedsit.

***

Soon after, I found myself travelling to that little village with Louis. I knew the minute I stepped off the coach that there was something special about the place. We stayed with a local family who spoke no English. They pointed to the church. They pointed to the hills. They pointed to the vineyards. They put every morsel of food from their land onto the table each evening and bowed their heads in prayer before each meal. They rose before us and went to bed after us. Though we couldn't understand their language, they spoke with kindness to one another and to each pilgrim.

From that first day in the village I had this urge to walk to the base of the highest mountain and climb as high as I could. They called it Križevac or Cross Mountain and we were told that within the white cross that sat at the top of the mountain there was a piece of the true cross of Christ.

The urge would not leave me as the days passed. So, while others chased the visionaries or waited for the sun to spin, I took off one day through the vineyards and along narrow paths until I came to the base of the big mountain. Here I met a young priest with no shoes on his feet who smiled at me. He had something in the palm of his hand, which he held out towards me. Silver rosary beads all tangled in a pile, the crucifix sitting on the top. I took them from him, thanked him and then began my climb.

I had nothing on my back, yet it felt heavy. Twice I had to stop and sit on a rock while I caught my breath. At one point I must have gone off course, because the path became less clear and the foliage more dense. I could see no one. My head started to spin and I longed for even a dribble of water. I fell back against a bush, closed my eyes and started to cry. 'Only a damn fool would try to climb a mountain without any preparation, Suzanne,' I heard my mother say in my head.

Wiping my eyes, I stood and climbed some more. Still I seemed to get nowhere. After some time I sat on a large rock and looked out across the village. As I looked at the fields below, it seemed like they were draped in a fine gossamer of gold. Just like on the mountain, I could see no people in the village below. It was as though everyone had disappeared. I was alone and yet, for some reason, I did not feel alone. In fact, I'd never felt more presence in all my life. I could have stayed there for an age. I'll never forget that sense of belonging.

'This is what it means to want for nothing,' I remember saying to myself.

I did not flinch when someone touched me lightly on the shoulder. It was the young priest who had given me the beads at the bottom of the mountain. He held out a bottle of water from which I drank.

'Father, will you show me the way?' I asked.

I didn't know if he spoke any English but he must have understood as he held out his hand and guided me the rest of the way up the mountain.

When I reached the top, I took a deep breath and made a decision that I would leave all my worries up there. Leave them in God's hands.

The priest walked behind me as I went down the mountain, his presence a constant comfort that someone had my back. I tried to thank him when we reached the bottom but he was already walking away. He paused by a statue of the Virgin Mary that stood in the garden of a nearby house and said, '*Totus Tuus*, Maria,' before disappearing down the dusty road.

That evening, after Mass, I sat on a bench in the grounds of the church and tried to make sense of how I was feeling. It was useless. It was something I couldn't explain. I wanted to bottle it and bring it home. I worried about how I would feel when I left the village. Would the feeling wear off? Would I forget my experience on the mountain?

I took the rosary beads out of my pocket, the ones the priest had given me at the bottom of the mountain. At first I thought it was the reflection of light; then, maybe, that that was the colour they had always been. The more I looked, the more I realised I was wrong. The beads the priest had given me at the bottom of the mountain had been silver. But just like the view of the fields at the top of the mountain, the beads that now lay across my legs were different.

They had turned gold.

I've been to the village twice now. Once before Sarah died and once after. I told her about it when I came back first. She said that maybe she would go there someday. Maybe Charlie would come too when things started to go right for them again, she added. But she never made it there.

Even I found it difficult to go back after she died. But it was where I found the most comfort. It was where I felt closest to her.

All I want is for Charlie and Jen to arrive there safely. To have some time away from Beauvalley, away from the house, the hospital, the main road. If Charlie could experience just one iota of what I experienced in that little village, then maybe, just maybe, he can find a way out of the hole he has fallen into. And I know it's Jen that I worry about most, but I can't ignore the fact that Charlie has been a wreck these past few months. There are times when I wonder if Jen will soon be an orphan. He is in such a self-destructive mode and time is running out. This feels like my last chance to help him. To help them both. And I'm not even sure it will.

All I can do is hope.

6

YUGOSLAVIA

IVA

I remember that day very well.

'Why must we get up so early, Mama?' I asked. 'It is cruel to make us suffer so. It is not fair!'

It was true that I was taking a risk by questioning Mama like this. Tata would surely have scolded me if he had heard what I said. But I was getting older, I was thirteen. And Veronika, my younger sister, always said I was the cheeky one. For me, I did not see it as being cheeky; it was more like standing up for myself and speaking my mind. We were told enough of what to do and what not to do by the communists and the milicija. Maybe if we stood up for ourselves and were a little bit braver, then things would be different.

'Don't be so stupid,' Veronika would hiss. 'You will cause more trouble for our family if you stand up to the communists. You should know this already.'

Deep down, I knew it would be foolish; I could never get away with it with the communists. But with Mama I could. Just a little. It was four o'clock in the morning, after all, and the air was so close in our small house that it was difficult to take a breath. I could feel the heat from Veronika's body as she lay beside me in the bed. My skin was sticky, even though we had slept on top of the bed sheets all night. Before Mama called me to get up, I had been dreaming of standing on a flat rock beneath the icy cold and rushing waterfalls not too far from our village.

'Hush, Iva,' Mama said. 'No more complaining. Have you not been doing this since you were only a few months old? You should be well used to it by now.'

I turned over so I was facing Veronika's feet. My sister had been poorly with headaches for two full days and so had been relieved from her duties in the fields. I did not know if Veronika had been telling the truth but as I looked down at her sleeping peacefully I knew that I would swap her headaches for even a couple of hours away from the fields.

Mama grabbed the tips of my toes and tickled the sole of my foot.

'Please, Mama,' I pleaded. 'Just one day off. I beg you. My legs are aching and my fingers are turning numb. I will get up tomorrow and work extra hard. I promise.'

Mama moved to the top of the bed. Her hands were cool as she wiped away the heat from my forehead. I knew that she didn't like to wake me so early, but it was a must if our family was to survive. Through my half-closed eyes, I could see her battle with her own conscience. But she didn't relent.

'Everyone is in the fields, Iva. Today will be a hot one. We must start early.'

'Why did you bring me to the fields when I was so young?' I asked, trying to gain more time. 'Surely a baby should have been left at home.'

'And who would mind you at home when everyone else was working in the fields? And anyway, you had fun with all the other babies playing in the soil!' Mama laughed. 'Come on. We don't want to be late. Even your grandmother has already left.'

My grandmother, Baba Ana, does not sleep at all any more, it seems, because she is the first one up every morning and the last one to bed at night. Old age has given her superpowers.

In my prayers that morning, I asked God to take the tobacco fields away. The sheep could stay grazing on the hills, I said, but the tobacco fields need to go. He must send a big flood to wash them away so that I do not need to get up so early in the morning any more. Then I will be happy, I thought, as I pulled myself out of the bed.

Mama walked ahead and I trudged behind, picking juicy grapes from vines and ripe figs from trees before stuffing them into my mouth. And on that day, I thought – even if God does not send a flood to get rid of the tobacco fields, I will not work there forever. Soon, I will go to Germany. Tata knew someone who could get passports for a good price. When I get to Germany, I will be a fashion designer and the rich ladies will all buy my clothes. It will no longer be necessary for Mama and Baba Ana to rise so early and walk three miles to the tobacco fields. And Tata will not need to work so hard. I will build a new house for them. One with a toilet inside and a bedroom for each of us. Anton will not need to sleep on the hard floor at night and Luka could go to university in Zagreb to study business like he always wanted.

As I moved up the line in the field, Mama said to me, 'There are still some flowers left on that plant. Start with that one, make sure that all the flowers have been removed and then start picking the mature leaves. We must get as many as plants as possible done before sunset, because that's when Anton will be here with the tractor to transport what we pick to the kiln for drying.'

***

Though it seems like a lifetime ago, more than two years have passed since that day – the day things started to change. As the morning drew on, Mama began to speak of a pain in her side that travelled up her spine. At midday she had to rest under the shade of a tree; hours later we found her still there, slumped in a deep sleep.

In the following days her stomach began to bloat to twice its size, even though she ate little, sometimes nothing at all. Baba Ana mixed herbs to try to ease her pain. Nothing worked. Soon Mama took to the bed for more hours than was natural. She became unable to rise at four to go to work in the fields. When she did follow on later in the day, she stood with her hands supporting her back, her eyes focused on the large cross that stood at the top of Mount Križevac. The same cross that her own father along with many others in the village had helped carry up the 1,700-foot-high mountain, which had been done to commemorate Christ's crucifixion.

Sometimes Mama complained of a burning heat within; at other times, her body shook as she shivered through the sunshine. Tata was away at that time, trying to get credit so he could buy some farm machinery. Baba Ana tried to nurse her as best she could. She mixed herbs fresh from the earth and stayed with her through the night when she cried out.

One morning, when the pain was so bad, Anton and Luka lifted her from the makeshift bed on the floor and carried her all the way to the doctor's clinic on the outskirts of the village. Doctor Marković's rooms were full of people with common ailments but when he saw Mama and the way her face was contorted with pain, he ushered her to the top of the queue.

'You need to take her to Dubrovnik immediately,' Doctor Marković said after he examined her. 'I will write a letter of urgency. They will do more tests.'

He said no more than that, but he could not look my brothers directly in the eyes and so they knew it was not good.

Only our neighbour, Ivan, had a car, so Anton asked him to drive Mama to Dubrovnik. In the blistering heat, we drove for three hours through the mountains. I sat with Mama in the back seat and held her hand throughout the journey. She lay as still as the terrible roads allowed. Her face had now turned a waxy shade of pale. Her breathing came in short, sharp pants. Her lids closed to mere slits but the blue of her eyes still shone through the small gaps. Anton willed the journey to pass more quickly. He looked back at Mama and saw a tear streak down and settle in the dimple of her cheek. When he reached back to hold her free hand, their fingers met and Anton told me afterwards that he felt a spark of electricity run through him. Mama inhaled deeply, closed her eyes and allowed her head to rest to the side. She passed away, just as Ivan pulled up to the doors of the hospital.

It is a strange thing to see your father cry. He did so for many weeks after Mama died. And if Baba Ana had not slept much in the past, now she did not sleep at all. She just sat on a wicker chair, drowning under the weight of her black clothes. She toyed with her rosary beads, moving them from one hand to the other. Just like Mama did in her final weeks, she too stared at the white cross that sat overlooking our village on the top of Križevac. If it was a sign she was searching for, it never came. Still she stared and mouthed prayers for hours each day.

After that, it did not seem so hard to rise at four o'clock in the morning any more. My eyes would open wide in the hope of seeing Mama at the foot of my bed, her black hair hidden by a white headscarf, the dimple in her cheek more prominent with her wide smile. The nights I dreamt of her were the most difficult. For in these dreams, she seemed so real. She walked about our house doing chores. Always smiling. Always in good health.

'Look!' Veronika said in one of these dreams. 'Mama is here!'

And there she was, sitting on a chair, her elbows leaning against the table with a mug of hot tea in her hands.

'But she can't be here,' I responded. 'Mama is dead.'

'I know she is dead,' Veronika said. 'But look, she is here!'

It was perfect. Mama said nothing, only smiled. One by one, each member of the family came into the room and stood around the table looking at her. We knew it was not possible, but we didn't care because she was there and we could see her.

When I woke, for those first few minutes – my mind trapped between the dream and reality – I believed she was still in the room. The pain of realising she was not there, and never could be again, cut through me like a sharp knife and left me weeping.

***

And now, still, the sadness remains. Still I cry. If I could just see her for one moment. If I could reach out, let my fingers sweep across her face. Oh, Mama, how I miss you. How things have changed since you have gone. This is the time I need you most. You would know what I should do. You would help me understand why all this is happening in our tiny village. And why it is happening to me.

I have no idea why I was chosen. On that first day, I attended Holy Mass and joined in with the procession for the Feast Day of St John the Baptist. As people returned to their homes, Veronika told me that my friend Marta was looking for me. She needed help bringing some sheep home. I found

Marta up in the hills and helped with her chore. Afterwards, we walked through the vineyards, hoping to see our other friends, but nobody was around. Everyone was indoors, preparing for dinner. But I did not want to go home. I did not want to be called on for any chores. So we walked some more and talked about sharing pizza later. Marta talked about becoming a teacher and about how she would love to write a book.

'You will need to be careful what you write about,' I laughed. 'If it is the wrong thing, those communists will put it on a pile and burn it so that the words never reach a single eye.'

We came to the hill of Podbrdo and rested on a small stone wall. Marta had her back to the hill but something caught my eye through the bushes. I saw a shimmering light that slipped through the gaps of the leaves.

'What are you looking at?' Marta asked as she turned around.

I did not reply.

'What is it, Iva?'

My eyes tried to focus and follow the trail of this light. When I stood up and began moving towards it, Marta followed me. The stones moved under my feet but a gentle force made my body feel lithe and I climbed without any difficulty. I could hear Marta behind me calling my name, but I did not respond.

When I came to a clearing, I had to blink three times to make sure my eyes were not playing tricks on me. This cannot be possible, I thought.

There before me, floating a few inches above the rocks, was the most beautiful young lady I had ever seen. A beauty that seemed too difficult to explain in words. Her long hair was jet black and her eyes were a brilliant blue, like the oceans I dreamed of seeing. Over her greyish-blue dress, a lily-white veil cascaded down her back and above her head was a crown of twelve gold stars. In her arms, she held a baby who did not move or cry.

'What are you doing up here?' I heard Marta call from behind.

Though I did not want to take my eyes away from this vision, I turned to Marta and said, 'Look. It is the Gospa.'

Suddenly I felt rain on my head as the wind rustled my skirt. Marta looked in the direction I was pointing and though her mouth fell open, no words escaped. My heart began to beat fast beneath my chest and I felt fear creep in.

'Do you see?' I asked Marta.

But Marta did not reply.

And I did not turn back.

I took Marta's hand and we raced back down the hill.

When we told our friends, they did not believe us. They chomped on apples they had picked from a tree and laughed when we spoke about what we saw.

'Do not mock us,' Marta said sternly and our friends suddenly grew quiet. 'Come see for yourself.'

And so the six of us went to the hill. Six of us saw the beautiful woman. Six of us moved with caution as she gestured at us to come closer.

'Now do you see?' Marta asked, but nobody answered.

All six of us turned around and ran down the hill.

We slept little that night and the next morning tried to go about our day as normal, though it was not easy. That evening, at the same time, we went to the hill once again and came face to face with the same vision. She gestured for us to come closer and we did. But this time it was different. This time she spoke to us.

***

They come in their thousands now. People who know that most of us do not understand their language but continue to talk nonetheless. Anton has taken to sleeping by the doorway at night. This morning, like every morning now, Veronika steps over his curled-up body and pulls the door ajar, just enough so she can count the heads outside.

'There must be fifty today, Iva,' she says as she rushes back over to the bed and climbs under the covers, pulling them way over our heads.

'Tell them to go away,' I moan. 'Tell them they have the wrong house, that it is further down the road. Show them Stela's house. Tell them she is the girl they look for.'

Veronika throws her head back and laughs. 'I don't think Stela's mama would be too happy with that.'

'Why not? Does she not love all this attention that has come to our village?' I joke.

For some time we lie on the bed as Anton wakes and goes outside to try and disperse the crowd. Veronika and I guess the countries they come from and wonder about how they live.

'I bet they live in grand castles and feast on turkey every single night,' Veronika says.

'I bet they have rooms full of clothes which they only wear once,' I say.

'Do you see their scarfs, Iva?' Veronika asks.

I know she is not just talking about the patterned scarfs they wear around their necks like American film stars, but also the bright T-shirts and colourful runners. Stela's mother has housed some of the pilgrims and Stela tells us of the pink soaps they wash with. There is no need for Stela's mother to queue for a meagre heap of coffee; the pilgrims bring jarloads with them, which they give to the families they stay with. They do not think twice about sharing. It is how they show their gratitude to the families putting them up.

Outside, Anton can only communicate with the pilgrims by waving his hands as though he is attempting to direct a herd of sheep. He shakes his head when they ask a question. 'No speak English. No speak English,' he says. After some time, they leave. My guess is that they have moved on to find the houses of my friends who also see the visions, hoping to get a better reception from them.

'What does she look like?' Veronika asks.

'I have already told you this a thousand times,' I say.

She is lying flat on the bed, her eyes are closed and she holds her knees close to her chest.

'Tell me again, Iva. Please.'

And I know that when I speak, it is Mama who Veronika pictures in her head.

'She is young.'

'Younger than Mama?'

'Yes. And she has long hair so black it is like the night sky without the stars.

'Go on.'

Veronika's eyes are still closed.

'Her eyes are like sapphires and she wears a greyish-blue gown with a long white veil.'

'Does she float, Iva?'

'Yes, I cannot see her feet but she floats on a small cloud. And on her head sits a crown of twelve stars.'

'What does she sound like when she speaks?'

'Her voice is soft. Her words are almost like music. And she is so beautiful, Veronika, so much so that I can never describe it properly. There are no words in our language – in any language – to describe her beauty. But she is beautiful because she loves so much. It is beauty of the soul.'

'Does she know I am your sister?'

'Of course she knows. What a silly question. She knows everything. And she loves everyone too. She says we are all her children – each and every one of us – and she says that if we knew how much she truly loved us we would cry tears of joy.'

Veronika is quiet. I see her swallow hard.

'Do you ask her about Mama?' she croaks, curling onto her side so that she faces away from me.

I lie down on the bed, wrap my arm over hers and nuzzle into the back of my sister's neck. If I hold her tight enough, the shaking will stop, but the tears that pour from her eyes flow fast and heavy down her face.

'Of course I ask her about Mama,' I say. 'Every time I see her, I ask.'

'What does she say?'

She turns her head so she can look me in the eyes. Within both our bodies there is a painful hollowness. It is the absence of our mother who no longer dries our tears or ties up our hair. That emptiness cannot be filled, no matter how many kind words pour in. It will always be there.

'She tells me she is happy. Although we are all sad, Veronika, Mama is happy. This is what she says.'

I stroke Veronika's hair and move my fingertips across her wet cheeks. Her body is exhausted, her eyes raw. Outside, there is no sound and Anton comes in to tell us that the last of the pilgrims have moved on.

'Now maybe we can get on with our day,' he says.

Veronika sits up. 'I wish I could see her one last time,' she says.

'So do I, Veronika,' I say. 'So do I.'

7

YUGOSLAVIA

JEN

Ma always said that she'd love to go on one of those package holidays. Mr and Mrs Baldwin went on one to Spain a few years back where they stayed in an apartment block taller than the Ballymun flats, only they had a view of the Mediterranean when they woke in the morning and not a burnt-out car in an overgrown field.

They brought their own powdered milk with them, because they'd heard from the tour operator that the milk over there had a funny aftertaste. Mrs Baldwin had been tempted to bring a pound of Kerrygold butter too, but Mr Baldwin told her there wasn't a hope in hell of her keeping that in the case with all the clothes. 'Sure, it would melt the minute we hit the tarmac in Malaga,' he said. 'I'm sure they'll have a bit of butter over there, anyway, Irene; it's Spain we're going to, not Kathmandu, for cryin' out loud.' Mrs Baldwin was especially relieved when our other neighbour, Mrs O'Driscoll, told her they sold plenty of cans of Coca-Cola over there. That's what she needed when she was lying on the sandy beach. Not for drinking, mind you. For her tan. Apparently, if you weren't bothered by the sticky feeling, you could pour it over your legs and arms and get a great colour. That's what Mrs O'Driscoll had done when she went to the Costa del Sol the previous year and came back browner than the locals. 'They were all speaking to me in Spanish over there,' she laughed. 'They thought I was one of their own!'

Ma had felt like the odd one out being stuck in the middle of Mrs O'Driscoll and Mrs Baldwin sharing holiday tips – 'Don't drink the water unless it's boiled' – and tanning solutions – 'Bring plenty of Sudocrem for the burns, especially on the shoulders. Last year I got one blister that was so big it looked like a fried egg. And when it burst, it took half the skin off my shoulder with it.'

'I'll throw you in a few brochures, Sarah,' Irene Baldwin said to Ma. 'They have some great deals through England if you book a year in advance.'

Ma would take the neon-coloured brochures and put them out on the kitchen table and she'd sit there for hours, sipping tea and turning pages. When Da came in from the shed in the evening, he'd pretend not to notice.

'Did you get the evening paper?' he'd ask, sitting opposite her.

'I forgot,' Ma would say. 'Why don't you have a read of these instead?'

'Don't tell me those aul ones have been barking on about their holidays abroad again,' Da would say. He'd barely glance at the brochure or the page it was opened on before throwing it to the far end of the table. 'Who would look after things if I was to go gallivanting off on a holiday? And where do you think I'd get the money from to pay for something like that?'

And so the conversation was over before it even began. Ma wouldn't mention it again, but she would hold on to Irene Baldwin's brochures, keeping them in the drawer beneath the cutlery. Months after she died, when we realised there was no coal, Da went to that drawer and took the brochures out to use for the fire. As the flames burned and stretched high, we watched tall apartment buildings, sandy beaches and crystal blue seas disappear forever before our eyes.

I think about these brochures as we arrive at Dublin Airport. Even though it is still too early for most, throngs of people stand inside the departures area, searching for check-in desks and ladies with clipboards. As we try to navigate our way through the people, Da stops dead in his tracks, which leads to people banging into him from behind. Above the noise, he can hear someone shouting his name. I can hear it, too.

'It's coming from over there,' I say, pointing my finger in the direction of a group of people huddled at the farthest end of the check-in desks.

'For the love of Chr–' Da says when he sees the group of people. Not one of them looks younger than sixty-five. 'What have I got myself into?'

'Da, you've got to move. You're blocking the way,' I say as people nudge their way around us.

'Mr Carthy! Mr Carthy!' a man calls.

It is Louis, Aunt Suzanne's friend, who is standing in front of the group with a brown cowboy hat, waving a placard with a crucifix in the middle of it.

Seeing him, Da turns around and tries to push his way back through the people, but I catch his arm and pull him towards the group.

'Not him,' he says. 'Of all people, not him.'

'Da,' I say. 'Come on. You promised. You promised you'd make an effort.'

'I can't do it, Jen,' he whispers. 'I don't belong with these misfits and religious freaks. And I certainly don't want to be within a foot of your man Louis. Your aunt has some explaining to do. She said nothing about him coming. Never mentioned it once. I'll kill her.'

The group are all staring at us thanks to Louis' shouting. It is obvious that Da is ignoring Louis' calls and my cheeks flush pink as I feel several pairs of eyes study us from afar.

'Please, Da,' I urge.

Closer to him now, I can smell the malt whiskey that lingers on his breath. I don't question him about it, because I know he will only tell me a lie, saying it's for a bit of courage, that he doesn't like flying.

When he nods I guide him slowly over to the group of pilgrims, who continue to just stare at us for what seems like an eternity. When we queue up in a line before the check-in desk, I notice two other people who are younger than the rest of the group. There is a woman with tightly cropped hair, maybe a few years younger than Da, and in the buggy she wheels ahead of her is a child of about two, who is sleeping soundly despite the noise in the departures area. I wonder if the over sixty-fives think that she and I have made a mistake and booked the wrong flight.

***

The plane shakes for the entire three-hour journey. Da presses his nose hard against the window and only pulls back from it when the drinks tray comes around. The landing is difficult, the plane rocking from side to side before bouncing onto a loose gravel-filled runway. Da seems disappointed that we have survived.

'Great,' he says sarcastically when the pilgrims begin to clap and bless themselves, 'we made it.'

Next up is a three-hour bus ride. At first, we pass through the city of Dubrovnik with its limestone streets and stony beaches. Then we glide along a narrow road on a rocky mountainside. Down below, beneath the rough cliffs, there is a glistening sea – the Adriatic, I hear the guide say.

As we travel inland, small villages sit on hilltops and look down onto the rough road on which we travel. At times, the guide tries to talk above the noise of the chugging bus, but her English is broken and the noise of the rocking coach means that most people give up trying to hear what she is saying and set about praying instead.

Da just sits at the back of the bus like a bold schoolboy. I tug at the sleeve of his shirt, urging him to peel his eyes away from his feet and look at the views outside our bus. But he just closes his eyes and turns the other way. I call over to him once or twice but he doesn't respond, though I know he is not asleep. My da doesn't sleep much any more. I overheard him tell Aunt Suzanne once that his dreams give him too much trouble.

Eventually, with the sun setting, the bus pulls into a narrow, dusty street in a small village. We are here, the guide announces. We all get off the bus and are led to the houses where we are staying. The one where Da and myself are to stay is bigger than our house at home and there are cats roaming around on top of the flat roof. A woman stands outside. She has hardly a word of English but she seems pleased to see us arrive and we go inside.

'*Molim. Molim.* Please. Please,' she says, as she points to the bread and tea laid out on the handmade lace tablecloth. In the corner of the room an old woman, all dressed in black, sits looking at the foreigners invading her home. She has few teeth but her eyes are wide and alive.

Louis comes over to where Da and I are standing. He will be staying in this house, too.

'Just to warn you,' Louis says as he grabs himself a cup, 'it's goat's milk.'

Da doesn't answer. He doesn't even look at Louis. He just picks his cup up from the wooden table and walks away, like he was walking away from a rotten smell. Louis fiddles nervously with the cowboy hat on his head.

There are seven of us staying in this house – on top of the actual family – and there is only one shower for us all to share. I hear someone say that the toilet is outside and is made of wood. When we go upstairs we discover that the shower is in the room next to ours. Outside, the church bells toll, and I see Da shake his head.

The walls in our bedroom are pure white and bare, except for a crucifix with the figure of Jesus, his body limp and helpless. There are two low, wooden single beds, with thin mattresses and one flat pillow on each. A window that only a four-year-old child might squeeze through is the only way the air gets in, making the room hot and claustrophobic.

We aren't in the room five minutes when Da leaves. He tells me he is going to find a bar, that he needs a drink. At least he's honest, I suppose. After he goes, I stare at the small suitcase that sits upright in the centre of the floor, still waiting to be emptied. It's the one I packed last night. I look around and think about emptying it out, but I notice that there are no drawers or wardrobes in the room. An old bedside locker with a Bible on top is the only piece of furniture.

As I stand here, in this tiny room, with the crucifix hanging on the wall and the Bible sitting on the bedside locker, I wonder how my da will find a pub in this tiny village, particularly now, with the sun having set. There is no street lighting to guide his way, after all, but I know he'll keep walking until he finds somewhere to get a drink.

I'm too tired to go after him. Not tonight. Not here.

Chanting slips through the small window as I strip to just my T-shirt and crawl into the low bed, pulling the white sheet up to my chin. My eyes are too heavy to keep open. Things will be better in the morning. Da will be different after this trip. Aunt Suzanne told me so.

It's too early to sleep but I'm going to anyway. I know there's no point worrying about him. He'll come back when he's ready, when the drink has taken hold and when his thoughts have been numbed. He'll lie down in the other bed, thinking I'm asleep, and I'll hear him talk to Ma.

'Why did you leave me, Sarah?' he will say. 'Why did you go out that night?'

And I'll keep my eyes shut tight, trying hard to slow down my breathing and stay still. Then, when I know he's sleeping, I'll whisper a soft prayer, asking Ma to make him better, to heal his pain, to bring him back. For I know my da left me around the same time as Ma did. And although I know that she's gone forever, my da is not.

8

YUGOSLAVIA

CHARLIE

If there's one thing I know, it's that a hangover is ten times worse in twenty-seven degrees of heat. That's twenty-seven degrees of heat at nine o'clock in the bloody morning. I don't know where I ended up last night, but the beer was strong enough to do what it's meant to do. It's damn hard to see in front of your two feet when everything is jet black. It's even harder when there are no pavements and no beginning or end to the road – and you have a good load of beer in you. And then there is the sound of those crickets chirping close by. You can't see them but you can feel it when they jump onto your shorts and slide down your legs.

I walked and walked for what felt like an eternity, possibly in circles. Somehow, I managed to find my way back to the house. I could have dreamt this but I've a vague recollection of your man Louis standing at the door of the house, his arms folded and eyes weary with the lack of sleep. His string vest was too tight for his upper body but his striped pyjama bottoms hung off his hips and swamped his skinny legs. He could have been standing there for hours for all I knew. Above the house, I could see that the sky was starting to change shades. A faint light was rising.

'I've nottin' ta shay to you,' I slurred as I brushed past him.

But he followed me all the same, trailing as I trudged up the stairs. When I stopped at the top, he pointed to the room where Jen was. He waited until I got inside and only when the door slammed shut did I hear the slap of his footsteps.

'Get up, Da, get up,' she roars into my ear. And me upside down and hanging off the side of the bed, fully clothed and practically frothing at the mouth. It's all right when we're at home and I'm in my own room and I've time to splash a bit of water on my face before she wakes. But we're sharing a room here, so that's a different kettle of fish.

I had asked Suzanne to get me a separate room, and sure you'd swear I'd asked her to walk on hot coals. 'What? Are you out of your mind, Charlie Carthy! You needn't think it's a singles holiday you're going on, for crying out loud. It's bonding with your daughter you need to be doing on this trip,' she said.

'But Jen is a teenager now. Maybe she'd prefer her own bit of space, instead of sharing with her aul fella,' I tried.

'Pffaw!' she said as she brushed her newly permed hair out of her face. 'Teenager is right, Charlie, and yet it's Jen that's chasing you out of the pubs and mopping up your vomit, not the other way round.'

It stung, all right. And I know Suzanne regretted it even before the insult left her mouth. Part of me knew that she loved to play the over-protective mother role, because she never had the chance to have any kids herself. Another part of me knew that she missed Sarah as much as I did and saw her live on through Jen: in her mannerisms, her looks and her demeanour.

The bedroom's a pokey room with no air. I suppose I'll just have to get used to Jen screaming in my ear just after that damn cockerel in the yard outside completes his morning wake-up call. Your man Louis is another matter. If I can keep my fists by my sides I'll be lucky. And I'll have to bite my tongue too. What I won't say to him if I get the chance.

The shower is icy cold with only a trickle of water spitting out from a hole. I let out a bit of a scream when the water first hits me; I'd say the whole house must have heard it, particularly given what Jen says when I meet her downstairs for breakfast: 'I told you we need to wake up earlier.'

'How much earlier could we possibly get up?' I ask as I sit down opposite Jen and look around the breakfast room at the sprightly sixty-five-year-olds devouring the food laid out before them: cuts of freshly baked bread, cubes of thick butter, luscious homemade jams and large eggs are all spread out on a handmade lace cloth. Jugs of freshly squeezed orange juice, the bits floating on top, and pots of strong black tea are placed down on each table by the woman of the house who looks like she hasn't seen a good meal herself in months.

'I know, I know. It's goat's milk,' I say when I see Louis approach.

Jen kicks me under the table. 'Da, don't be rude,' she whispers.

I keep my eyes low and crack my spoon off the side of the egg, but he stays there, peering down at me. The egg is runny, though I prefer them hard. I begin to eat it anyway.

'How are you feeling this morning?' he asks.

I keep my head hung low, hoping he'll move on, but he's still standing there. Still talking.

'I hope the room is all right for you both,' he says and then his voice goes quiet, like he doesn't want anyone else to hear. 'I know it's basic but then again it's not a five-star cruise we're on. It's a pilgrimage. And with pilgrimage comes sacrifice.'

A piece of egg gets stuck in my throat, causing me to spit it out onto the table.

Sacrifice, he says. *Sacrifice.* The word just hangs in the air, looming above my head, mocking me.

'Maybe you'll both join us this morning for a walk through the vineyards?' Louis continues. 'After that, we'll be going up to the small mountain for some morning prayers,' he says, focusing his attention on me. 'It might clear the head a bit.'

'We would love that,' Jen pipes up, and I'm wondering how it came about that my fourteen-year-old daughter began answering questions for me.

'Are you out of your mind?' I say after he leaves. 'The last thing I need for company is him of all people.'

But she says nothing, just gets up from the table and walks out the door.

***

Outside, the heat is intense. It hits me the minute I step out. When I turn my back on the sun, the glare of it stings the small patch of baldness that has sneakily found its way onto the back of my head over the past few years.

Louis throws a beaten cowboy hat in my direction, one that looks uncannily like his. 'I always bring a spare one.'

'For the love of ...' I mutter, catching it.

'Da,' Jen pinches me on the elbow, 'put it on and don't be so rude.'

And Louis is looking at me in such a way that he seems to be pleading with me to wear his hat.

'Thanks,' Jen says to Louis as I put it on my head. I can see the relief in her face that I haven't embarrassed her too much on this trip, just yet.

We trail behind the group, the dust rising up around our legs. Some shuffle their feet, others slide through the dirt, but Jen and I stomp at the ground as though digging for something buried. Five or so minutes later, we stand at the start of a maze of vineyards, beyond which fields of dry grass stretch on as far as the horizon. As we begin to move through the vineyards, I feel like we're almost gliding along a lush green sea.

Ahead, the chanting of prayers mixes with the lyrical chirping of sparrows. As we follow in the footsteps of those who go before us, we pass an old woman sitting on a plastic crate. Her body is draped in heavy black clothes but there is no perspiration visible on her brow. In her hands she has some knitted boots and mitts that might fit only a newborn baby. She holds out her wares to the passing pilgrims, who smile and nod but buy nothing. Behind her, a girl about Jen's age stands protectively over the old woman, a steely look in her eye that tells me she is unimpressed with the influx of strangers to her small village.

Louis runs back from the top of the line and places a dollar bill in the old woman's hand but refuses to take the small knitted boots that she is holding out to him.

'Have you ever seen her?' he whispers to the old woman kneeling beside her.

The old woman smiles and answers back in Croatian.

'Of course she see her,' the girl says in broken English.

'Has she ever seen who?' I ask Jen as Louis makes his way back up to the top of the line of pilgrims.

'I don't know,' she says.

'The Gospa,' I hear the girl call out to us as she offers the old woman some water from a cup. 'She say, yes, she see the Gospa.'

The air fills with bell tolls, the sound travelling over from where the two steeples of a church can be seen rising high above the green landscape.

'The church of St James,' Jen tells me as she flicks through an information leaflet she found on the breakfast table earlier. 'St James is the patron saint of pilgrims.'

Though the church stands tall, imposing itself on the small village, it's the mountain behind it that dominates the scene. Rising high, it hosts a large cross on its peak. I can just about see people who resemble small dots as they make the steep ascent.

'Maybe we'll climb that while we're here,' Jen says with more enthusiasm than I want to hear.

'Have we much farther to go?' I ask, running my tongue across my lips, trying to put some moisture into my mouth. The sooner I get to the bottom of the smaller mountain, the sooner I can leave Jen with the group and slip off for 'the cure'. I can already taste the strong yeasty flavour of the local beer flowing down my throat. And it will only take a few sups before my shoulders relax, the fresh drink mingling with the dregs of the previous night's to fizz and sparkle inside me. There's a mighty comfort in the deadening of thought that it brings, when surrounding sounds become muffled and faces blur. I'm at my happiest then, if there even is such a thing, when the world is a mere glimpse through a narrow keyhole of a locked door.

I still don't know how I managed to end up here in this strange land of limp fairytales where few words are spoken, English or otherwise. The locals have little, yet give what they have to us – invaders of their once-quiet farming village. In some of their eyes I see suspicion. I see a contempt brewing towards every new arrival. Others are too entrenched in prayer to notice, even if they were to loosen their grip on the wooden rosary beads or raise their heads from staring at their feet.

The country is under communist rule and yet I'm told they flock to the church, to the mountainside and to confession. It seems their faith is only strengthened by the threat from those who want to take it away. And I'll admit I'm envious of their defiance, their bravery. I'm sure I possessed those traits some time in the past when I had an ally by my side and confidence in my step. But that was before I tripped and fell. I haven't gotten up since. And I don't think I ever will.

9

DUBLIN

SUZANNE

I was worried about sending Charlie off to the village. He is a sceptic at the best of times, though it wasn't like I was trying to shove it down his throat. I just felt it would be time away from the house, time he could spend with Jen.

Louis' jaw dropped when I told him he was going. He paced around the shop floor of The Humble Jumble and told me he wasn't sure he could look him in the eye, let alone spend a week with him. Not after everything that had happened. At the same time, he said he felt a responsibility towards him, and to Jen.

The past year hadn't been kind to any of them. Not Louis, not Charlie, not Jen.

'I just don't want him to hate the place,' I said. 'And I want him at least to make the effort. If not for himself, then for Jen.'

Louis told me not to worry, that he would leave him be for the most part, while keeping an eye on him all the same. 'I've seen it all before, Suzanne,' he added. 'They're only short of being dragged there kicking and screaming, and their first thought when they step off the bus is how the hell they are going to get out of there. I've seen the eyes roll in the head, heard the tuts and sniggers from under their breath. I've seen the way they look at other pilgrims, as though they belong to a different species. They'll avoid the mountains, turn their backs on the church, and if they fail to find the only bar in the village, then they'll sit in their rooms for most of the day staring at the white walls as though this will somehow make the time go quicker.'

It doesn't last long, though, he added. Something always changes.

'Don't ask me why,' he said. 'But I've seen more transformations come halfway into the week than any other time. Maybe it's something to do with the third day. And it's best if you leave them to their own devices. If they don't want to stick to the programme, then let them be. They'll find their own way eventually, that's for sure. And the road they came in on becomes very different to the road on which they go home.'

And Louis certainly knew what he was talking about, as he has already visited the village several times. Sure, it was his initial excitement about visiting the village that got the pilgrimages from Ireland to Yugoslavia off the ground. He was convinced he had to visit the village as soon as we finished watching the videotape that time.

The following Monday, he asked me to open up The Humble Jumble while he took the bus into the city centre. Just off O'Connell Street, down a side street not far from the River Liffey, Louis found a small travel agency run by a giant Russian man whose thick arms looked like they might burst out of the shirt he wore.

'You want go where?' he asked Louis from behind the small chintzy desk that was piled high with brochures and foreign-worded documents. A glass ashtray overflowing with chewed butts sat on top of the pile. The odd one was stained with red lipstick but, other than that, Louis couldn't see any sign that anyone else worked there.

'It's a place in Yugoslavia,' Louis told him, 'beside Hungary and Romania.'

'I know where is, for goodness sake,' the Russian snapped back and Louis was sure he got a faint whiff of vodka from his breath. 'Why there?'

And so he explained it to him, as best he could, while the Russian sat there with his thick elbows resting on the desk and his fingers rubbing the stubble on his chin. He didn't interrupt, even though his eyes seemed to lose focus at times. The office was so dark and small that he had a large lamp, the light of which found its way onto Louis' face. There was a brief moment where he wondered if the Russian was going to pull a tape recorder out from underneath his desk, as if this were an interrogation. When Louis stopped talking, the Russian continued to stare, as though he was expecting something more from him.

'I can't get you to this place,' he said after a while.

'What do you mean you can't get me to this place?' Louis said. 'Surely there must be a way to get there. It can't be impossible.'

When he stood up from behind the desk, the Russian had to stoop so his head wouldn't touch off the low ceiling. He tried to squeeze through the gap between the desk and the wall, and when he realised it wasn't going to be possible, he pushed the desk out so it almost hit off Louis' legs. On his feet, he wore steel-toed army boots that were polished so well Louis could almost see his reflection in them.

'Mr – what your name, please?' the Russian asked.

'Louis,' he replied.

'Mr Louis,' the Russian began.

'No, just Louis is fine.'

'Mr Louis,' he said again and Louis decided not to correct him, 'I would love bring you on flight and take you to place you talk about. That is my job. That is what I do. But I cannot take you to place because there is no route convenient and there is no price that is affordable for journey. Maybe you go to Spain like all other Irish people. It is less complicated than Yugoslavia. No regime over there.'

Louis wondered if the Russian had listened to anything he'd said to him since he came through the door.

'You don't understand Mr – what is your name again?'

'Boris. My name is Boris.'

'Of course it is. Okay, you don't understand Mr Boris.'

'No, just Boris.'

'Sorry, Mr Boris. You don't under–'

'No. Just BORIS.'

'Boris. Sir,' Louis pleaded, even though he was tired of talking in circles. 'You must have some information about how I can get there. Even if you can't get me there yourself, you must know someone who can.'

Later, when Louis was recounting the meeting to me, he told me that he could have sworn the room grew smaller at that precise moment. Seemingly, he had touched a delicate nerve when he mentioned that maybe someone else could organise travel for him to Yugoslavia.

'Are you say I cannot do job right?'

'Now, I never said that,' Louis said holding his two hands up in the air.

'But you instituted it, no?'

'Instituted? Ah, you mean insinuated.'

'Yes, that's what I said. *Instinuated* it.'

Louis felt a migraine coming on.

'Boris, I'm not suggesting for one minute that you are incapable of doing your job, but the simple fact is that I want to travel to a destination that you say you can't bring me to. It's very simple. If you can't put me on a flight to this place then I will find someone who can!'

Boris walked back over to his desk and reached underneath. The sound of glass bottles clanging together explained the faint smell of vodka. He tugged and pulled, ducking his head down every so often. When he surfaced, it was with a large rolled-up piece of paper that he clutched tight. Then he brushed his arm across his desk, sending all its contents, including the mound of ash and cigarette butts, spilling onto the floor.

'Now,' he said as he rolled the map of Europe out onto the table, using heavy tumbler glasses to hold down the four corners. 'Show me where you want go.'

The Russian pulled the lamp down lower so it illuminated the map. From his shirt pocket, Louis took out his glasses and let them sit low on the bridge of his nose. His finger moved across the page until it landed on Yugoslavia.

'It is big country, no?' Boris asked. 'What part?'

Both men ran their fingers around the outline of the country, moving from east to west. When they had settled on the area in question, Boris flopped down onto the chair and rubbed at his chin. Louis had set him a little challenge. Outside, people strolled by: men in suits nipping out to the GPO nearby to mail a letter or purchase a stamp; women window-shopping for clothes they could never afford while pushing babies in wide prams. Not once did anyone turn their heads in the direction of Boris' travel agency, nor did the bell on the door jingle to announce a new customer. Louis' guess was that he sat alone for most of the working day, taking this map out every so often and waiting for someone to enter so he could show it to them. Boris raised his hands to his temples as he closed his eyes. Then he sat upright with a bolt.

'Okay,' he said, pointing the stubby index finger of his right hand up to his head. 'I have idea.'

'Go on,' Louis urged.

The Russian pulled his chair in tight under the desk and grabbed at Louis' wrist to pull him down low. 'I will get you to this place,' he began.

'Wonderful!' Louis replied with a grin that showed off too much gum.

'I will get someone to fly plane to Yugoslavia.'

Louis felt his jaw lower. He was beginning to regret ever stepping into Boris' office. 'I beg your pardon?'

'I will get plane,' the Russian continued. 'Charter plane. I will charter plane.'

'Ah,' Louis said, feeling somewhat relieved.

'But you must fill plane for me before it flies.'

'I beg your pardon?'

'You must find seventy, no, eighty people to fly on this plane and we will get you to village.'

'How am I going to find eighty people to come with me to this place?' Louis asked.

'I don't know,' Boris said as he raised two hands up in the air. 'You speak so wonderfully about this country and what is happening there, surely everyone wants to go, no?'

A part of Louis wondered if Boris was simply amusing himself to pass yet another monotonous day. Maybe he thought Louis was just another frustrated retiree, who had nothing better to do than hop from travel agency to travel agency across the city centre enquiring about the most unusual Eastern European countries he could possibly think of. Both of them stood there staring, trying to gauge each other's genuineness.

'How much will all this cost?' Louis eventually asked.

'I cannot tell you that yet,' Boris said. 'I must negotiate with contacts. But I know it will be small aircraft, possibly eighty seater, because I'm thinking it best to fly into Mostar, a military airport. The runway is not big enough for larger plane, so we charter small one. And Mostar, this is closest for where you want go. Only thirty minutes to village from this airport.'

'Just a few minutes ago you were acting as though you had never even heard of the place,' Louis said. 'Now you're talking about hiring an aircraft to fly into the most convenient airport!'

'Please, Mr Louis,' Boris smiled to reveal a mouth of perfectly straight teeth, all white bar a gold one in the back of his mouth. 'I read newspapers, too. And I'm travel agent, for goodness sake. It is my job to know these things. If you fill me planeload of pilgrims, I will make sure you all arrive there safely.'

Initially, Louis thought it would be impossible to convince that many people to fork out their hard-earned cash on a trip to a place of which they had never heard. But somehow, things just came together. Father Dennehy, the local parish priest, let Louis put an advertisement in the weekly parish newsletter.

'Anything that keeps them coming to Mass on a Sunday,' Fr Dennehy said. 'Sure, I haven't been on a pilgrimage since Lough Derg in seventy-three. To be honest, I swore I'd never go on one again after that. The fasting nearly killed me. But Yugoslavia sounds a bit more attractive, now that you mention it. Do you happen to have a spiritual director to accompany you on this trip?'

'I don't, Father,' Louis said. 'Would you be interested in coming along yourself?'

Word spread quickly and those who were supposed to go on the annual pilgrimage to Knock pulled out at the last minute, hearing there was something new on the cards.

Then the phone calls began to come in from outside of Dublin. Word had spread around the towns and cities as to what was going on in Yugoslavia. Copies had been made of the video Louis had watched with me and they were distributed to parishes around Ireland. There was hysteria in some of their voices as they rang the shop phone and plied Louis with questions. But he couldn't answer them all and there was a sigh down the line from a lot of people when they heard the cost of the trip.

'Maybe not this year,' some said with an air of disappointment. 'But you'll let us know how you get on over there when you come back, won't you?'

A woman called Celestine, who lived on the outskirts of Galway, called to say she had thirty-five people from her parish and surrounding areas who wanted to travel. She was planning to get the bus over from Galway later that week with the cash for the trip strapped around her waist and secured with brown packaging tape.

'You look after the Jackeens, boy,' she said across the phone line, 'and I'll look after the Tribesmen.'

I told Louis I would go on this trip with him too, and before he knew it, we were all packed into a Russian eighty-seater plane with one middle-aged air hostess with no English and a fairly dishevelled-looking pilot who quite possibly could have been her son. The seats were covered in cigarette burns, the air stale and musty. No safety demonstration was provided, but sure enough, just as Boris the Russian promised, we made it to Yugoslavia.

That first trip was to become the first of many for Louis. He told me that, for him, the place has this strange magnetic pull.

'Once I go home,' he said, 'all I can think about is going back.'

When we were discussing Charlie going, Louis told me that it's on the bus there, among the pilgrims – the ones all caught in a soft trance with the chanting of prayer – that he always sees one who is slumped in the seat, almost drowning with each decade recited. They won't make eye contact, Louis said, nor polite conversation. In their heads they are wondering where they can get some of what we've been eating. Such joy shouldn't be found on faces. 'What has God ever done for me?' they'll say.

When they all properly meet in the little village and stories are shared, these reluctant pilgrims can see that they are not alone. But their transformation takes time. Things don't get rushed out there. There is a sense of urgency to arrive but once there, the days move slowly. It allows your body and mind to absorb the surroundings, something that is becoming less and less possible to do back home each day.

The same will be true for Charlie, Louis reassured me.

'He's a good man deep down inside, Louis,' I said to him the day before they left. 'And sure you know Jen yourself, she is just a gem of a child. Her little heart is broken since Sarah died. Smashed to pieces, it is. And her having to look at her da like that, too.'

Louis knows what it is like to lose someone, even though they are still physically there. He said he used to think that there were those who wanted to be helped and those who didn't. But he realises now that he was wrong. Everyone wants to be helped, he said; some just don't know how to ask for it.

10

YUGOSLAVIA

CHARLIE

I heard someone say that it's much hotter here in August, though I find it hard to believe it could get any warmer than this. To be honest, I think it was your man Louis that said it, the walking, one-stop travel shop. Everywhere I turn, he's there – his mouth open like he's ready for a conversation. It's like he has swallowed an encyclopedia on this place, though I doubt the village even makes it into any book. It's too insignificant to be worthy of a place on any map.

There's no hint of a breeze to give me a break from the clammy air. *Muggy*, my ma would call it, or *clammy*. If I'd any sort of respect left for myself, I'd be embarrassed at the wet patches on my T-shirt. Jen had to remind me earlier today to take a fresh one out of the case. And I did it because it seemed that it would mean something to her, that it would make her happy – though I didn't pick the Bowie one that Sarah bought me for my thirtieth birthday.

Even though your man Louis is really getting on my wick, I'm picking that stupid-looking hat up from the floor every morning and not taking it off till I go to bed. The fella behind the bar has my pint pulled before I walk in the door, and I'm sure it's because he can see the brown cowboy hat bobbing down the road before he can even see the rest of me.

We are three days here now. Every day, more and more people arrive. Not just the aul ones you'd expect on the average pilgrimage, but people younger than that. Even younger than me. You would wonder what could be dragging these kids out of their countries, out of the comfort of their beds. But then I think of back home and the lack of jobs. Sure, why wouldn't they want to throw on a pair of hiking boots, heave an over-sized backpack over their shoulders and start searching out miracles? Beats standing in the line for the scratcher every week, looking at the same old faces singing the same old tune.

But they're closing in on me all the same. Everyone is too close, too *in* on you – even here in these strangers' homes. I feel like one of those people who doesn't like crowds and who prefers to stay inside with no one for company but themselves. There are times when the vineyards are empty, I've noticed. It's usually around now, when the sun is at its hottest and those with any sense have gone inside. So I tell Jen that I need to get some time away on my own. And she looks at me as if to say, 'But Da, you are always on your own.' So I tell her that I'm just going to have a walk through the vineyards, to try and make it up the base of that small mountain. That would clear my head, I say. And I'll be back for food later. They serve the dinner at four o'clock in the house we're staying in, and I've a feeling that the family eats the leftovers once we're done. I don't even think they are sleeping in their own house. If they are, it's on the floor in the kitchen or on a makeshift bed in the shed out the back. They must sleep near the chickens and the rooster or close to the black cat and her litter of kittens.

The vineyards are only a few minutes away from the house. When I reach the gap at the start, I walk at a slow pace, pulling Louis' hat down over my eyes and letting my feet guide the way. The track is narrow with mounds of sandy-coloured earth at the edges. The leaves that grow on the vines are as green as the grass back home but more rubbery to touch. Small ants form long lines in places and keep me company as I walk. When I stand on a cockroach, the sound of his back snapping makes me wince. I stop there for a few seconds, listening for other sounds, and when I look down to the ground the cockroach has multiplied and they are all scurrying away from the path.

Even though I can't see them, I can hear the birds singing. They hide in faraway trees or on the ground beneath the shade of the vines. Their song fills the air. It's hard to tell how long I've been walking for; each twist and turn of the path looks the same. The mountain in the distance never seems to get closer. And I have a thirst on me like no other.

Eventually, the track ends like it began – abruptly coming to a dusty road. Up a slight hill is a cluster of small houses, one of them painted a deep blue. In places, roses grow out of the ground and climb up stone walls, even though there is barely any earth to nourish the roots. Ahead, I can see a small group of backpackers looking in the direction of the sun. The four young men and two women speak with thick Scottish accents and interrupt one another as they talk. Their fingers point to the sky before they reach for the Polaroid cameras around their necks. One of them kneels down on his bare knees, not caring if the stones tear his skin. They ask each other to confirm what they see. If they are all seeing it, they say, then it can't be their eyes playing tricks.

'Can you see it?' one of the lads asks when I come up from behind.

'Not a thing,' I say, even though I don't know what he is talking about.

I am eyeing up a small stone wall. It's just the right height for me to sit on for a bit. I can feel my feet swelling inside my runners and want the relief of ripping off the shoes and letting them breathe.

'Can you see it, Fergus?' one of the Scots asks again for the umpteenth time.

'I can, Malachy. It's unbelievable,' his friend replies, 'it is a brilliant white. So perfectly round. And it's spinning so fast, over and over again.'

At the stone wall, I peel my socks off. The man named Malachy looks at me with arched eyebrows.

'Can you really not see that?' he asks again.

'No,' I reply, even though my eyes are cast down to my feet.

They move on after a while, towards the mountain with the white cross on top. When they are out of sight, I look up to the sky, but all I can see is the fiery orange ball of the sun slipping in and out of thin clouds. Already I had heard the other pilgrims talk, especially after dinner, when they were walking in groups towards the grounds of the church and there was an audience gathered. Some spoke of spinning suns that turned a brilliant white, resembling the host they received at Mass. Others talked of rosary beads made of the cheapest metal turning gold in their hands. Suzanne had told me about something similar happening to a pair of beads that some priest gave her on one of her trips here. I didn't care to look when she put them on the table.

Some people claimed to have had their own personal apparition of some religious icon, be it Padre Pio or the Virgin Mary. There was one fella who said he could only see grey in the sun when everyone else saw white. 'That's because you haven't gone to confession yet,' someone suggested, and the poor gullible fella headed straight for the church. I'd said nothing as they rambled on. But I could see Jen watching them as they spoke, letting the nonsense fill her young mind. I'll be quick to tell her they're nothing but fairytales and theatrics when I get the chance. She might be a quiet young one, but she's no fool. At least I hope she's not, anyway.

There is a house across from the stone wall where I sit, with a boy sitting cross-legged on the doorstep. He reminds me of a young, dark-haired Francis Nelligan, the way he is looking at me. It's as though he is wondering what it would be like to be someone else for a day. His eyes bore into me and after a few minutes he leaps up and runs into the house. When he comes back out, he walks across to where I am sitting with a cup in his hand. He holds it out and I don't pause to think about what it is as I gulp it down. It's wet and cold and that is all that matters.

Twice the young fella runs back into the house, each time returning with a fresh cup of water in his hands, which he holds out to me with great urgency. The base of his feet are white from dust, I notice during his sprints back towards the house, and his tan scrawny legs are bare except for a pair of high-leg shorts. He is only a slip of a thing, but his eyes are wide and clear and his face bright. He probably spends his days sitting on the doorstep of his house, looking at all the foreigners walk by, mesmerised by their curiosity and awkwardness.

'Podbrdo,' he says with his finger pointing over my head.

I realise then that I have been sitting at the bottom of the small mountain all this time. Apparition Hill, they call it. Or so I'm told. The boy fills the cup up for the last time and then goes inside his house, closing the door behind him. And he likely thinks that by giving me the cups of water, he has prepared me for the climb – one I have no intention of doing.

My socks are soggy, even though I have tried to squeeze out the excess water. When I go to put my left foot back into the runner, it is as though the runner has shrunk a full size. I wonder where all the people are until I hear the bells ringing from the church in the distance and realise that they must have flocked to Mass for the second or third time that day.

Behind me, the small mountain waits. My intention had always been to walk to the base, just so I could tell Jen when I got back to the house. She might get off my case then, stop telling me I should be doing more while I'm here.

I don't know the time. Those bells have rung several times throughout the day. I try, but I can't get my feet into the runners, so I pick them up and turn to face the small mountain.

'It's more of a hill,' I mutter. I think about turning around and heading back the way I came, but something is urging me to go on.

As I ascend the hill, the terrain changes from the rough concrete of the road to small stones of different colours, shapes and sizes. It is easier to walk when I place the ball of my foot down first and only slightly let my heel touch the stones. The climb is steep for the first while. There is no obvious path but I concentrate on keeping my eyes down to search for any flat rocks on which to step. Wild bushes with prickly leaves grow on either side of the route I follow. Loose stones move beneath my feet and the beating of the sun makes the back of my neck sting. I have no company as I climb, everything is silent bar the singing from the unseen birds.

For the first time in a long time, I have space in my mind to think. I don't want the thoughts to come, though, because when they come, they stay for an age and chip away at my insides like a chisel. As I climb, her face returns to me. It is so vivid. When I close my eyes, she is smiling like she is the happiest girl in the world. 'You make me happy, Charlie Carthy,' she used to say. 'And you make me laugh too. Sure what else would a girl want?' She didn't know back then that all those times I made her smile would count for nothing when the tears came.

'I hate you, Charlie Carthy,' she told me the first time I'd gone missing after a day of drinking. 'I wish I'd never laid eyes on you.'

She tried to understand what it was like when the work dried up. I was barely scraping by on the funds my old man had left in the business account when he died.

'I could get a part-time job up in Cadbury's,' Sarah said one day, when I hadn't got the money for the weekend groceries. 'That will give us a boost. And I'll have loads of free time with Jen starting secondary school next year. There'll be no minding in her then.'

I wouldn't hear of it. It was my responsibility to look after them, not Sarah's. Things would pick up, I kept telling myself. Even though they never did.

I wasn't entitled to a penny from the dole. Self-employed, I was. Never paid a stamp in my life. Don't think I could've faced the embarrassment of going down there, anyway. It was bad enough my wife knew I couldn't make ends meet, but to have some young one behind a counter who was ten years my junior know too would have finished me off altogether. So I did the same routine every morning: let Sarah get the brew on until the tea looked like tar and go down to the shed at the back of the garden to stare at the books on the shelves for the day. No one came near me, except Jen when she came in from school, as I'd long since stopped hearing from the regular customers. They disappeared, just like the bricks of the old premises when it was demolished. I could have tried to negotiate a lease on a new premises but a huge part of me was terrified to enter into something in case I messed it up. I should have learned more on the business side of things from my old man instead of focusing so much on the craft. His ledgers were always impeccable, his handwriting so neat it could have belonged to a woman. Everything balanced at the end of each month. He had it all down to the last penny before he closed over the red ledger and placed it safely back in the drawer of his desk.

It was like they all talked about it behind my back but said nothing. Suzanne kept things aside from The Humble Jumble that she thought would fit Jen. Sarah started selling miracle creams from a catalogue from which she got a pittance of commission when people bought something. Her ma often came up to the house on a Thursday with blue plastic bags full of fresh meat. 'Ma said she bought too much, Charlie,' she'd lie. 'She said it would only go off and end up in the bin.'

At the weekend, Sarah fried stale bread in chunks of white lard and scolded when Jen complained that she was sick of it. 'Well, you should count yourself lucky, young lady, that you're not living over in Africa where they haven't got a morsel to put into their mouth or a dribble to quench their thirst.'

'Can we not talk about things like that,' I'd mutter and then wish I had never opened my mouth.

'You can't sweep everything under the carpet, Charlie Carthy,' she would say. 'Things are happening all over the world. Really bad things. And you can't pretend they're not.'

At this point, I would scrape the crusts from my plate and into the bin, grab the paper and head out the door, not caring that it slammed behind me.

It might have been a pittance that we were living on, but somehow I always had enough for a few scoops in The Beauvalley House at the weekend. There was something at the bottom of a freshly pulled pint that made the troubles lie low and disappear into the background for a while. And that suited me just fine.

Sometimes, they had poker sessions at the back of the pub. When I lost my shirt, I would come home early enough and hope that the stairs didn't creak as I walked up them. On the nights when I thought I was on a roll, that's when I stayed out all night, only to always lose everything before the sun came up. My old man's saying about only betting what you can afford to lose never really registered with me.

Sometimes, Sarah acted like she didn't notice or care; other times it would creep up on her like a fright and she'd lose the plot with me altogether. Every name under the sun, she would call me. I was reminded of what a worthless piece of crap I was, and how my father would be turning in his grave if he knew what I was up to – throwing away a business it took him years to build up and spending my weekends knocking back pints like they were going out of fashion. I was a disgrace, she told me. A mess and a disgrace. To her, to Jen and most of all to myself.

You wouldn't want to have feelings, would you?

For the first time since I started my climb, I lift my eyes up to see how I've progressed. The ground has levelled out a bit and there is a wide clearing ahead. In the centre stands a white statue of the Virgin Mary. Makeshift crosses are scattered around her. Petition letters with blue and black ink lie in folds under rocks and rosary beads dangle from her hand, outstretched as though it is reaching for another hand to clasp. To the right of her bare feet lie a bunch of red roses, their green stalks devoid of thorns. The eyes in her alabaster face look downwards, and I am grateful that I don't have to meet her gaze. 'I'm not all bad,' I want to tell her. 'There's a bit of good in there somewhere.'

I am standing here alone. It's just me and the statue, the rocks and stones, and me not knowing what to do. If I had been a praying man, I would have fallen to my knees, just like the Scottish man who saw the sun spinning in the sky. My old man was a church-goer, never missed a day.

Even during the week, he would leave me minding the shop and skip up to morning Mass. He said it was good to start the day with prayer and that it was like having breakfast in the morning. It set you up for the day. I never had what he had with the church. Never saw the point. They had knocked the fear of God into us as children but children grow up and become adults. They get sense eventually. At least some of them do. I did, anyway.

It is only when I turn my back on the statue and look down onto the village below that I realise how high I have climbed. I see countless fields with square houses dotted in between the greenery, and people as small as ants moving about the streets. The two steeples of St James' church point high up to the sky and I wonder, like everyone else wonders, I imagine, why they built such a large church for such a small village. For a moment it looks like it is drenched in gold, but then everything looks illuminated from up here.

I turn back around to face the statue. My feet ache from the climb but there is something soothing in the mild pain. No prayers come to my lips, so I just stand there watching her look at the ground. For a moment I feel something stir inside. Not a want to start reciting decades of the rosary or for some sort of sign to appear before my eye. It is a compassion for the woman who the statue represents. There is sorrow in her eyes. A pain I can identify with.

I stay there for too long. The sun doesn't start to spin, nor does the hand on the statue move, but the sun begins to sink lower in the sky and for the second time since I reached the mountain, the bells toll from St James' church.

On the climb down, I pass pilgrims starting their ascent. They too keep their eyes on the ground, watching for any dangers that might cause them to trip and fall. They ignore the thirty-something-year-old man with the sweat stains on his T-shirt and the tears streaming down his face.

'Time is a great healer,' I've heard the do-gooders say. And though I know they mean well, I also know they've never had to suffer like I have suffered. Or like Jen has suffered. Or Suzanne, or Sarah's parents, who never in a million years thought they would have a child die before them.

I'm the only one sailing down the mountain as the rest of them climb. Different currents, different tides. I wonder what in God's name they could be thinking about as they stub their toes off sharp rocks and fight the muscular pain in their legs. Then I think of what I've been doing for the past few hours. And I realise that deep down we are all the same. All searching, all questioning. And I realise something else: we'll never know the answers.

There was a point on the small mountain, I'll admit, as I stood in front of that statue, when my shoulders felt less heavy. At the bottom, though, just as my left foot hits the flat slope that leads out onto the road, my load returns.

The little boy runs out of his house and tugs at my arm.

'Gospa!' he shouts and his eyes are so wide. 'Gospa!'

'No,' I tell him as I pull my arm away, 'no Gospa.'

And I don't look back once as I walk down the dusty road. Yet his face stays in my mind, right up until I walk into the only bar in the village and pick up the freshly pulled pint that is waiting there on the countertop for me.

11

YUGOSLAVIA

JEN

On the morning of our third day here, I go to Mass with Louis and the group. The Masses are different over here than back home. For a start, there's not just one priest on the altar, but sometimes as many as five. They go on all day long, giving Masses in Croatian, English and Italian. Louis said that you can go as many times as you like and that you can take the holy bread more than once too. When it comes to the homily, a priest stands up on the altar and talks to the congregation like they are his best friends. They tell stories that would be too personal to share back home. Stories about their lives and the lives of people they meet. And they listen over here, not like back home. When we stand to say the 'Our Father', people hold hands. At the sign of peace, they hug you instead of offering a weak handshake.

After Mass, we hang around the grounds of the church for a while. Priests in thick robes hear confessions on chairs in the fields. I have never seen so many priests in one place before: young ones and old ones, ones who wear brown robes with hoods that are tied at the waist with a white rope, and others who are dressed in dark shirts with white collars like the ones back home. Pilgrims kneel down in the tall grass and don't seem fazed that they have to look their confessor in the eyes. One woman finishes and then bursts into tears. Another woman finds a quiet corner in the shade after her confession where she stays and prays for a while.

In the distance, behind the church, I can see Mount Križevac with the white cross. Louis says it contains a piece of the true cross that Jesus died on and that the locals started building it back in 1933. I can't imagine how they managed to climb up so high with all the stone on their backs. Louis says the climb is similar to Croagh Patrick and points out that the best way to do it is to get up at about five in the morning. Not only would it be cooler at that time, he says, but we would also beat the hordes of Italians who flock there every day.

Louis has some of the group huddled under a wide umbrella and so I go to join them. He points from big mountain to small, from fields to houses, and over to the Franciscan priests' house, where the visionaries have their apparition every day. The milicija have stopped them from going to the small mountain where they first saw her appear. It is safer close to the church, as the children are under the protection of the Franciscan priests there, Louis tells us. We will go there tonight, he says, at half past six. No one will be allowed inside, only priests and the sick, but we can wait outside the door for when she appears at 6.40 p.m.

Underneath the only wide-branched tree in the church grounds is a wooden bench. The young woman I had seen at the airport and who is staying in our house is sitting down in the shade, gently rocking the pushchair where her child lies sleeping. Like me and da, she doesn't talk much within our group. The woman's eyes are grey and shaped like almonds. She looks sad as she sits there, so I walk over.

'Hi,' I say, when I get closer. 'I'm sorry, I've forgotten your name.'

'Connie.' She smiles, moving over on the bench so I can sit down. 'Well, it's Constance really, but everyone calls me Connie. And this is Christopher. You're Jen, right? I see you with your da.'

'He wouldn't get up to go to Mass this morning. He got in too late last night,' I explain as I sit on my hands and swing my legs under the bench.

'Mass is not everyone's cup of tea, I suppose,' Connie says.

Christopher is actually awake in the pushchair, I realise, but he is lying very still. When he stares it is at nothing in particular. I haven't seen him out of the buggy since we arrived. He must be over two years old but he wears no shoes on his feet.

'He can't walk,' Connie says as though she is reading my thoughts.

'Oh, I'm sorr–'

'Don't be,' she says, almost too quickly. 'That's only one thing in a long list of things that Christopher can't and never will be able to do. God knows the doctors told me enough times.'

As I sit there, looking at her and Christopher, she explains how it is impossible for her to do many of the things Louis has organised. She tells me how the wheels of the buggy get jammed with chunks of earth when she tries to push it through the narrow path of the vineyards. The church is so packed at Mass times that she stands outside the entrance door, although sometimes someone will hold it ajar so she can listen in from outside. A mountain climb is also out of the question, she tells me.

'Are you going tonight?' I ask. 'To the priest's house where she will appear.'

Connie sniffs a laugh. 'I suppose I will,' she says. 'There's not much else to do.'

We walk back to the house together. Connie lets me push Christopher half the way. Stones from the road and the uneven paths mean we have to twist and turn the pushchair every few minutes. Christopher doesn't flinch or let out a whine as we bump along the road.

'Is he always this quiet?' I ask Connie when the house is in sight.

'Yes. Always has been and always will be, I think. That's why I knew there was something wrong with him after he was born. He never cried like all the other babies in the ward. Even at night, I had to wake him for feeds. When the public health nurse called out to check on him, she said it wasn't right for a baby to be so listless. No kicking of legs or movement of arms. No slapping together of lips longing for a sup of breast milk. Even his head never moved position in the Moses basket he slept in.'

I bend down to grab the strap at the front wheels and lift the pushchair up the step of the house.

'It's a pity Christopher's da couldn't come to help you,' I say. 'Then maybe you would get some time on your own to climb the mountains or walk through the fields.'

Connie just sniffs a laugh once again.

'Christopher's father isn't around any more,' she says.

'I'm so sorr–'

'Don't be,' Connie cuts across me again. 'It's just me and Christopher now. And it's better that way.'

When we reach the door, the man of the house appears from the kitchen and, in one swoop, lifts Christopher and the pushchair and carries them up the stairs.

'See you later then?' Connie asks me as she follows him up the stairs towards her room. 'Maybe your da will come too?'

'Maybe,' I say.

I stand at the bottom of the stairs for a while, thinking about Connie and Christopher. I think of Francis back home and wonder if he is sitting in the woods all alone. Maybe the old homeless man will stay a bit longer and they can talk for a while.

When the man of the house comes back down the stairs, I ask him for some breakfast to take up to the room.

'My da slept it out and he'll be starving,' I say.

I pretend I have a cup and saucer in my hands, which I bring up to my mouth before saying 'Tea' to him. Then I mimic someone buttering a slice of bread, shoving it in their mouth and rubbing their stomach while saying, 'Mmmmm.'

He disappears inside the kitchen and comes back with a cup of black tea. 'No milk,' he says as he hands it to me. In the other hand he holds a plate with two slices of freshly baked bread smothered in blackcurrant jam. '*Dobar tek*,' he says, which I think means something like when the French say, '*Bon appetit*.'

'*Hvala,* thank you,' I say back to him.

Upstairs in the room, Da is sitting up in the bed, rubbing his bloodshot eyes.

'Where were you?' he asks, like I was the one who had been out all night.

'At Mass,' I say, handing him the tea and bread.

'You should have called me.'

'I did.'

'I never heard you.'

'I know.'

'What time is it?' He's looking around the room, searching for a clock.

'Late,' I say.

'Late, as in?'

'It's eleven.'

'That's not late, Jen.'

'It is over here.'

His jaw cracks as he bites into the crust of the bread. In between chomps, he sips the tea and doesn't complain that it has no milk in it. When he's finished, he stands up and the crumbs fall from his shorts onto the floor.

'That will bring in the ants,' I say, but he doesn't reply.

'Right then, at least there will be no queue for the shower. I'll have a quick wash then I'm going to head off on my own for a while. I might go look at one of those mountains everyone talks about. Throw me a towel out there from the suitcase,' he says.

When he returns from the shower, I see the razor blades I packed for him still in his washbag, and notice that he doesn't spray on the deodorant I left on the bed. When he goes to put on the same T-shirt he has slept in and has been wearing since we left Dublin, I tell him he needs a change. And as I stand there watching my da dress himself like an awkward child, I realise that Ma never had to chastise him like this when she was alive. He always made the effort for her – well, at least until the work dried up and The Beauvalley House became his second home.

After he leaves, I bring the plate and cup downstairs. There is no reply when I knock on the kitchen door and I don't want to go in uninvited, so I place the cup on top of the plate and leave it by the door. The house is quiet. Everyone seems to be out somewhere. Or maybe some are having a lie down now that it is close to midday. I think about what it must be like for Connie in the room all alone with Christopher. Maybe she is here looking for a miracle for him. I know that lots of things are possible but I don't think something like that is.

If Francis were here with me, we would go off for the day. We could have trailed through the fields and climbed the mountains together.

Francis would likely have picked a different route, one where we could do our own exploring. He'd have found a way to slip away from the crowds and I know he'd have discovered things that others would have missed. When we got to the top of the big mountain, the one with the white cross at the peak, Francis and I would have sat on the rocks and thought of our mothers. And we would be up so high, almost touching the clouds. Closer to them both.

Around the back of the house, there is a yard with a wooden shed. During the day, you can hear the chickens cluck about. They roam around on patches of grass, flapping their feathers against the heat and pecking at grains that lie scattered. Nobody is around. I can hear a noise come from the shed and I move closer. Although the door is ajar and the sun bright, I can't see inside because of the darkness. Maybe we aren't allowed in the yard, but I edge closer and try to keep my footsteps light. When I reach the frame of the door, I see the silhouette of a woman dressed in black. In her hands she struggles to hold something down and when I move closer, I can see she is wrestling with one of the chickens. She gets a grip on its neck with her left hand and, still in the crouched position, with her right she reaches to the ground for an axe. The blade shines as she holds it up high and when I see her weathered hand, I realise it is the grandmother of the house. The chicken clucks loudly, as though sensing what is about to happen. It flaps its feathers one final time before the decisive swoop of the blade. She holds its fat body as it jerks around, right up until the point where it stills. I run from the shed and out of the yard, my hand held up to my mouth. For the rest of the day, I stay in my room, staring blankly at the four white walls.

***

Connie knocks gently on my door in the late afternoon. When I open it, she looks around the room and over at Da's vacant bed.

'I thought you could do with some company at dinner time,' she says. Sniffing the air, she adds, 'It smells good, whatever they're cooking. I wonder what it is tonight.'

'Chicken,' I say, before peeling myself off the bed.

Downstairs, Louis reminds the group that we should try to get to the priest's house as soon as possible once dinner is over.

'I don't suppose your da is going,' Connie asks me as she spoon-feeds Christopher. His lips move with no great effort as mashed potato drips down his chin.

'I haven't seen him since this morning,' I tell her.

'You can come with us,' she offers. 'I imagine we will be stuck at the back of the crowds, though. But at least we'll be there.'

'Okay,' I say, excited now. 'Let me get washed and then we'll head over.'

We leave after Louis and the rest of the group. Connie seems happy to stay back from the others. She says she gets fed up repeating and explaining things to people. Most times, people come up to Christopher in his buggy and start cooing and chatting to him. When they don't get the response they expect, they look nervously from child to mother, not knowing what to say. Most times, Connie says, she just turns the pushchair around and walks off in the opposite direction. It isn't that she is being rude, she says, or that she doesn't realise that it might be uncomfortable for the person; it's that she just hasn't got the energy to talk about it any more.

The grounds of the church are empty but for a Franciscan priest. His wide, black-rimmed glasses match the colour of his hair, and he walks with great urgency as he mutters under his breath. For a brief moment, he glances over at us, his eyes lingering on Christopher. Then he continues on his way.

Further along the road, a crowd has gathered at the steps that lead up to the priest's house. In the middle, I can see the top of Louis' hat. Like the others, he chants prayers. At times, there is a swell from the back that pushes the crowd forward, causing those at the front to cry out in protest and shake their hands in the air.

'It might be best to just wait here on the outskirts,' Connie says.

The main difference between here and back home, I find, is the birds and the songs they sing. Though the crowd chants and murmurs to one another, it is the birds that can be heard the loudest. And I only ever hear them in the church grounds or in the vineyards. I do not know their name, but they are small, like the robin we see back home without the red breast. Sometimes they hide in the branches of the trees, watching the world go by. Other times they swoop to the ground and remain there for a brief moment before flying back up high. It is as though they want to be heard, need to be heard.

People up front begin to shriek and wave their hands in the air. Soon the entire crowd rocks like people standing on the deck of a ship as it moves with the swell of the sea.

'I think the children are coming,' Connie says. She stretches her head high above the crowds but only catches a glimpse. 'Follow me,' she says.

The wheels of the pushchair knock off people's heels as Connie tries to turn. I hold on to the back of her blouse, shuffling behind her as she leads the way. People call out and raise their hands high to the sky, begging to be allowed closer to the children. Connie moves along the edge of the crowds until, somehow, we are close to the bottom of the steps.

There we see the children climb one by one. When they walk it seems to be in slow movements, their heads kept down as they focus on their feet. At the top, there is a tall, dark-haired boy of about seventeen. Four girls, maybe a year or two younger, follow behind. One has hair so blonde she looks German. The others are sallow-skinned with chocolate-brown hair. One of them has a tight-cut hairstyle and boyish frame. The girl with the blonde hair turns around twice to look at the boy who walks up the steps last. He is not even ten years old. He raises his head for a moment and when the girl smiles at him, he looks a little less afraid. He smiles back at her and then tilts his head down once again, focusing on his feet.

At the top of the steps, the door is ajar. From the darkness, a figure in brown robes emerges.

'That's the same Franciscan we saw earlier,' Connie says.

He gently touches the arms of the children as they pass into the church and then scans the crowd of people gathered below. Some pretend to faint but quickly gather themselves when they realise no one is paying them any attention.

Christopher stirs in the pushchair and, as he does, the Franciscan turns his gaze to Connie. From where he is standing at the top of the steps, he stretches out his arm so that the sleeve of his robe hangs deep and low.

'Come,' he says, pointing to her.

I don't know how we got to the bottom of those steps. Or how the Franciscan managed to choose Connie out of all the begging and pleading people in the crowds. Connie just stands there with her hand on her chest and asks, 'Me?'

'Go, Connie,' I say, pushing gently at her back.

'I can't go,' she cries, 'what about Christopher?'

The Franciscan moves down the steps with speed and picks up the pushchair. Connie follows him as he moves back up the steps. She has time to glance back down at me once, her cheeks flushed, before he ushers her inside and closes the door behind him. I hope that she saw the smile that covered my face.

I stand here, at the bottom of the steps, watching the look on the people's faces now the children have gone from sight and the door has been firmly shut. Some weep into their hands, others go back to their prayers. The birds keep singing and more people gather.

Then, in an instant, there is a hush.

It is the absence of birdsong that strikes me first. It is as though they have been swallowed up into some large sinkhole. Then the people go quiet. They move their hands up to their faces and close their eyes. Rosary beads dangle between their fingers but make no sound. I don't think I have ever heard something as powerful as this silence before. It is almost deafening.

I look at my watch. It is 6.40 p.m.

Everyone is deep in prayer, but all I can think about is Da – where he is and what he is doing. With all the quietness, I want to scream out his name. I want to shout it loud enough so it will soar above the mountains and travel on the wind. And if he could hear me, then maybe he would come. Come running. Come fast. Wrap his arms around me tight in a big bear hug like he used to do. We would walk away then, from the crowds and the spectators, and we would go home hand in hand.

I stay here, dreaming about what once was until the sound of the crowd pipes up again. Shortly afterwards, the door creaks open. One by one, the six children come out. At the top of the steps the Franciscan stands, tapping each one of them on the shoulder as they leave. They have lost the nervousness of when they first went in. Their cheeks are flushed with colour and they smile at one another as they move down the steps. Once or twice they glance down at the crowd. The blonde girl even gives a little wave. But they also move with haste, as if they don't really want to stay around to greet those who have been standing here for close to an hour.

At the bottom of the steps, I am close enough to reach out and touch them as they pass, but I don't. So many of those gathered try to grasp at their legs or get a feel of the cotton skirts the girls wear.

On the second last step, it seems that someone in the crowd has succeeded in their attempt. A woman reaches out to grab the ankle of one of the girls. In doing so, she pulls too hard and the girl's foot gets caught. It happens quickly and there is no time for someone to catch her. She tumbles down the concrete steps.

'Iva!' her friends cry out.

She is slumped at my feet, crunched into a ball. I crouch down and slide my arm under hers before lifting her up from the ground. Though her hair is tied up in a ponytail, stray strands fall around her face. In her pierced ears silver glistens and I think she has the deepest brown eyes I have ever seen. Before her friends help her move out of the way of the crowds, she smiles at me and mouths some words in Croatian and I recognise *hvala*, 'thank you'.

'Jen,' Connie calls from the top of the steps. Her eyes are wet, her cheeks tear-stained.

I take the steps two at a time and grip the strap on Christopher's pushchair. He looks the same as before he went in. Vacant eyes, lethargic limbs. And I wonder if this is why Connie looks upset. That she didn't get her miracle.

'Are you all right?' I ask when we get to the bottom, but she doesn't answer.

On the way home, she lets me take control of Christopher's pushchair. I don't ask her what happened, and she doesn't volunteer to tell me. We walk in silence until we reach the house and the man comes out to help her carry Christopher and the pushchair up to her room. It is still early. Too early for sleep.

'Goodnight, Jen,' she says anyway and leaves me at the bottom of the stairs.

I'm left on my own, not knowing where to go or what to do.

***

It's almost midnight now. Da is still not home. If I listen hard enough, I swear I can hear the singing of a drunken song in the distance. So I know he must be near. When he wakes up tomorrow, I'll tell him about the old grandmother chopping off the chicken's head and about Connie going into the priest's house to see the vision. I'll tell him about the children, and the girl who fell and spoke to me in her own language.

He might just listen, my da. Even if he thinks it's all a load of rubbish. As long as he listens, I don't mind what he thinks. Once he is here. Really here.

12

YUGOSLAVIA

IVA

I have been many times to different doctors, not just Doctor Marković. All six of us have been. 'There is nothing wrong with these children,' the doctors say. 'They are healthy. They are not sick.'

Still, some of our neighbours are not happy. Our friends say that their parents tell them it is all nonsense. 'Why would the Gospa appear to these teenagers?' they say. 'Were they not just out having a walk and smoking a cigarette? What was in those cigarettes they were smoking?'

Others believe us. They have flocked to the hillside with their own children by their sides.

'Ask the Gospa what she wants us to do,' they call out to us.

'Pray for my sick auntie.'

'Ask her to send some rain.'

The communists do not like so many people getting excited about these things. That is why they have sent the milicija to the village – to tell everyone not to go to the hill. This all has to stop, they say. It is pitiful to see the villagers starting a revolution against the regime. Have they no shame?

Stela told me that they threatened her father and told him that he would not have any more work if her mother continued to go to the hill with her children.

'Maybe you should stay away from there for a while,' Stela's father said, but his wife was not impressed.

'I will not stop going to the hillside, nor the church, nor the village,' she told him. 'I will not abandon my faith because of some threats from a godless regime! If there is no work, there is no work, Marinko. But God has never let our family go hungry. He will always provide.'

Father Petar decided that it was best that we stopped going to the hillside for a while. There has been so much commotion in our little village. Every day, more and more people arrive. Father Petar said it would be safer near the church and so we went to the priest's house.

We once heard Father Petar argue with the bishop when he came from Mostar to speak with us. After he had taken us into separate rooms to interview us, he met with Father Petar in another room. And it was impossible for us not to put our ears up against the door to try and hear what he said. 'Disobedient' was a word he used a lot. He, like the communists, did not believe what we were saying.

In my head, I often thank those police for taking Father Petar's passport from him; otherwise he may not have stayed and who would we have had to turn to? Sometimes, I feel like he is the only one who is our true friend and that he understands what this is really like for us.

But now they have told Father Petar that he must close the church. That he must put a stop to this revolution. He will be put into prison if he doesn't, they said. 'Who would look after the children then?' they asked, while laughing in his face.

But Father Petar is strong. He is not afraid of the communists. I wish

I had his strength. I try to be brave but sometimes, even though my face might look defiant, I am shaking inside.

Stela's brother, Dominik, thinks that it is all fun. He sells melons by the roadside and charges one dollar for a slice. The pilgrims are so thirsty from the heat that I don't think they care how much they pay.

As I think about this, my sister calls to me from where she is standing at the front door: 'Iva, Iva. They are coming! So many this time. Hurry. You must hide.'

The clock on the wall tells me that it is three o'clock. I have not had a chance to lie down for a rest today. There is a rumbling noise coming from my stomach. It has been too many hours since I ate bread for breakfast. Where do these pilgrims get their energy from? Always moving, always searching. I wish they would just stop and live in the moment instead of trying to chase me.

'Iva!' Veronika calls again.

I leave through the back door, moving through the scattered tents that are pitched in the field. Thick clouds that are full and grey move across to shadow the sun, but the heat stays intense. I can feel the sweat dripping down my neck. It moves into the creases and folds of my skin and soaks the back of my knees. Stiff blades of grass slice at my feet, insects crunch into the earth and my skirt whips at my bare legs as I go.

Run, run, run, I repeat in my head. *Run to the farthest end of the vineyards and hide beneath the ripened grapes.*

Up ahead, I see an old carthorse pulling his load, the farmer sitting on top of the bales of hay, daydreaming of a life where a man of his years can rest. He takes his flat cap off his head and tips it in my direction. Still I run. As fast as I can, knowing that soon I can stop and take a breath and lie hidden where no one can question me or pull at me.

In the vineyards my feet get tangled and trip each other up. And then I am face down on the ground, my hands grazed, and I'm sure I have torn my skirt. I try so hard to hold it in by scrunching up my nose and holding my breath. Then something clicks in the close air and I begin to cry like a five-year-old child who has had a fall in the schoolyard.

'Are you all right?'

A shadow floods the ground I lie on. I open my eyes to see a pair of worn trainers with long laces that are mostly undone. A thin arm reaches down to hold my wrist before lifting me off the soil and bringing me to my feet.

'Thank you,' I say in English.

I recognise the girl who helped me when I fell down the steps yesterday.

'Thank you,' I say again.

'What are you doing here?' she says.

We have learned some English in school but it is Father Petar who has taught me the most. He knows I want to travel someday, maybe even as far as America, just like he did. But I need to do more reading, Father Petar has told me. He said that it is only by reading that my English will improve. Although I imagine speaking to a native speaker will also help.

'I hide.'

'From who?'

'Pilgrims.'

'I'm a pilgrim.'

'Yes,' I say. 'I no hide you.'

She laughs just a little, then stands up on her toes and looks around.

'Come,' I say, taking her hand and walking her through the greenery.

'Where has the sun gone?' she asks as we walk. 'The sky looks more like it does back home, just before it pours.'

She talks too fast and I don't fully understand but I get enough to know that she is asking about the weather. Isn't that what people talk about when they have nothing else to say? There hadn't been a cloud in sight for the past few weeks, just one big ball of fire burning in the centre of the blue sky. Each day gets hotter, temperatures almost too high for this time of year.

'Rain,' I say, pointing to the sky before putting my hands together. 'Prayer … for rain.'

There are no more words spoken but she keeps a tight hold on my hand as I lead the way. Maybe she is the same age as me, I think. She is skinny too, like me. Her eyes are blue and wide and her hair is the colour of a field mouse. On her back she has a small green rucksack.

'Here,' I say as we come to a halt. 'Sit.'

She takes a glass bottle filled with water out of her rucksack. 'You first.' She offers it to me, and I gulp it down so fast there is barely any left for her to drink.

'I sorry,' I say, but she doesn't seem to mind.

'I helped you yesterday, when you fell,' the girl says as she sits cross-legged on the dusty earth.

'How old you?' I ask.

'Fourteen. And you?'

I try to remember my lessons from school as I count the numbers up in my head.

'Fifteen. Do you have brother? Sister?' I ask as she rummages through her little rucksack again, before taking out some bread and jam wrapped in some torn tissue.

'No. Do you?'

'Yes. Big brothers. Little sister. My tata, eh, father, and Baba Ana.'

'Who is Baba Ana?' she asks.

I try to think of the word and after a minute, I remember.

'Grandmother!' I say as though I have just answered a million dollar question.

We both laugh, almost choking on the bread.

'And you?' I ask.

'I have no brothers or sisters. Just Da and me,' she says.

'Da? What Da?'

'Father,' the girl explains, 'tata.'

I search my head for something else to say.

'Work. What work your father?'

'Nothing really,' she says. 'He used to make old books look like new again. But he doesn't really do that any more. Does your mother know you are hiding? Your mama?'

I smile. 'Maybe.'

'Won't she be angry?'

'If she angry, I don't know,' I say, toying with the dry soil. 'Mama ... dead.'

The girl's eyes widen. 'So is mine,' she says.

We let the words linger. The reality of it all washes around in the air above our heads. There is no need for weak words of sympathy, for we feel it within one another like a bolt of electricity – the pain that consumes every part of us.

'Is it real?' the girl asks eventually when the silence becomes too much.

'Real?'

'The visions. The apparitions. The Gospa. Is it true? Do you see her as clear as you see me?'

How do I explain what so many people ask me to explain to them every single day? Always the same questions and nobody is ever fully satisfied with the answers. They always want more.

'Of course is true! Why lie? Why no true?'

'Is she beautiful?'

'The Gospa?'

'Yes, the Gospa.'

I nod. 'Beautiful.'

How can I describe the vision in another language when I cannot describe it in my own?

'Do you miss her when she goes?' the girl asks.

And I'm wondering if this foreign girl can read the thoughts in my head. If she can feel the pain of loss that I feel when it all ends. For the time the Gospa is with me, I feel close to Mama. I have two Mamas by my side. One so clear before my eyes, and the other invisible but undeniably there too. Sometimes, I count down the hours until I will see her next.

'Yes,' I say. There is a want in the girl's eyes. If just for one minute I could show her what I see every day, then maybe the emptiness inside her could be filled. I know her sorrow only too well. How it cuts like a sharpened knife.

I wonder about her life and what it is like to be unknown and go about your daily business unnoticed. It seems so long ago now – when things were simpler and only my family, cousins, neighbours, teachers and friends knew my name. Now people I have never seen before call out my name from afar. They shout it as though they are long-lost friends who have found me after years of searching. But I do not know them. I don't get time to ask their names. They have too many questions. Too many requests.

The sun has moved far across the sky. I stand up and reach my hand out to the girl so I can pull her up from where she is sitting. 'I must go,' I say. 'Baba Ana will look for me. She old.'

I point across to the small mountain.

'Come. Podbrdo,' I tell her.

'Now?'

'No. Podbrdo. At night.' I hesitate, counting in English in my head. 'Ten o'clock.'

I bring my finger up to my mouth and make a shushing sound.

'Quiet. No milicija. Secret. Yes?' I say.

The girl doesn't speak but nods.

'Light too,' I say.

'Light?'

I pick up the bottle of water and hold it out as if it were a flashlight.

'Ah, light. You mean torch,' the girl says.

'Torch!' I shout and we laugh once again.

'Can I bring my da?' she asks and her eyes are wild with excitement. 'My father. My tata.'

'Tata, okay. No more,' I say.

'What about Connie?' she asks.

'Who Connie?'

'Friend. Connie is a friend.'

'One friend,' I tell her.

'What about Louis?'

'Louis?'

'Another friend.'

'Two friend,' I sigh as I start to leave. 'No more.'

'What is your name?' she calls.

'Iva,' I say. 'And you?'

'Jen!'

I leave her standing alone in the maze of the vineyards surrounded by full red grapes hanging from rich leaves. She no longer looks lost or sad.

Her lips have curled into a smile and those blue eyes are getting wider by the second. I have seen it in the faces of many. It is something people wish for and we yearn to have in our lives. It is what helps us get out of bed each morning. It is buried so deep beneath the skin that it is sometimes hard to comprehend that it even exists. But it is there, if you search hard enough. If you open your mind and your heart. It is there, waiting patiently to be grasped. It is what we need most in this broken world.

It is hope.

13

YUGOSLAVIA

JEN

There is no point in trying to talk to him. I don't think Da will really listen if I speak. But if I write it down for him – how I feel – then maybe, just maybe, he will understand. There's always the threat, though, that he won't return from the pub in time, or when he does he will fall onto the bed without seeing the note, or that he'll just crush the paper in his hands before throwing it onto the floor. But I have to try.

Ma used to say that the written word is more powerful than the spoken one. She said you absorb the words more when they are printed before your eyes. You can't close your ears or let your thoughts stray when they're jumping off the page at you. Every day, at break time in school, I would open my lunchbox and find little notes tucked in under the tinfoil that covered my ham sandwiches. Me and Francis used to have competitions to try and guess what they would say.

'I bet it's "You are smart" today,' Francis would say. 'Or wait! Wait! Bet you it's "You are sweet like sugar."'

Sometimes, he was right. Other times, Ma would surprise me with a new one.

'Look at this one, Francis. "Be kind to yourself." I wonder what she means by that.'

Francis would tap his dirty finger against his cheek before saying, 'I think it means you should do something for yourself instead of for others.'

Ma also sometimes left notes on little pieces of coloured paper for Da after they had a row. 'Bad night, didn't sleep well. Sorry for snapping.' Or, 'Didn't mean what I said, just angry. Think Jen is upset. Could you talk to her?'

The notes came after the big rows, like the time she smashed the teapot against the back wall of the kitchen, or when she took the scissors to his trousers before she stuffed them in a bin liner and threw them out the bedroom window. And she didn't care that the curtains were twitching or voices were tutting on our small cul-de-sac; they could all go to hell for all she cared. They didn't have to put up with what she had to put up with, I heard her say.

The rage never lasted too long; it always died away. Afterwards, she seemed satisfied to have gotten it all out of her system, to have released the anger inside.

'You drive me mad, Charlie Carthy, sometimes,' she'd say a day later as she nuzzled into his stubbly chin.

And then everything went back to normal.

Louis keeps asking me where Da is, and I'm not sure what to say, though I know that he's found a bar down a side street, only a few minutes from the house. I've seen him in there, leaning over the counter with a cold glass in his hand. Part of me wants to run inside and shout at him and tell him to stop. But the other part of me hopes he will stand up and walk out himself. Of his own free will. But I can't tell Louis this, and I don't want to lie either. When I lie, my words get jumbled up and my palms go sweaty.

So I don't bother saying anything. I don't see the point any more. People can see through you when you are lying. *I'm okay*, I used to tell them. *No, Da is fine too. He has just popped out to the shops. He'll be back real soon.* And the way they looked at me, all pitiful with arched eyebrows, told me that they didn't believe a word that was coming out of my mouth.

Dinner has been over for hours. I go outside to the front of the house to where Louis and Connie are. The air seems a little cooler than previous evenings. Maybe the rain that Iva prays for will come tonight. Connie is still walking around in circles, I see; she's been doing this since after dinner this evening – when the woman of the house told that her she would mind Christopher tonight while she goes to the hill.

'But I've never left him with anyone else before,' she says, her face contorted.

'You won't get an opportunity like this again,' Louis tells her. 'We only have a few more days here and there's no telling when you'll get back again.'

When he says it like that, I wonder where the time has gone. The day we left Dublin felt never-ending: Mr Baldwin's car, the airport, the plane, the coach ride and the arrival into this strange village. But the days since just seem to have rolled into one another – the vineyards, the church, the apparition and now the mountain tonight. I've almost lost count of how many days we have left. Connie scratches at her head just as the woman comes out from the house. Then she looks from Christopher, who is still in the pushchair, to the woman to Louis to me.

'If I get him to sleep first then I'll go,' Connie says. 'I would be happier if I knew he was down for the night and wouldn't give her any bother.'

The woman shrugs her shoulders, puts her hands in the air and mutters something in her own language, which I imagine would translate to something like: 'Whatever you want, lady. I'm only trying to help.'

A stray black cat with green eyes scavenges for leftover food on the road. He sulks, meowing every so often. There are no stars out just yet but the moon is there already, covered by a grey veil. Soon, I think, when the night falls properly, the cat will only be visible by the glint of his green eyes. Already, I can hear the song of the night crickets, loud and constant. In the direction of the church, the sound of tyres crunching into the gravel on the road can be heard, followed by the rev of a car engine as it drives away.

From behind me, Connie comes out to where I am standing. Louis too.

'You got him settled then?' Louis asks.

'I only rocked him for a few minutes in my arms and he was out like a light,' she says.

'Okay, let's go,' I say.

The small torches Connie and Louis hold as we walk down the road give off a faint glow that attracts tiny white flies. Louis also carries a stick that reaches as high as his hip and on his head he wears the same battered cowboy hat, even though the sun is gone. Connie wears a light cardigan over her shoulders, the stray hairs from the wool glistening in the faint light. She runs her fingers through the strands of fringe that stick to her brow, trying to free them. She is jumpy, I can tell. Maybe anxious.

The sky turns a deep blue as we walk down the street. Soon, stars will appear but for now, I can still see a faint glow on the horizon behind the church. Some lights in the windows of the houses are left on. Most of the villagers have settled in for the night even though it is not even ten o'clock. When we reach the vineyards, everything is still and quiet. Connie's fingers brush off my hand; I grab hold of her. I think of Francis and the fear he has of darkness, how it blinds him and makes him cry. He's too big now for the cupboard underneath the stairs where Old

Man Nelligan used to put him when he got angry. Now he grabs him by the scruff like a bold pup and stuffs him into the hot-press, closing the chipped wooden door tight so that he has to lean against the over-sized rusted tank. Then Old Man Nelligan pulls the mahogany cabinet from his bedroom, the one with seven years' bad luck cracked into the mirror, dragging it across the bare floor until it blocks the hot-press door. And no matter how hard Francis bangs, or shouts, or cries, no one comes. No one releases him. The only sound is the dripping inside the water tank and the scratching of the rats as they scurry around the attic floor overhead.

'Will your da follow us?' Connie asks.

'I don't think so.'

'Do you think the others will mind that we didn't tell them about it, Louis?' Connie asks.

'Most of them wouldn't be able for the climb. Not at this time,' he says as he tries to navigate a way for us through the fields. 'It's hard enough for them during the day, let alone at this hour of the night.'

For a time, we think we are lost and that we've done nothing but walk around in circles in the vineyards. Even though he's not saying it, I know that Louis is wishing we had stuck to the road we started out on – though we had to leave it, really, to get to where we want to go. It's kind of nice, I find, just walking between the two of them – Louis leading in front, tapping at the ground with his stick, and Connie behind. Now I see why they all walk around in groups. It's comfortable. Secure. Makes you feel a little safer.

I always had the comfort of Francis by my side when we were in primary school. There never was a morning when I woke up, looked out the bedroom window and didn't see Francis sitting on the kerb. When I tapped at the window, he would lift his head up from where it was stuck between his knees and bare his overcrowded teeth.

'I'll be down shortly,' I'd mouth and Francis would raise his thumb high in approval.

No one seemed to protest when we chose the table made for two at the back of the classroom next to the window that was left permanently open. Sometimes Miss Fleming would go out of the room and then return with a bottle of something in her hand. Then she would march down to where Francis and I sat, point the bottle over our heads and spray till there was nothing left in the can.

'What's that for?' Francis used to ask me.

'Fly killer,' I would lie.

'I didn't know fly killer smelt so nice,' he said, smiling.

All the parents loved Miss Fleming, with her layered hair and drop-down earrings. Ma said she looked like one of the actresses that appeared on the television in *Dallas*.

'Do you know her first name is Priscilla?' I heard her tell Da one evening when they sat down to watch it. 'Imagine naming your child Priscilla. It's awful exotic, don't ya think?'

And though she looked good, she was as nasty as the women on *Dallas* too sometimes.

'Francis Nelligan!' she roared one day. 'What in the name of God do you call this?'

The shoulders of her white jumper were stiff with pads and had tassels hanging off the ends that swayed as she stood up. Between her thumb and her index finger, she held the corner of Francis' homework copy-book. The page was only a quarter full with writing, the rest of it stained with dirt.

'You'll be lucky if you get a job sweeping the streets!' she roared as everyone in the class turned full circle to face Francis.

'I don't want a job sweeping the streets, Miss,' he piped back. 'I want to work with horses when I'm older.'

'You'd be better suited working with pigs,' Git O'Connor said while holding his nose.

Everybody burst out laughing.

'Don't mind them, Francis,' I whispered, even though he couldn't hear me over the noise. 'You can be anything you want to be.'

He often told me that he wouldn't have bothered going to school if I wasn't there too.

'Sometimes the mocking is worse than the beatings,' he said.

***

Connie jumps when a roll of thunder breaks the air. Droplets spray down on our shoulders and the tops of our heads, but only for a brief moment. Then it's dry once more. There's light up ahead, little dots of white moving slowly up the hill. They sparkle like the cat's eyes that are dug into the roads back home.

'Look, Louis,' I call a little too loudly.

He shushes me with his finger. 'The milicija.'

We spill out of the vineyards and onto a road, banging off one another as we do. The road slants upwards, steep but smooth. Louis breathes in deeply before the small climb, as Connie and I link his arms on either side. Further ahead, people appear on the road. They come out of the nearby houses with small children by their sides. Black scarves that have been worn over their heads during the day now sit around their necks and cover their shoulders. Silver-haired women with long dark clothes sit on the stone wall at the bottom of the mountain, toying with the brown wooden beads in their hands. Carefully knitted shawls with intricate detail are draped across their upper bodies and the thick shoes they wear are barely visible beneath the full skirts. A little boy comes running over to us as we get near, offering us a drink of cold water from a jug before we climb. He runs back to the open door and gets a stick, like the one Louis has, and offers it to Connie.

'No,' she says. '*Hvala.* Thanks.'

There is room on the wall beside the old women but Connie sits herself on the ground and takes the sandals off her feet. When she stands back up they dangle between the fingers of her right hand and she wears a smile that makes her face glow in the night just like the little lights on the hill.

'Will it not hurt?' I ask as she lets her feet sink in between the loose stones on the ground.

'I suppose we won't know unless we try it,' Connie says and smiles.

I slip my left foot out of the runner, holding onto Connie's shoulder for balance. I feel my skin breathe and the bones in my toes stretch.

'Leave them at the bottom here,' Connie says as she places her sandals down behind the wall. 'Nobody will take them.'

I don't want to tell her that they are my only pair, so I nod and place them next to where she has placed hers. The boy appears once again with two lit candles in his hands and offers them to us. We shake our heads and show him the torches in our hands. He looks disappointed that we have refused his small gift and so we put our torches down beside our shoes and reach out to take the candles. I see Connie's eyes linger on him for too long and wonder if she's thinking of Christopher back at the house.

'You're a good boy,' she says and he smiles at her in a knowing way.

'Are you both ready?' Louis asks.

We nod.

We climb, guided by the lights that go before us. The stones are loose and cold but most are smooth on the feet. My body feels so close to the earth, it is like I was born to climb mountains barefooted. It's so easy and self-satisfying that I feel I must be doing something wrong. I overtake Louis and Connie and rush past those who were already on the hill before me.

'Wait, Jen,' Connie calls. 'I'll lose you.'

'You won't lose me,' I call back. 'Meet me at the top.'

Prayers fill the night, soft and rhythmic. I lean my body forward when the hill becomes steeper, and soon I am touching off rocks with my free hand and sweeping past small bramble-like bushes dotted along the side. Connie is way behind, Louis even further, but I can hear the sound of his stick as it scrapes the rocks and can feel the whisper of locals as they murmur prayers. I'm not praying as I climb, no thoughts are in my mind. It's just me and the rocks and the black and the glow of the candlelight all scooped up into a perfect bubble.

The moon pushes through the grey clouds to shine down on the climbers and lights up the coal-black sky. There is a clearing a few feet ahead and I can just make out the white statue through the people that have gathered. Some sit cross-legged on the stones. Eyes closed, they seem lost in a trance as they sing to the moon, the clouds and the stars.

Beside the statue, the six children stand at a greater height than the others. As I move closer, I see Iva looking around, her mind far away from the prayers the others are whispering. I'm stretching high on the ball of my foot, like a ballerina, as I wave in her direction.

'Excuse me,' I say as I step over women and men who are lost in prayer.

Pages of petitions lie folded underneath the stones. A tiny makeshift crucifix with a photograph of a young child tied on with a white ribbon sits alone at the edge of a large rock. Booklets of novenas that have been said many times over and which show pictures of saints are scattered in places. Bunches of red roses, the petals trampled on and the stalks crushed, are placed in a pile near the small bushes that grow on the mountainside. Down below, only the tiny houses that have left their lights on are visible. And the church.

Silence gathers on the mountain as the Franciscan priest stands on top of something, high above the crowds. Once ready, he leads the people in a prayer in his native tongue. Iva has stopped looking around. The children all have their heads lowered and eyes cast down.

I try to concentrate but I can't pray.

I want my da here beside me, holding my hand.

A clap of thunder can be heard, closer than when we were down in the fields.

Raindrops splash against my forehead and the people gathered pull hoods or shawls over their heads; some consider putting up umbrellas that had earlier been used as walking aids, though the sound of the nearby thunder makes them hesitate. Soon the rain turns heavy and people start to rise from where they are sitting. Prayers get closer as they try to compete with the sound of the falling rain. The brightest flash tears at the darkness, looking like a giant tree with white branches. Someone cries, and then others. Thunder again. Closer. Feet slip on the rocks and people stumble as they try to move.

'Sshh,' I hear a lady say. 'It is time.'

The children are no longer praying. Their heads are raised high, their lips moving, the white in their eyes so brilliant. Everyone is quiet again, even as the rain continues to fall, soaking every fibre of my clothing, every patch of uncovered skin. And I don't know what to do, so I just stand where I am, looking at Iva even though she can't see me.

I'm alone again, despite there being so many around me.

The sky lights up once more and I swear I see Ma's face in the glow. And I crumble to my knees, not sure what are tears and what is rain on my face. I want to call out his name from the mountaintop. He'll have to hear me from up here, I think. I want to cry out but I can't.

Da, I call to him in my mind. *Where are you? I need you.*

14

YUGOSLAVIA

JEN

'Maybe he couldn't get up the mountain because of the crowds?' Connie says on the way down the hill.

I always thought that the journey back was meant to feel quicker, but the end of the hill still seems a long way away.

'I doubt he even bothered trying,' I reply.

She doesn't disagree.

Connie doesn't treat me like I'm a child. She doesn't look at me with sad eyes or whisper 'God love her' under her breath. I think Ma would have liked Connie. She didn't have too many friends, apart from Aunt Suzanne.

'Anyway, men aren't worth the hassle, if you ask me,' she says after a few minutes' silence. She is thinking about something because her eyes look out into the darkness of the fields and never once drop down to check what her feet might be stepping on. Her ankle buckles as she slides on a greasy stone and when I catch her by the elbow, she loses the glaze that had coated her eyes.

Louis puts his arm around Connie's shoulder. 'We're not all that bad,' he says.

As they move down the mountain, I trail behind. Ma always said that it was rude to listen in to conversations. She used to say that you only ever get one side of the story. But, in this case, I can't help but listen.

'I'm not as bitter as you think,' Connie says to Louis. 'I guess it just would've been nicer if I had a crystal ball a few years back. Or the slightest bit of foresight. Only fools fall in love. Isn't that what they say?'

Louis hugs her. 'It's good to talk sometimes,' he says.

Connie turns around and looks at me but I keep my eyes down towards the ground and pretend I'm not listening. He asks her about Christopher's da.

'Now you can tell me to mind my own business, by all means,' Louis says. 'But at the same time, if you want to get it off your chest, work away. I promise I won't judge. Just listen.'

And although I get the feeling she doesn't like Christopher's da very much and that he might have done something bad, she doesn't seem to mind talking to Louis about him.

'It was well into September, but we were having an Indian summer after three months of non-stop rain. Rain not too unlike tonight,' she says. 'I was working as an air hostess and Dessie surprised me at the airport when my shift finished. When I came out of the arrivals hall, he threw his jacket on the floor and got down on one knee. The box was big. The ring a bit small. But then he wasn't on a manager's salary just yet at the Esso station, he told me, even though half the people in the town thought he owned the place. He liked to think he did own the place, all right, but he only worked there. He was fifteen when they offered him a job. Weekends to start off with while he finished school. Then full-time when his parents told him there wasn't a high hope in hell he was going to college. Streetwise, his da called him. Not a bit academic, he said. "Sure, he would be wasted in college, our Dessie,"' Connie says, as she mimics some aul fella with a thick country accent.

Louis laughs at her impression.

Connie continues. 'My ma tried to hide it when I told her he proposed, but she was gleaming from the inside out, like she had just won the draw on the prize bonds. "And he just appeared there after work?" she asked me, "Totally out of the blue? Had you even time to put a bit of rouge on your cheeks or rob a spritz from the duty-free perfumes? Oh, you'll need to look after yourself more, Constance. You wouldn't want a man like Dessie Mahon to stray just because you let yourself go now, would you?"'

'Did you like working on the planes?' Louis asks.

'Not in the slightest!' she says. 'That day he proposed to me, for example, my shift started on the first flight to London and I was back and forth all day. Climbing to cruising altitude before levelling out over the choppy Irish Sea. Ears popping, stomach dipping, plane shaking. I should have been used to it after five years of trolley-dolly flying. Truth was, I hated flying. Always had. Still do. "Don't make eye contact with any of the passengers when the turbulence hits, Connie," Dessie used to tease me. "If they saw the look on your face they would think it was the end." Says him who has never been on a plane in his life,' Connie sniggers.

'So you were an air hostess who was afraid of flying?' Louis says.

'I suppose so,' she says. 'But I couldn't help how I felt. I was nervous. I just couldn't shake that feeling that at any minute the plane was going to drop out of the sky. I always thought it was a possibility. Even though Dessie told me it wasn't. "Planes don't just drop out of the sky, Connie," he said. Of course I told him that they did and had before. And I could see him rolling his eyes and muttering something through his teeth. He told me I should "get over myself" and stop fretting about little things that are never going to happen. Me fretting over things! This from a man who spent so much time holding two small oval mirrors in his stubby hands as he tried to evaluate the seriousness of the ever-growing bald spot on the back of his head.'

Louis laughs so hard at this that people look over in their direction. 'Did you know he was going to propose?' he asks.

'Not really. I mean, we had been going out a while and he was part of the furniture at home but I wasn't prepared for it. If I had been given a chance to think about it instead of being caught off guard, then things might have been different,' she says. 'He had stayed over the night before. Ma never seemed to mind, once he stayed on the couch downstairs. Not that she would have said anything if he did venture up to my room. No doubt she would have turned a blind eye. Sure butter wouldn't melt in Dessie Mahon's mouth. He could fall into manure and come up smelling like roses, in Ma's eyes. The son she never had, he was. And a right lick too; mowing the lawn for her when he stayed over, cutting back the overgrown hedges that pushed at the fencing around the garden. Once the mugs of tea kept coming along with the salty rasher sandwiches, golden boy Dessie would hang around long after I had gone to work. Even Mr Connolly from across the road with his gammy leg waved to him when he was out in the garden, as if he were waving to my da, God rest him. Sure they all loved him. Ma, the neighbours, the customers at the Esso station. And why wouldn't they?'

Connie takes a deep breath in and tries to brush off the raindrops that hang from her cardigan.

'It was all my fault we split up, Ma said. The shame of it. A separated mother with a sick child. How would she cope with it all? "Oh Jesus, Mary and holy St Joseph. What will I say to Father Dennehy?" she cried.

And I told her that another separated couple in the parish was the least of Father Dennehy's worries at the moment. There were horrible things being said about his predecessor, Father Keogh, and what he had allegedly been doing to the altar boys a few years back. That should have been enough to keep him awake at night without my marriage failure getting in the way, I told her. She said that I should have been more understanding towards Dessie. That it wasn't his fault the child was born like that. And all I wanted to shout at her was that it certainly wasn't my fault either.'

I can hear the anger in Connie's voice. I can feel the regret. I want to run to her and hug her tight but I don't. Louis is listening. Louis is there.

'It was Ma and him who discussed what our living arrangements would be after we married. She told him there was plenty of room in the house until he got on his feet. She said she wouldn't get in our way at all. And that we wouldn't even know she was there. I remember her saying this while scooping a dollop of creamy mash onto his plate before topping it with a juicy ten-ounce piece of sirloin. I stood there watching him shovel it into his gob and tell Ma how he loved her mash because his own ma only used the packet stuff and there was nothing like the taste of a real spud. Then he told her we would be delighted to stay in the house.'

'Did you ever get your own place?' Louis asks Connie.

'No. We never got the chance,' she says. 'We were only married a wet weekend when I found out I was expecting. I was told I was making the passengers nervous with all the vomiting on such short flights. I packed the job in and spent the next seven months mostly in the bed or in a horizontal position. It was the only way the nausea seemed to subside. I only moved to the couch when Dessie came in from work every evening and went to sit down.'

'It was Ma who missed him most after he left,' Connie says and I see her bite at the nail on her small finger. 'I think she missed the chats they had before dinner, as he hovered around the cooker sipping tasters off the wooden spoon. And how he would make her a cup of tea after she had washed the dishes. A little milk, two sugars and in her favourite Royal Tara fine bone china teacup, the one with the shamrocks scattered around the top. "I'll have one if you're making another, Dessie," I would say from the far end of the couch. "It's you who should be making your husband a nice cup of tea after a hard day at work, Constance," Ma would scold. "Don't bother then," I would say. And he wouldn't.'

Connie moves her hands down to her stomach. 'The labour was intense. Forty-eight hours in total. I thought I would die from the pain. I remember hearing about a woman from our area that died in that hospital a few years back. Imagine dying in childbirth in this day and age? I heard people say she was a tinker. As if that made any ounce of difference. Didn't she have the cop on to give birth in a hospital instead of in some campsite on the side of the road? The poor woman. God rest her,' Connie says.

I wonder if she is talking about Francis' ma.

'"Don't be so dramatic, Constance," Ma said when I told her about my fears of going through labour. "Just ask them for the epidural and you'll be grand. There was nothing like that when I had you. I've never been the same down there since. Backside first you came out. Destroyed I was."'

Louis clears his throat. I don't think he wants to know about things like that.

'So I did. I asked for the epidural, but not until the forty-seventh hour. The midwife told me that I'd gone this far and would I not just do without. No, I said. I wanted the drugs. The anaesthetist wasn't at all impressed when he arrived and I swear he gave me a weaker dose just to spite me because it never kicked in until after I had given birth. I got out of the bed to ring Dessie and collapsed onto the floor before I realised I had no feeling in my legs. It took three of them to lift me back into the bed.

'They said that during the labour the umbilical cord was kinked and the baby didn't get enough oxygen. I knew straight after he was born that he wasn't right. His limbs didn't move as much as the other newborns in the ward. Other times, his body would start to jerk before he turned weak once more. The nurses tried to fob me off at first. I often wonder if they knew something was wrong and just weren't saying anything. But I pushed and pushed it with them. Even after I brought him home, all swaddled up in a pale blue blanket that Ma had knit for him, I still called the hospital every day insisting on seeing a paediatric specialist. They eventually got sick of my calls and I got my first appointment. After the tests, they told me that Christopher had hypoxic brain damage caused by a lack of oxygen during the birth. I could always put him in a home if I wanted, the consultant told me. Babies like him weren't usually suitable for adoption, he said, so a home would be where he would live out his years.'

Louis reaches over and takes Connie's hand. I can't see, but I imagine he is squeezing it tight. I want to tell her that it's all right to cry. That sometimes it helps.

'On the bus ride home after the consultation, I took Christopher out of the pram and held him tight to my chest, afraid that if I took my eye off him for a second someone would take him away. I stroked the thick black hair that trailed down the back of his neck, and I kissed his plump little lips over and over again. His eyes stayed closed; he was exhausted from the day. I don't think I ever saw eyelashes that long on a baby. Any girl would kill for those eyelashes, I remember thinking. And I let the people on the bus coo over him and tell me what a beautiful baby I had. They didn't need to know that someone had just told me to give him away, to put him in a home for unwanted babies where he would never feel his mother's embrace again.

'Dessie and Ma were sitting at the kitchen table when I got in. A ham and cheese sandwich cut into neat triangles sat on a plate in front of Dessie. It's funny the insignificant things you remember in certain situations, but his hair was gelled back off his face making his forehead look too large. "Well. What did he say?" Ma asked as she topped up his cup up with some fresh tea. But it was as though they already knew what the consultant had said. It was like they had gotten the news before me and had had the time to sit down and discuss it before I came home. I spoke anyway. Told them everything I could remember the doctor telling me. I left things out and got most of the medical terms mixed up. The gist of it was right though. I managed to hold it together too, right up until the last sentence came rushing out of my mouth. "And then he told me I should put him into a home," I said. Neither of them came near me as my shoulders collapsed and I cried. They just looked at one another with arched eyebrows waiting for me to get myself together so we could discuss the next step. And then Ma reached her hand across the table and brushed her fingertips against my knuckles. "You have to look at all the options, love," she said and all I can remember after that was how I stood up and ran out of the room, and how Dessie never came after me.

'The weeks that followed rushed in and out. Conversations were brief. Sometimes they were in whispers. At night, I would toss in the bed, my mind swelling with fearful thoughts of the future. At the worst of times, I hoped that Christopher would die before me, and then I wouldn't have to worry about what would happen to him after I was gone.

'Dessie grew more distant. Then one day, he said to my ma: "Nothing like this ever happened on my side, Mrs Farrell. I checked with my ma.

She had a distant uncle who went a bit soft in the head later on in life. Suffered with his nerves, she said. Ended up in a mental hospital on the north side of Dublin. He's still there, I think. The wife put him in and died a few years later. Ma said no one ever thought about claiming him out. But now that she thought of him, she said she'll make a point to visit him someday soon. That's if he's still alive. Which she thinks he is."

'Oftentimes, I would long for night to fall, when Dessie and Ma were asleep and it was just Christopher and me,' Connie says. 'I would stay there listening to his breathing against the still of the night. I would pick him up out of his Moses basket and creep down the stairs. There I would sit on the couch and watch as he suckled on the teat of his bottle and sigh after every few ounces. At times, he would fall asleep and I would gently rub the side of his cheek until he started to drink again. Dessie never offered to get up. But I didn't want him to either. The odd night, Ma would creep down the stairs, thinking I couldn't hear the creak in the second last step. She would stand in the doorway, peeping through the gap, looking down on her only grandson. "Is that you, Ma?" I'd say. And she wouldn't reply, yet I would hear her sobbing all the way back up to bed.'

Connie straightens her back and holds her head a little higher. 'I didn't have to tell them that I wasn't giving him up. They knew by the way I held him.'

I think of Connie and they way she looks at Christopher. How she caresses his cheek.

'Dessie left that September. Two years to the day after he proposed. He left a letter for Ma and one for me. They were both written on Esso headed paper blotted with tea stains. He didn't bother with an envelope, just folded them in half and left them under the sugar bowl in the centre of the kitchen table. *Constance* it said on the front of mine. Not Connie. *Constance.*

'In it, he said he was sorry and that he loved me with all his heart. It wasn't my fault, he said. It was him. He just couldn't bond with the child. And he couldn't be responsible for someone with so many challenges. He wasn't equipped to deal with it. The child. It. He never mentioned Christopher by name. Ma was shocked, at first. "He has gone back to his own house," she said when she finished reading her letter. "Thanked me for everything over the past few years. He says he is sorry it has come to this." I remember how she sniffed back a sob, folded the letter back to the way it was and then threw it in the bin. "I guess it's just the three of us now, Constance," she said.'

'And that was it?' Louis asks. 'He just walked out and never came back? Not even to see Christopher?'

'The next time I saw Dessie Mahon, he was sitting on the wall outside the Esso station giggling with a young one in white spindle heels and neon leg-warmers who looked like she had just finished her final year in the convent secondary school. She was all leotards and short-cropped hair with bad highlights. And he looked at her like the sun was shining out of her backside rather than his own.

'Ma came round after a while, once the shock of Dessie leaving got out of her system. "D'ya know, he wasn't all he's cracked up to be at all, Constance," she said one day as she gently bounced Christopher on her knees. "He destroyed my rose bush that time he was hacking away at the garden, and all my spring bulbs were dug up too. And the smell of Old Spice from the bathroom every morning was enough to bring on the worst headache. Sure we could be worse off, I suppose." I liked the way she said "we". It was like the three of us were in this together. "I mean, did you hear about all the young fellas getting hooked on drugs and destroying their families and their lives. That would be enough to send you to an early grave," Ma said.'

Only now, does Louis look away. Only now, does he slow down so that he is behind Connie.

'I'm sorry,' Connie says. 'I wasn't thinking. I didn't mean to ...'

'Please,' Louis says, once again reaching for her hand. 'It's not your fault. It's no one's fault.'

Da doesn't like Louis. He says he can't bear to look him in the eyes. I'm not sure if I'm supposed to feel the same way. Thing is, I don't.

The lights in the houses at the foot of the hill are closer now. Down on the road, I can see people begin to walk in different directions. All weary but content. Ready for home.

'I know what happened last year,' Connie says to him. 'And I can only imagine what you and your family have been through. It can't have been easy for any of you,' Connie says.

I had heard Ma and Da talk about all the drugs from the city that had found their way closer to our home.

'I knew your son, Philip, growing up,' she adds. 'Your daughter, Linda, was in the same class as me in school. And everyone knew him because his style would change like the seasons. I always remember how he blended from a mod to a punk and then into a skinhead all in the one year. Wasn't he even an altar boy at one stage? The only altar boy ever to wear eyeshadow, I think! But sure wasn't that all the rage. Still is.'

Louis doesn't answer at first. He just nods his head. Eventually, he says, 'He found it hard to get work after he left school. I tried to get him a job in the civil service but jobs were scarce everywhere. Then he started to hang out up at those flats they built near the shopping centre not a half hour's walk from the house. The ones where the sulky ponies roam on the small patch of grass.'

'I know where you're talking about,' Connie says.

I see Louis' shoulders shake.

Connie moves closer. 'The last time I saw Philip was when I was walking up past those flats towards the shopping centre. I remember him shuffling towards me. I didn't recognise him at first.'

'It's hard to recognise someone whose eyes are grey and sunk back into their head,' Louis says.

'He asked me for a loan of money,' Connie continues. 'But I didn't have it. Times are tough for us all, I told him, and so he went on his way.'

'Sometimes I don't know why I come to this place,' Louis says. 'I suppose I come looking for answers, looking for change, looking for peace. Peace in my life. Peace in my family's life. But is it all worth it? I just don't know. All I can do is keep trying. For now, anyway.'

'Hey,' Connie says. 'Don't think like that. Look at the amount of people you have brought here. And I'm here, aren't I? If I hadn't gone into The Humble Jumble that day looking for baby clothes I wouldn't be here now; I'd still be at home worrying about my life.'

'It was your mother, really, I was thinking about when I gave you the leaflet about the trip,' Louis says. 'I didn't think you would be interested at all.'

'Do I give off that attitude?' Connie laughs. 'A sceptic?'

Louis shrugs his shoulders.

'You would be surprised how many people think I'm nuts!' he says.

'Well, Ma was a bit surprised when I came home and showed her the leaflet. "Oh, I don't know about that, Constance. I'm surprised Father Dennehy is endorsing it. More times these things turn out to be hoaxes," she said. "It's not moving statues that we're talking about. That's a communist country, for God's sake. You would think Louis McNamara would have more sense. And Father Dennehy too, for that matter."'

'Did she say that?' Louis asks, surprised.

'She calmed down after a while. I told her a break might be good for her – and for me – and I can remember how her eyes softened. She knew how tired I was, so exhausted that I could barely function some days. Christopher woke up, so she unfolded her arms and lifted him out of the pram. When he let out a whimper, she rocked him gently and sang a lullaby. Then she told me it was me who needed the break, not her. And here I am,' Connie says.

'Are you glad you came?' Louis asks.

'I was a bit worried when I got to the airport and saw the old biddies who were closer to Ma's age than mine – no offence, Louis. And you'd swear they were going to Butlin's for a week, the way they were going on. Seeing Jen with her da made me feel a little less awkward.' She laughs.

I run so I am closer to them. 'I like it here,' I butt in.

'Me too,' Connie replies. 'I think so, anyway. Most people keep to themselves. I suppose each one has their own secrets, their own baggage weighing them down.'

'That's for certain,' Louis says.

'You're a good man, Louis,' Connie says. 'You don't deserve what you've been through. No one wakes up in the morning and decides they are going to be an addict. I hope things get better for you. Better for us all.'

I wonder if that's what happened to Da. If he just woke up one day and became what he is now.

'It's the quietness here that I like the best,' Connie says. 'Life is simple, the way I imagine it was in Ireland some years back. Small stone houses dotted around the vast fields. It reminds me of the Gaeltacht in a way. Generations living together and looking out for one another as they work the land. A want for little and contentment in having just enough to get by. And a genuine thanks for what they have, knowing things could always be worse.'

'Do you believe in it? Do you believe in miracles?' I ask, and she stops for only a few seconds before answering me. Louis stops too and I know he wants to hear her reply.

'I didn't think about it much on the plane journey, or on the bus ride into the village, but deep down I suppose it was always there at the back of my mind. After all, if it was true and so many great things were happening over here, then maybe Christopher would get better. Maybe he could be the next miracle they all talk about.'

Neither Louis nor I say a thing; we just let her talk.

'I don't know why that Franciscan looked at me the way he did or why he picked me and Christopher from a crowd of so many and brought us into that room in the church. I tried to remember what it was like to be a teenager again, as the children all stood around the little altar at the top of the room. The youngest one became distracted when they began to say the rosary. And why wouldn't he, I thought, I don't know any ten-year-old who could lose themselves in such intense prayer.'

I think about how hard I find it to pray, but then I remember how Ma used to always tell me that a good thought is a prayer.

Connie frowns. 'And then, in a moment, they were on their knees. They fell in unison and raised their eyes to focus on a spot above the altar. As they stayed in their own personal ecstasy, so many thoughts ran through my head. Thoughts of Ma, of Dessie, of Christopher, of the years ahead, what will be or what will not. But I could see nothing through my own eyes, no hazy vision or brief apparition. At the back of the room, I saw a young priest with clean-cut hair and blue eyes that were brimming with tears. When he closed his eyes and lowered his head, the tears streamed down his cheeks. The weight of Christopher in my arms didn't seem so intense.'

Connie starts to cry when she speaks next. She wipes the tears away but they keep coming. 'I had so many unanswered questions after his birth. Why was he born that way? Why did it happen to me? What did I ever do to be given a handicapped baby? When I met a new mother on the street, I wished that she would tell me that her baby also wasn't perfect. That she was in the same boat as me. But I never met those women. The ones I met all had healthy children and their only worry was whether or not they would be blessed with another child again soon.'

I want to say something helpful but the words won't come out. Instead, I stroke her arm, right down to the tips of her fingers, just like Ma used to do to me when I was upset.

Connie sniffs, rubs her nose. 'I will say this. Those children were all looking and speaking with someone. All six of them witnessed something that no one else in the room could see. When they came out of the trance, there was not only relief in their eyes, but a sorrow that whatever they had experienced was now over. I don't know what people prayed for or what was on their minds, but everyone there felt something. In all that time, while the children had been kneeling, I stood in that small room with my child in my arms, and instead of asking for a miracle for my son, I found myself asking that I be able to accept him always. Just as he is.'

Finally, we reach the bottom of the hill and put back on our shoes. Standing out in the middle of the road, I look up at the tiny stars that begin to appear one by one across the night sky, as I continue to move my hand up and down Connie's arm. Then, realising something, I move my hand across her shoulders and down her back.

'Feel your clothes,' I say. 'Feel mine too.'

I'm running my hands all over my body now from my legs right up to my chest. Connie does the same and we both look at one another in shock.

Louis does the same.

'My clothes,' Connie says. 'How can that be?'

'I don't know,' I say.

We look around to search for others and see if they have noticed it too. Everyone has disappeared from the road. Connie, Louis and I link arms as we begin to walk. We don't say a word but I know that all three of us are wondering the same thing. How our clothes, which had been drenched from the rain as we climbed down the mountain, are now completely dry.

15

DUBLIN

SUZANNE

Louis told me there were times when he wished his eldest child dead. Times when he pictured his coffin being lowered into freshly dug ground, in a pit with space for two more. He said that it was only when he imagined the final shovel of sod filling the grave that he released the breath he has been holding for the last few years.

As my time working for Louis continued, we came to confide in each other more. We often told stories and shared snippets of our lives outside of the shop. One day – it had been a slow day in The Humble Jumble – he sat there allowing the tea to grow cold as he opened up to me about his son.

Louis said that he spent years ignoring the reality of it all, hoping that one day he would wake up and his eldest child would appear at the end of the bed with bright eyes that oozed sincerity. '"That's it, Da," he would say to me as he stood tall and clean-shaven. "I've had enough. That's it. No more. Never again,"' Louis said.

As I listened, I remember thinking that at least he could face it. Sarah had always said that there's nothing worse than a man who can't bring himself to see his own failings. Worse still is a man who can't admit that the wheels have finally come off the cart.

'Philip never gave us an ounce of trouble as a child. The teachers told us he was way ahead of the curriculum and that there were times when he became distant in the classroom just out of sheer boredom. He didn't make friends easily, though. Always drifting from one person to the next. He never seemed to bond fully with any particular child. Like his classwork, they bored him too after a while. But he never gave any cheek to Joanie, nor did he fight with his younger sister, Linda. If I had to call him anything as a child, it was placid. Well-behaved, too,' Louis added.

I didn't have any advice to offer to Louis. I knew better after Sarah. I had tried giving advice to her when the cracks first began to show with Charlie.

'Nip it in the bud now, Sarah,' I used to say to her, referring to his disappearing acts.

'He's only letting off a bit of steam,' she said. 'It hasn't been easy for him of late. Times are hard enough, Suzanne, without me breathing down his neck.'

That was Sarah. Always seeing the sliver of good among all the bad. She would see the goodness in a rat, our Sarah. In the dirtiest, filthiest rat.

So I stopped dishing out the advice. It was falling on deaf ears. I learned that I did more good just by listening. If she wanted to strip him down and tear him apart then she was entitled to. Not me. My job was to listen. Not to comment. And that's exactly what I did with Louis.

'When Philip was in recovery the first time, he told me that he felt like he never fit in anywhere; that he never belonged,' Louis said. 'When he injected the junk, as he called it, it put things right for him. Made everything seem all right. I tried to think back and identify the warning signs. I used to worry that he didn't have many friends, but that was until he fell in with a bad crowd. And then Joanie. Poor, poor Joanie. "Isn't it great that he has such a variety of friends?" she would say. She was oblivious to the reality of it all.

'When we spoke to the counsellors they told us that Philip didn't really fit the profile of a heroin user. Most of the addicts came from broken homes where their lives lacked consistency and routine. They asked us if he had ever shown signs of being depressed, but Joanie was quick to respond by telling them there was nothing like that in our family. No, Philip didn't fit the profile of the stereotypical heroin user, but he possessed every last trait of them once he got caught in the net and couldn't get out.'

'How did he get into it?' I asked.

Louis buried his face in his hands and shook his head. When he faced me again, his eyes were raw. I suggested we stop talking about it. But he said he wanted to keep going, that there were few people he could open up to about it. Even Joanie couldn't bear to talk about it any more, he said.

'There was no work around. Not in the suburbs, nor in the city centre. You know the underground passageway up near the flats where the young fellas hang out all day decorating the walls with graffiti and getting stoned on the funny stuff to pass the time? Well, Joanie would use the passageway as a shortcut to get to the shopping centre. The young fellas never bothered her, but when she noticed the used needles on the ground mixed in with the usual rubbish she stopped going that way and chose the longer route instead. We all knew about the drug problem that had gripped Dublin. Every week on the news we were hearing more about how out of control it was,' Louis said.

'Then one day, someone told Joanie that some of the locals had cleared the junkies out of there and that the passageway was safe to use again. She still avoided it for weeks, though. Sometimes, her nerves got the better of her. You know how it is,' he said. 'Then one morning she woke up in great form and told me she was going to head off for the day and make the most of the fine spring air,' Louis said.

Spring has always been my favourite time of year. You can see the green stalks of daffodils stretch tall from beneath the soil in the garden; people on the street opening windows that have been shut for months, and women waving children off to school who no longer needed coats on their backs.

Louis continued to unload. 'Joanie told me she was going to get a nice bit of minced lamb for the dinner to make a shepherd's pie. I went to work as usual only to be told, just after the eleven o'clock tea break, that there was an emergency call from my wife. When I picked up, I couldn't understand a word she was saying. She was nothing short of hysterical. I went home to find her standing over the sink, her face contorted with pain and her body trembling with a fear I had never seen before in my life. After I sat her down and made her drink a small brandy, she began to talk. She said she wished she'd never got up that morning, that she'd never set foot outside the door of our house. It turned out that Joanie had taken the usual route through the Grove, up past the Rise and out onto the mile-long road that led up to the butcher's in the shopping centre. And in the distance, she could see the entrance to the passageway where someone had planted flowers of purple and yellow and red along the edge of the freshly cut grass. It seemed like the locals were taking back what was once theirs, and instead of taking the long road up to the shopping centre, Joanie stepped over the low wall and walked down the sloped grass until she reached the opening of the passageway. She told me she was blinded at first, after coming into the tunnel from the bright sunlight. But she could hear footsteps up ahead, a sound of high heels scraping off the gravelled path and this put her more at ease – to know there was someone else close by. It was when she was three-quarters of the way through that she said she felt there was something amiss.'

Louis told me that she could see a faint stream of sunshine tumble into the passageway up ahead, which cast a light on two men who lay slumped over one another against the wall. When she got closer, she could see that one of the men was Philip. There he lay in a pool of his own urine, surrounded by empty cans and used needles. Louis said she just stood there as her screams echoed through the passageway, making birds fly away. At the time, Philip came and went as he pleased at home. Sometimes he would be away for days. When he came home, he would say he had been looking for work and crashing in a mate's house. But when Joanie saw him that day, she realised exactly what he had been spending his time doing and who his so-called friends were.

'The counsellor told us that most heroin users don't live past their thirties. Unless they get clean, of course. Then there is hope,' Louis said. 'She told us this after Philip's second time in recovery. At that point, I had taken the hard road and locked him in his room for a full week to let him go cold turkey. Linda moved out after the second night to go stay with a friend. She said she couldn't take the screams any more or him crying out her name and begging her to help him. On the days when I thought he was subdued enough, I would unlock the door and creep into the room. And there he would be, lying with his thin bare legs crunched up to his chest, his whole body trembling. He complained to me about the pain in his head and how it felt like it might explode. On the floor beside him lay a pool of vomit and untouched food. And I knew he wasn't sleeping because if it wasn't the screaming and the pleading and the begging I was hearing, it was the sound of him rocking in the corner of the room. His bones knocking and his joints clicking. That hollow, hollow sound of pure emptiness.'

I refilled the empty cup in Louis' hand. He nodded his thanks before continuing. 'He stole from us too. More times than I can count. The dole money wasn't enough for him. It wasn't enough to feed the habit, to pay his debts. When the vigilantes ran him and the other users out of the underground passageway for good, he moved into the inner city where he was close to his dealer and other so-called friends. They squatted in an abandoned bedsit near the Five Lamps and took turns injecting each other in whatever vein hadn't collapsed. Philip had been using it so much that he ended up injecting himself in his right eyeball when it wouldn't work anywhere else.'

I wanted Louis to stop talking. The pain of his story was too much. And yet still he spoke. So I continued to listen.

'The little finger off his left hand is missing now,' he told me. 'The dealer had only taken the tip off but Philip didn't get it seen to for a few days so gangrene set in. The heroin had numbed the pain, but when the drug wore off and he had no money for more, he decided to pay a visit to the emergency department. They didn't even ask permission before they took the whole finger off in the operating theatre. Or if they had, Philip wasn't in his right senses to give it. He was just another junkie. No one important at all.'

Louis sipped on the fresh tea, keeping a firm grip on the cup.

'The counsellor told us they could only help Philip if he wanted to be helped. "I do want help," Philip said when I unlocked the bedroom door and sat at the end of his bed after he had gotten through the worst of the cold turkey. I pretended not to notice the stench or see the stained sheets that lay in a pile on the floor. He had knocked over the slop bucket in a fit of rage and smeared the walls with its contents. Scratch marks covered his unshaven face and the black of his teeth was prominent against the paleness of his face. But there and then, I didn't care what he looked like or the state of the darkened room. My son was telling me that he wanted to get better. And stay better. For good. Or so I thought.'

Louis said the next few months were the hardest.

'He never finished any programme he was put on. The doctors lost interest and their sympathy – if they had any in the first place. The dose of methadone, which was meant to act as a substitute, didn't work and he returned to the bedsit and continued to shoot up. Three times he was resuscitated. Once by a pregnant girl who hadn't taken her hit just yet, but who injected herself once she knew he was all right. Once by paramedics who were called to the bedsit by his dealer, who only wanted him alive so he could pay back his most recent debt. And once by me when I came home from work to find he had robbed Joanie of her wedding and engagement rings and so had gone into the city centre to find him. He had made it to the pawnbroker's before me, cashed in and bought himself enough heroin to last him a week. When I arrived to the bedsit, he was on his own, slumped up against the peeling wallpaper in the corner of the darkened room. His eyes were half open, his mouth too. The room was icy, but his breath was not visible. It was not visible because it was not there.'

Louis started to cry, so I reached out and squeezed his free hand.

'I couldn't tell you how long I worked on my son that day. From the moment I peeled him away from the cold wall and laid him down on the bare floor, I begged and prayed that I could save him. I cursed myself for all the times I'd wished him dead.

'We had given him all the chances in the world and tried to help him as best we could, but nothing worked. Philip couldn't control the drugs.

They controlled him. At times, when he was trying to get better, I would see the optimism of a young child in his eyes. He would talk about going to college as a mature student. Or starting an apprenticeship in some trade. But those simple dreams weren't enough for him, and he just never won the battle he tried to fight. The odds were always stacked against him. Not only have I lost my only son, but I've seen my family crumble before my very eyes. Joanie – always outgoing and chatty, who everyone knows – has pretty much stopped setting foot outside the front door. The doctor prescribed her Valium, but I think it has only made her worse. Linda has lost her brother and a lot of her friends. It's not cool to have a junkie for a brother; their parents don't have to tell them that.'

'I'm so sorry, Louis,' I said.

'Don't be sorry. Just be thankful,' he smiled. 'No one ever thinks something like this can happen to them. Well, we just blinked and it did.'

As I stood up to go and boil the kettle, Louis inhaled deeply and let the air whistle out through his lips. My listening had helped him, if even for a short while. Lord knows, a lot more has happened even since that talk.

If I close my eyes now, I can see him standing in the grounds of St James' church, his eyes closed tight and his face pointing up towards the sun. With his lips, he will mouth many prayers.

Always for others, never for himself.

16

YUGOSLAVIA

CHARLIE

I've made a decision to do more with Jen on this trip. In all honesty, as I sit here in the only bar in the village, I see that it's the least I can do. She doesn't ask much of me any more. Or maybe she does and I just don't hear her. Maybe she has given up. But the intention is there now, so that should make it all right. That's what Sarah would say if she were still here. It's what she used to say to me when I never did the things I said I'd do.

'At least the intention was there, Charlie,' she would say, and the guilt would slide off me like butter off a hot knife.

If I go with her to the vineyards and the mountains over the remaining few days, then maybe I will be able to say the words that I never seem to be able to say any more. I never had to give it much thought when Sarah was alive. Words came easy. They would spill out of my mouth with little effort.

Urgent.

Meaningful.

True.

'I love you, Jen. More than I can ever explain and more than you'll ever know.'

I used to say it to her most nights as she settled into bed. But then the great world turned on its axle and spun and spun, throwing all the perfect contents away. And when I opened my eyes, everything was wrong. Nothing was in its place. Things were missing. Important things. Precious things.

Stolen.

Absent.

Gone.

At first, I tried to make sense of it in my own head. Retrace the steps of the day and see where things went wrong. It seemed right not to speak so much. My mind could process things better that way. If there was some sort of mistake, then maybe the nightmare would be over. Maybe it wasn't Sarah the two gardaí were talking about when they stood at the front door with no shelter from the pouring rain. The one who talked first was only a whippersnapper, just out of training. By God, he would get some rap on the knuckles from the sergeant when he heard that he told the wrong man that his wife was in a bad accident, I remember thinking.

Yet when he spoke, it was with conviction. Like he knew what he was doing. And his facial expression was bang on: the lips unsmiling, the brow furrowed. He'd been trained to do this sort of thing. This was his big moment.

His big moment.

My worst moment.

They told me to talk to Sarah in the hospital, even though her eyes were closed and the machines were the only thing keeping her heart beating and her lungs working. Even then, the words got stuck. They lodged like thick apple chunks at the back of my throat and made my eyes sting with salty tears.

I had only ever cried twice in my life before that. Once when I was fourteen after going three rounds bare knuckle with Shavo Nelligan. He was not only five years older than me but a good three inches taller and he wore his da's steel-toed boots even though they were too big for him. I held my own for the first two rounds until he jabbed me slyly in the kidneys, which made my legs go from under me. My knees had barely touched the concrete road when I felt the dusty leather of his old man's boots crack the bone in my nose. Everyone knew that Shavo had to win every fight, because the hiding he would get off his old man if he ever lost one would mean he would never be able to bare his fists at anyone ever again.

I see Shavo Nelligan the odd time now. Still as dour, with bullish hands and a heart so dark it's a wonder it's still beating. But then again, sometimes it's the hate that keeps people alive.

Jen hangs around with his son, Francis. The poor young fella doesn't stand a chance.

The second time I cried was just after Jen was born, when I held her in my arms. I'd never held a baby before. The white walls and fresh flowers in the hospital ward and the smile on my wife's face should have been enough to make me feel calm. There were others in the room but we might as well have been alone. Just the three of us – me and Sarah and this tiny baby who needed us more than anyone else in the world. Sarah had looked at me funny when she held her out for me to hold.

'What's wrong?' she asked me as I took a step back. 'Don't you want to hold your daughter?'

'I'm afraid I'll drop her,' I said with my arms tightly folded.

'Don't be silly, Charlie,' Sarah whispered. 'Sit down on that chair and relax.'

When the dinner ladies came, they didn't try to move quietly as their trolleys scraped off the hospital floor. They clanged and banged and pulled back curtains. They didn't seem bothered that they were disturbing new mothers and screaming infants.

'Cup of tea, love?'

'No thanks,' I said.

'Not you,' they laughed. 'You're not the one who has just given birth.'

And the whole ward laughed too.

All I had wanted them to do was leave so I could pull the curtain back around the bed again and spend forever looking at my daughter.

'Sit back into the chair,' Sarah instructed.

Dark shadows lingered beneath her eyes. Her skin was pasty and limbs weak. She had been cradling Jen since the moment I walked in, kissing the top of her forehead and stroking her long arms. I sat back into the chair and held my arms out far, as though I was about to catch a falling child.

'Relax,' Sarah laughed as she gently placed our newborn daughter into my arms.

I pulled Jen tight to my chest to let her hear the beating beneath, and I wanted her to know right there and then that I would never stop loving her, not even after the beating had stopped.

I made a silent promise to myself that day that I would never let her down. That I would always be there for her. And that's why I've made the decision to do more with Jen on this trip. I can remember that moment in the ward. I can remember that promise and even though I've broken it too many times since Sarah's death, maybe, just maybe, it's possible for me to mend it. I've still got a conscience dug somewhere in the back of my head, you know. My entire soul hasn't disintegrated just yet. I want to be there for her, to show her I am making the effort.

I only sip the pints this time. I even skull back a glass of water in between. But you don't see the hours ticking by when you're lost in your own thoughts. So I'm surprised when I look outside and see that it is dark. In the distance, a clap of thunder can be heard, which puts a smile on the barman's face.

'Rain. *Kiša,*' he says as I walk out the door. '*Hvala bogu.* Thanks be to God.'

I decide to leave before the rain arrives.

Inside the house, the grandmother sits in a corner, her stubby fingers twiddling her rosary beads. The woman of the house paces around the floor as she rocks a young child in her arms. Under the dim light, the man of the house sweeps around the women. He places the brush against the wall when he notices me come in.

'She gone,' he says.

When he speaks, he throws his hand out in front of him, as if brushing away some dust that lingers in the air. As I stand in the centre of the room with the heat of the light bulb warming my head, I wonder why the three of them are all looking at me as though I am obliged to give a response. No one says a word. The woman stops rocking the child in her arms and places him into his pushchair. It is the first time I have seen the child without his mother and, as he lies sleeping with a light blanket draped over his legs, I can see the same pureness that I remember seeing in Jen's face when she was that young.

'She only child,' the man pipes through gritted teeth and I know he is talking about Jen.

'I'm aware of that,' I say, but he just stands there with arms folded and chin raised high.

I wonder if they have held some sort of meeting while I was out where they discussed the man who spends all his time in the bar while leaving his daughter with a bunch of strangers.

'It's amazing the amount of English you have when you want,' I add.

The grandmother whispers prayers and the woman rubs the head of the child in the pushchair.

'Taking us all for fools, you are,' I tell them. 'One big hoax is all this is.'

No one speaks back. The man picks his brush up and continues to sweep at nothing on the floor. I slam the door shut as I leave the room, causing the child to wake and cry out for his mother. I can hear the thunder roar outside and the rain come down in buckets, making whipping noises as it bounces off the warm ground. Each step I take feels laboured and stiff. Inside my mouth is stale and I have a thirst for some cold water. I think about going back to the bar, about walking through the torrential rain and arriving there soaked and feeling sorry for myself. But the energy isn't there. It is like they have sucked it all out of me in that room. Like they took every last ounce of strength I have left.

Upstairs, the bedroom doors are closed tight. Everyone else is either sleeping or outside getting drenched to the skin and searching the sky for miracles. Christ, I never knew people could be so stupid, so goddamn gullible. And people ask if I have no cop on?

The bedroom is dark and I flick at the light switch but the bulb must have blown because no light comes on. After I trip over the suitcase and smack my knee off the wooden bedpost, I feel around until I am lying on the unmade sheets. I'm not sure what feels worse: the hangover that is starting to drill at my head, the pain in my kneecap or the memory of the look on the faces of the three people who sit in the room beneath me. At least I have the darkness, I think. With any luck it will swallow me whole.

As I shift on the bed, I hear the crumpling of paper beneath me. I reach under and pull out a page that is folded in two. An information leaflet, most likely. In the darkness, I fumble it onto the locker beside the bed.

When I try to sleep, it feels like a thousand pins are scratching at my eyes. The shadow of the crucifix that hangs on the wall seems to twitch in the dark. Every time I hear a footstep out on the street below, I wait for Jen to walk through the door. But she never comes. In my mind, I picture her lost in the village, no light from the moon or stars to guide her way. She won't act frightened but I know that deep down she will be. Jen has a way of masking things that bother her. She would never let on that anything was up. She thinks people have enough on their plates without listening to her little problems.

I know I should get up out of the bed and go look for her, but my legs are heavy and there's a whirring noise inside my head. I can't think straight. The pressure won't abate. All I can think about is waking up tomorrow morning, grabbing Jen and getting the hell out of this village with its crazy stories and far-fetched dreams.

I have seen the local men turn their battered cars into taxis to offer rides for cheap fares to lost tourists. I'll get up early and flag one down. They will take little or nothing for a ride back to the airport, and I'll stay there all day and night, if I have to, until there is a plane back to Dublin.

The sound of the rain stops around the same time that I slip away into a fitful sleep. In my dreams, I see my wife holding my daughter, her face proud and smiling, and Jen's skin smooth and pale like alabaster. Sometime during the night I wake at the creak of the door and watch as a shadow walks in and comes over to my bed. The figure stands there watching over me as a cool wind blows in my face. And yet my eyes will not open fully. I can't make out if it is Jen. All I know is that it is familiar and soothing and calm.

***

When I wake again, it is morning.

The sun burns through the small window of the room, making the air stale and musty. I look over at Jen's bed and can't tell whether she has slept in it or not. The pillow is plumped and the sheets tucked neatly under the mattress. But then, she has made her bed every morning since we arrived.

In the morning light, I pick up the piece of folded paper that still sits on the bedside locker. *Da* is scrawled on one side. I pull myself up until I am sitting. Even though I stopped drinking much earlier than usual the previous night, my head still throbs.

Dear Da,

I know we haven't been spending much time together lately and I thought this trip might give us time to do that. I'm glad we came here even though I know you really didn't want to. It might sound a bit silly, but I feel close to Ma over here. I picture her face so clearly. I see it in the sun and the sky and the fields and the leaves of the vines. When I see her, she is always smiling. She never looks sad. Sometimes I cry because all I want to do is reach out and touch her hand. Things feel different over here, Da. I don't really know how to explain it. Maybe it's just because we're not in Dublin and we have more time to think. I find it hard at home sometimes. Everything there reminds me of Ma. The curtains, the couch, the kitchen, the garden. And it's not that I don't want to be reminded of her, it's just that the house feels so empty without her, like a hollow barrel. I met a new friend over here. One of the locals. She has lost her mother too. Some of us are going up to the mountain tonight. We've heard that something special might happen there. I don't know what they mean by this but Louis and Connie are coming. I like Connie. She's kind and gentle but strong too. I think Ma would have liked her. I want you to come to the mountain too. Bring a torch so you can find your way. If I'm not at the bottom then it means I've already started to climb with Connie and Louis, so follow us up. And we can sit there, Da, you and me. We don't have to talk too much. Once we are close, I don't mind if no words are said. We can sit on the top of the mountain and who knows what wonders we might see.

Love always,

Jen

I stare over at the empty bed and then hold the paper close to my lips. When I inhale, I can smell the scent of her perfume, the smell of her jumper. Not Jen's but Sarah's. Woody musk with trails of florals from the fabric softener she used on the clothes. And in a moment, the page becomes fragile with the wet pouring out of my eyes.

Downstairs, I can hear the movement of feet shuffling around on the hard floor. The bells of the church chime and birds erupt into song. I fish a clean vest out of the suitcase and run my fingers through my knotted hair. Outside the bedroom there is no queue for the bathroom, so I go inside and splash water on my face, then race downstairs to find my daughter.

The house is empty except for the young woman and her child.

'Are you looking for Jen?' she asks.

'I am.'

'She left about an hour ago,' she says, as she rocks the pushchair with one hand. 'I'm Connie, by the way.'

'Charlie.'

'I know.'

'Where did she go?' I ask.

'To the church for morning Mass and then Louis is bringing the group on a day trip to the waterfalls,' she says. 'They should be back before dinner.'

'Aren't you going?' I say.

'No,' she says. 'It would be too long a day for Christopher.'

'Where are these waterfalls?'

'I'm not sure. About thirty miles or so from the village,' she says. 'If you run up to the church you might catch up with them.'

I stand there with my hands stuffed into the pockets of my shorts, not knowing what to do. If Jen didn't wake me to tell me about the day trip, then chances are that she doesn't want me to go along. I think about the note on the bedside locker and how she would have seen it there this morning. She must have thought that I had read it and not bothered to follow them up the mountain last night.

'I think I'll leave her be,' I say. 'Maybe she needs a bit of space.'

Connie laughs sarcastically through her nose. 'Or maybe she doesn't,' she says.

The woman of the house appears with a cup of hot tea and a plate of bread and jam, her expression stern. '*Dobro jutro*,' she says as she hands them to me.

'Good morning, Ana Marija,' Connie says.

Ana Marija smiles at her, then bends down to kiss Christopher on the cheek. Then she turns on her heel and goes back into the kitchen without so much as another glance in my direction.

Connie looks puzzled.

'We had a few words last night,' I explain. 'Well, not so much with her but with that husband of hers.'

I wait for Connie to tell me that she doesn't like him either. That there is something suspicious about him. Something funny. But instead, she seems surprised at what I have told her. 'Oh,' she says, 'I see.'

She fixes Christopher's posture in the pushchair so that he isn't so slumped.

'I'm heading out for a walk up towards the church,' she tells me. 'You're welcome to join us if you want.'

I weigh up my options.

I had made a promise to myself last night that I wasn't going to touch a drop of drink for the next two days. I glance at my watch. It's eleven o'clock. So far so good.

I know that I can either go back up to that pokey room and stare at the four walls all day, or I can get out and see a bit of this village before Jen gets home for dinner.

Connie watches me slurp the tea and take small bites out of the bread.

'I could leave it if you want to go now,' I offer.

'No,' she says. 'It's not right to waste their food. They have so little as it is.'

Outside in the blazing heat, I think about the cowboy hat that Louis had given me at the start of the week. Truth is, I'm not sure where it has gone. For all I know, it could be sitting on a bar stool, mourning my absence, or lodged in a gutter awaiting my arrival.

'We haven't seen much of you since we got here,' Connie begins.

'Ah, I've done a bit,' I say. 'Climbed the small mountain the other day.'

'Did you?' she asks.

'Yep,' I say. 'And I've been spending time with the locals.'

'You mean *in* the local,' she says, eyebrow raised.

I suppose I deserve that.

We walk along the dusty roads. Me with my hands shoved into my pockets and Connie with her hands clasped onto the handles of the pushchair. People pass by and nod a 'hello'. We must look like a couple with a kid. I try to keep my eyes from staring at my feet so I focus on the steeples of St James' church instead. The bells chime once again, which tells me it is noon. Connie pulls the shade of the pushchair over Christopher's head and lets a small white sheet drape down so he is protected from the sun's rays.

'They're probably well on their way now,' she says. 'Louis was going to organise a few taxis to take them there.'

At the very least, I am glad that I don't have to contend with Louis and the way he looks at me every time our paths cross.

'Sounds like he has it all worked out,' I say without trying to hide the sarcasm in my voice.

'Don't be like that,' Connie says. 'He hasn't had it easy, you know.'

'And I have?' I say.

And we leave it at that.

The roads move from one dirt track to the next until we circle the church and cross over into the fields. We are greeted by a sea of tents, all pitched at a comfortable distance from one another. Some vacant. Some filled.

I tell Connie to park the pushchair, then pick Christopher up and let his head rest over my shoulder as I carry him through the fields. Birds swoop down low and hide between the long grasses for a moment before shooting up into the blue sky once more. Young men rest their heads against rolled-up sleeping bags whilst others strum soft notes on acoustic guitars. Girls with sun-kissed faces gather in groups and sit cross-legged as they whisper stories to each other.

'I've heard the milicija were here again last night,' Connie says. 'They told them to move on, though there's no sign of that happening at the moment. But they'll be back later, I imagine. If they want the place cleared then they'll clear it.'

'Where would they even go?' I ask. 'There are so many of them. How did they even get here?'

'I've heard Louis say that most of them come over land. A busload of

Austrians arrived in the other day. Not one of them was older than twenty. They just hopped off the bus with their heavy backpacks and mountain boots,' Connie says.

'I'm not sure I would have been that curious at their age,' I say.

'Maybe it's the times we live in,' she replies as she looks across the vast fields. 'So much war in the world today. So much pain.'

'There's always been war and pain,' I say. 'You're just protected from it when you are a child. It's when you reach adulthood that your eyes are opened and you see the world for what it really is.'

We spend the afternoon like this, talking about things in fits and bursts with small nuggets of idle philosophy thrown in for good measure. After we leave the fields and Christopher is once again settled into his pushchair, we walk around the vineyards and along the path towards the mountains. The boy from the house opposite Podbrdo comes rushing out and hands us two glasses of cold water. He winks at me before running back inside.

'It's time we were getting back,' Connie says. 'They'll be back from the waterfalls soon.'

'You're right,' I say as we turn full circle and head back. 'I want to see Jen before dinner. There are a few things I need to say to her.'

***

It's evening time when we arrive back to the house to see that they are already back from the waterfalls.

'Where is she?' I ask Louis as I try not to look into his dopey eyes.

'You mean Jen?' he says.

'Of course I mean Jen. Who else?'

He lifts his battered cowboy hat up and scratches at the side of his head.

'Is she not with you?' he asks with squinted eyes.

'She was with you for the day,' I say, 'at the waterfalls. Connie told me.'

'Yes. Yes. She was with us all day,' he says. 'I sat behind her in the taxi back to the village. We had hoped to get back for the time of the apparition but we were too late.'

'So where is she now?'

He starts to rub his chin.

'Well, I thought she was with you,' Louis says.

Walls close in. The air stops circulating in the room. People cease talking.

'Do you mean to tell me that my fourteen-year-old daughter is missing?' I say as I curl my right hand into a fist. 'What in God's name is wrong with you?'

Louis lets his eyes fall to his feet. 'I'm … I'm …'

I don't wait to hear what he is trying to say. I am already halfway out the door and charging up the street by the time he finishes his sentence.

For the next few hours, every area is covered, every street re-walked. Connie has gathered pilgrims to help look. We search and search. But we cannot find Jen. When the moon starts to rise it is full and yellow, just like the sun was earlier. And though I continue to search the crowds for the face of my daughter, all I can see are the faces of strangers. Though there seems to be fewer and fewer foreigners as the darkness takes hold. The fields are emptying out and many of the tents have disappeared. Around the streets there is a sense of urgency as people move at a quicker pace.

It is then that I hear the stomping of what I know to be polished steel-toed boots. Many of the people scurry away, eager to avoid making eye contact with the men that approach. They want to get as far away as they can. Away from the milicija.

The milicija do not care about her safety.

'Go home to your countries,' they say to those of us who remain on the unlit streets, searching for Jen. 'There is nothing here to see.'

I bury my head in my hands. I scream out her name. She's missing. The only person I have left in the world is missing.

And it's all because of me.

17

YUGOSLAVIA

JEN

Iva pulls me away from the church grounds as soon as I get out of the taxi. Her eyes are raw and I can tell she has been crying.

'What is it?' I ask.

I have never seen the church grounds so empty since I arrived in the village a few days ago.

'Father Petar,' she says, 'go to prison.'

I remember the Franciscan who brought Connie and Christopher into the room with the children. He seems too good a man to have ever done anything deserving of prison.

'My friend, Stela,' she says, 'they hit Dominik, her brother. He go to hospital. Beaten. Very bad.'

Iva leads me along the side of the church out towards the fields where people are collapsing their tents and packing up their belongings.

'Why? What has happened?' I ask.

'The milicija,' she said. 'They do this. Do all this. They hear about mountain. They say we disobey regime. They say no more pilgrims. They take Father Petar to prison. After the Gospa come, the milicija come.'

'And what happened to Stela's brother?' I ask.

Iva buries her face in her hands and starts to sob.

'The milicija. They say no more melons. They take his dollars and keep,' she says as she pushes her hand deep into her pocket.

'They say it is revolution,' she says.

Iva takes a deep breath, trying to gather herself.

'What will happen to Father Petar?' I ask.

'I do not know. Father Petar gone,' Iva cries. 'They take him from church. Tie hands. Put him in car. No one can stop them. "Where are you go?" they ask. But milicija spit at their feet and leave.'

Iva puts both hands on my shoulders before asking a question that I can't answer.

'Who take care of us now?'

We wander around the streets and fields. People walk in different directions but everyone keeps their eyes focused on their feet. They try to ignore the milicija who roam around, kicking at stones and looking at things that are none of their business. No one notices Iva. They don't pay any attention to the girl and her foreign friend.

'You need to go home, Iva,' I say once the sun begins to fall behind the mountain. 'Your family will be worried.'

'And you?' she asks. 'Your father worry?'

When I don't answer her, she pulls at my arm.

'Come,' she says. 'You come my house. Eat. Pizza with pineapple. My sister Veronika cook. We share.'

***

I sit between Iva's two brothers at the dinner table and listen as the older one leads with the prayers. When he is done I try not to make noises as I chew on the pizza. Veronika keeps looking at me but the boys seem uninterested. Their hands are covered in earth and their shirts damp from a hard day of work.

'Thank you, Veronika,' I say when we are finished eating. 'That was delicious.'

Veronika smiles and then lowers her eyes.

'You eat pizza at home?' Iva asks.

And I think about the food Da tries to cook for me. Aunt Suzanne often calls by with a pound of mince on a Monday. I've heard her call it 'versatile'. It sits in the fridge for a day or two before Da has a go at it. He heats the pan and watches as the dirty lard that has been used too many times melts. When the pink meat has turned brown, he'll go to the cupboard and take out a tin of spaghetti and tip it into the saucepan before mixing it all together. On a good day, he'll chop an onion. On a bad day, he'll burn the pan.

'Not so much pizza,' I say to Iva. 'More spaghetti bolognese.'

'Come. I walk to you house,' Iva says once the plates have been cleared and washed. 'It dark soon.'

Her home is only a short distance from the small mountain. She leads me over walls and into gardens of neighbouring houses and down narrow side streets that I never noticed before as the darkness quickly fills in. She keeps looking over at the two steeples of the church and I know that is the direction she wants to go, even if it is too dangerous.

'Maybe they will let Father Petar go,' I say as we come closer to the church. 'Maybe he is already home.'

But we can both see that there are no lights from inside shining through the stained-glass windows. There are no priests around and few pilgrims. But there are many milicija. Too many milicija.

One of them notices us. He points over. When he shouts, two others move beside him and squint in our direction.

'They see,' Iva says. 'We must run.'

And so we do. We run through the streets and hide in sheds and gardens. When we hear a noise, we jump up and leave for somewhere new. Somewhere hidden. Somewhere safe. There is no sound around the village, only the noise of heavy boots and angry voices.

'We go to fields,' Iva says.

***

We run fast and heavy through the fields, further and further from the village, our fingers brushing against each other and our bodies almost colliding. Somewhere in the distance behind us I can hear the sound of a dog's bark. There is a rush and a thrill within as we disappear into the safety of the darkness. I stop first, bending my body forward and placing my hands on my knees. Up ahead, Iva is still running. She cuts through the long grass with ease, her head always lifted up towards the stars. I try to call her name but the words can't escape. I breathe in deeply through my nose and out through my mouth. All I want right now is the feel of cold water sliding down my throat.

'Iva,' I croak.

And though it is too quiet to be heard, even in the silent fields, she stops dead in her tracks and turns around.

'Jen,' she whispers, and it travels on the tips of the long grass back to where I am stooping.

She trips and falls as she tries to sprint back to me. When she is finally beside me, I reach up and place my hand on her shoulder.

'I have a stitch in my side,' I say.

'A stitch?' Iva asks.

'A pain,' I say, pointing to my right side. 'A sharp pain.'

'No sit. Please,' she says as she crouches down close to the earth. 'They come. Milicija come.'

She holds my hand and pulls me along and we continue on until neither one of us can go any further. Our legs are too tired. We stop together and, as I sit, I think about how I'm not even sure where she has brought me. It is all happening so fast. I try to remember when the afternoon turned into night. It seemed like only a few minutes ago when I was watching the rapid rush of a great waterfall.

Panting too, Iva sits cross-legged in the field beside me. Everything is quiet and I can hear my heart thumping beneath my chest. When it slows to a normal pace, I lie back into the long grass and look up at the thousands of stars that fill the sky.

'Did you see her tonight?' I ask and Iva knows who I am talking about.

'Yes, I see every day,' she says. 'Even when day is bad for me, still she comes.'

'Why does she come?' I ask. 'Why does she keep coming? Isn't once enough?'

'I don't know why,' Iva says. 'Maybe we do not hear. Too many wars. Too much hate. The Gospa, she say "Peace"! But we do not listen.'

'Why do they do this?' I ask of the milicija. 'Why would they want to destroy something that is good?'

'The milicija no understand,' Iva says. 'They only understand the regime. It is not possible to think different. Too dangerous for them.

People no want trouble. My people not have much. Just God and fields and mountains. But they strong. They have faith. That is why the Gospa comes to here.'

A gentle breeze floats by, making the grass rustle and the crickets wake.

'What do we do now?' I ask.

'For now, we must wait,' she replies as she lies down beside me. 'Just wait.'

18

YUGOSLAVIA

CHARLIE

Too many hours have passed. There is an eeriness in the air. It looms above my head and darkens my path. My feet ache and yet they have an urge to run however fast and far it takes until I reach my little girl. People gather around me, strangers that I've never met before. Backpackers due to go home throw their bags on the side of the road when they hear about the young girl who has gone missing. How can they help? Where should they go? Once they were intimidated by the milicija; now they will not leave this village, they say, until the girl is found.

We have now dispersed into smaller groups. Some head for the small mountain. Some the big one. Others mount the small walls that separate houses and run through backyards and rummage through sheds. Locals come out of their houses. The mothers raise their hands to their mouths and the fathers go back inside to fetch their sons when they hear the news. Then they begin to search through the maze of vineyards and sweep through the tobacco fields in search of the missing girl. And I think that if there was someone up there sitting on the moon, watching the world at night, they would be dazzled by the tiny lights that flutter around this little village in communist Yugoslavia.

I must have walked every twisting path and winding road ten times over and still I end up back at the same place on the same street by the small mountain. I feel someone tug at my shirt. It is the little boy from the house up the road. Still he wears no shoes, even though it is too dark to see what he might step on. He reaches out and hands me a bottle of cold water, which I drink in one gulp. Then he rubs at my arm and runs away. Connie is behind me. She walks with Louis, who shakes his head and weeps.

'We are looking for a young girl,' Connie says to a milicija, who is leaning against the stone wall of a farmhouse. 'Please can you help?'

He looks her up and down, then nudges his comrade who is drinking a bottle of beer. They talk in Croatian to each other then start to laugh.

'Why not ask Gospa for help?' he mocks. 'She will find, no?'

Jen is gone and they couldn't care less. There is a smugness to their expressions. *You pitiful fools*, it says, *go home to your own countries.*

Connie comes up behind me and holds onto my hand.

'Don't worry, Charlie,' she says, 'we'll find her.'

***

I think about the time that Jen ran away from school when she was seven years old. Sarah had been worried that she wasn't mixing well with the other kids, I remember, as no one ever invited her to their house to play and Jen just shrugged her shoulders when Sarah asked her who her friends were.

'You need to make friends, Jen,' she urged. 'School is so much more fun when you have a friend. Just go up and talk to someone. There must be other children in the yard who look like they could use some company.'

The next day at lunch break, Jen saw Francis Nelligan sitting by the bin in the corner of the yard, picking out orange peel and the crusts of leftover sandwiches while the other children chanted songs or skipped over thick ropes.

'You can have some of mine,' she said as she offered him a custard cream biscuit.

She told me afterwards how Francis had taken his head out of the bin, looked at her and smiled.

'Did you lose some baby teeth?' she asked when she saw the gaps on the right side of his mouth.

His face turned red and he shoved his hands in the pockets of his torn trousers.

'My da said they were coming loose anyway,' he said as he rubbed the side of his swollen cheek. 'Best not to bother him for any food for lunch in future.'

Sarah was thrilled when Jen came home from school that day and told her she had made a friend. Until, this is, she heard his name.

'I don't want her hanging around that house, Charlie,' she said that evening after dinner. 'That man's a monster. The way he used to treat that poor wife of his, God rest her. He's an animal. I've nothing against the child, but I don't want Jen anywhere near that house.'

I told her she had nothing to worry about, that I didn't think there would be any invitations to play in Shavo Nelligan's house.

'She has found a friend, Sarah,' I said. 'And someone she likes. Isn't that enough for now?'

Sarah didn't even have to call up the stairs to wake Jen up most school mornings after that. She would already be up and dressed before Sarah had the kettle boiled.

'I'm going to walk to school with Francis, Ma,' she told Sarah that first morning when she came downstairs.

'Well have your breakfast first,' Sarah said. 'I'm sure Francis won't be here for another while yet.'

'He is here,' Jen said. 'He's been sitting on the kerb since before the sun woke.'

Sarah pulled her housecoat tight around her neck and ran out to the front door to fetch the milk bottles from the doorstep. Just as Jen had said, Francis was sitting on the kerb with his head on his knees as he played with the gravel and the dirt.

'Come in here, Francis,' she called. 'I've a bit of toast left over from the breakfast if you want a bite. There's some homemade jam in the cupboard too.'

Sarah said she never saw a child hop up so quickly.

To be fair, Francis seemed nothing like his father. And so Sarah became happy, knowing that everyone else was happy.

Except we didn't know what was going on after they left for school each morning.

A group of older boys who were in the class above and who lived around the corner from Francis used to gather by the school gates each morning at the time. One of them had kicked a football over Shavo Nelligan's back wall a few weeks earlier and Shavo had thrown it back burst. As a result, they taunted Francis every time he came out of his house and this continued when he entered the school gates each morning. When he began walking with Jen, they jeered him even more. None of the parents who left their children at the gate, nor the teachers or the principal who watched the children like hawks, ever intervened when they heard the taunting. So Jen put her arm around Francis' shoulder and stuck her tongue out at the boys.

Later, there were a few weeks when Francis wasn't in school. When Jen asked the teacher where he was she said he'd had an accident with some boiling water that spilled out of a falling kettle. The burns were bad, but they would heal, she said.

Without Francis to taunt, Jen became the target of the boys. At lunch-time in the yard, they would surround her. Sometimes they threw banana skins and orange peel, aiming for her hair. Other times, they would call her the same names they called Francis: a tinker, a gypsy, a knacker and a tar baby born in the dirt on the road.

'I'm not that,' she cried.

'You must be,' one of the boys shouted back. 'If you hang around with one then you must be one too.'

She held it in for a while but then it all became too much for her. Sarah waved her off to school one morning and set about cleaning the grey ash from the fireplace. I went into town to buy some supplies, both of us none the wiser that Jen hadn't made it to the classroom.

Mid-morning, Sarah noticed that Jen had left her lunch on the kitchen table. When she arrived at the school to hand it in, she couldn't understand why the teacher looked so puzzled.

'But Jen's not in today, Mrs Carthy,' she said.

The sandwiches fell to the floor.

It was lunch hour by the time I got the bus home from town to find Sarah and several of our neighbours scouring the streets and back gardens of the houses.

'Don't tell me it's Jen,' I said with my hands clasped at the back of my head. 'Don't tell me something bad has happened.'

Sarah ran into my arms. When I went to caress her hair, I noticed that it was tousled. She must have been pulling at it with frustration.

'We can't find her, Charlie,' she cried. 'She never showed up at the school this morning.'

All I could do was squeeze her tight and whisper that everything would be all right. Even though I wasn't sure that it would be. It was the first time in a long time that I uttered a prayer. I looked to the sky and made promises I knew I would never keep. I begged and pleaded and said prayers I hadn't said since I was a child. And as I held my shivering wife, a thought struck me.

'Did anyone check our back garden?'

'Of course we did,' she snapped. 'I went into your shed. She isn't there.'

Even though I thought she might collapse to the ground, I let go of Sarah and ran towards our house. I didn't look back as Sarah called my name but instead charged through the front door, hallway and the kitchen until I was out in the back garden. I stood still in the centre of the garden and when all was quiet, I closed my eyes.

And there it was – a sound, faint but real.

It came from the coalbunker beside the shed. I couldn't mistake the small whimpers of my only child. A child who never let anyone see she was upset and who never wanted to worry anyone with her problems.

Sarah came bolting through the back door just as I was lifting the wooden lid off the coalbunker. I bent down, scooped Jen up and wiped the black off her tear-stained cheeks.

The three of us remained there, wrapped in a tight embrace for what seemed like an age. In my arms, her shoulders jerked and I said nothing as she sobbed.

'I'm sorry,' she eventually said when she raised her head, 'I didn't mean to scare you.'

***

This is the image implanted in my head as I walk around this strange place. Seven-year-old Jen covered in black, telling me she is sorry that she frightened me. Wherever she is now, I picture her as this small child and not the teenager into which she has grown. The pain of not being able to get to her is too much.

The world has gone quiet and I'm standing here, staring into nothing but seeing everything all at once. I see Jen stepping over me as I lie slumped at the bottom of the stairs. I see her try to wake me in the mornings before she goes to school and then giving up when I don't respond. I feel the hunger in her stomach when there is no food to be cooked. I see her sit at the back of the classroom staring out the window as she tries to choke back the tears. Then I see her in her bedroom, letting them all flow out. I see a child who needs her father now that her mother is no longer here. And I see how she has tried and will never stop trying to pick me up from the hole I've fallen into. It's all there before my eyes and I'm down on my knees in the middle of the street with my head hanging in shame.

Over to my left, I see something half buried beneath loose paper and stones. It's battered and broken and fit for the bin, and though I want to leave it to rot and disintegrate, I reach over and grab Louis' cowboy hat. I place it hard down onto my head and look up to the vast sky and I ask myself over and over: *what on earth have I done*?

19

YUGOSLAVIA

IVA

'Talk me about your land. Your home,' I say to Jen.

We have been hiding here for hours. We pull at the grass and try to make a bed from the piles, but still we feel the rough ground beneath our bodies. Though I am tired, I do not feel like sleeping. Jen feels the same, I think. We talk and talk, telling stories about our families, about our lands.

Everything is serene in the fields tonight. A soft breeze has found us where we lie. For a while we had tried to count the stars that litter the sky but too many times we lost count and broke into laughter.

'I miss Francis,' Jen says. 'He'll be missing me too, I think.'

'Francis. Boy? Girl?' I ask.

'He's a boy,' Jen says.

'Ah. Boyfriend.'

Jen jumps up. 'Francis! My boyfriend? Are you mad?'

'Mad?' I ask and Jen spins her finger in circles, pointing it at her temple.

'Yes, mad. Crazy. Loco.'

'Ah, loco. *Lud!* Yes, maybe. A little, some people think,' I joke and we fall back down to the ground with laughter.

I think I will miss her when she goes home. I do not have too many friends apart from those who share the visions. People want to be my friends, but not for the right reason. I can see through them; it's like looking through a clear pane of glass. Jen is different. She does not like me because of what I see. She likes me because we are almost kindred spirits and she too feels lonely. Even when there are so many people around.

'You miss your mama, yes?' I ask.

I don't want to upset her but Father Petar always tells me that it is not good to bottle things up or keep them hidden. 'You must talk about the things that pain you, Iva,' he always tells me. Though it is hard, I often do as Father Petar says. And it makes the heavy air around me feel a little lighter. Even if it is only for a short time.

Jen picks at the long grass, splitting the blades and then tying them together in a chain. 'I miss everything about her,' she starts. 'How she would creep into my bedroom and open only one curtain so that the morning light wouldn't be too hard on my eyes. How she used to have breakfast on the table when I came downstairs and how she would watch me eat from where she stood by the cooker, sipping on a cup of hot tea. I miss how she used to have my bed all made for me when I went back into my room. And how she used to have the front door off the latch for me when I came home from school. I miss the dinners she made, even though Aunt Suzanne is a better cook. I miss the multicoloured wool and different-sized needles that she used to buy for me at the Saturday market, even though I knew she had more important things to spend her money on. I miss how she used to cut my toenails after a bath because I could never cut them right myself. And I miss how, when I was sad, she wouldn't push things with me if I didn't want to talk about it. I miss the way she didn't scold me when I didn't do well in a school test because she knew I was giving Francis some extra help with his reading. I miss the way she used to fight with my da and then make up with him. I miss her smell, her smile, her long hair and her misty eyes. I miss them so much at times that I feel like my body will explode. And I have this want inside of me, so, so bad. To touch her, just to hold her for one last time. Even if it is only for a few seconds. Just so I can feel her and tell her how much I love her and miss her.'

I do not understand all of what she says. But I know that she speaks with much love. I stretch my arm out and place it on Jen's shoulder in the hope that it will stop the shaking in her body. When she cries, the long grasses sway as if they are mourning with her. If I hold her for long enough, then maybe the pain will ease a little and the tears that stain her cheeks might fall less and less. I hold her, like I hold Veronika, and somehow this eases the heavy burden that presses down on my own shoulders. And in my head, I start to remember all those things that people with good intentions said to me after Mama died.

'Time is a great healer.'

'She is in a better place.'

'Thank God you still have your father to look after you.'

I think about saying them to Jen, but I know that they will have the same effect on her as they had on me. They will do nothing to comfort her. Not now. Not anytime soon.

'It is good. Friends are good, yes?' I say as I lift her chin up with my finger. 'Francis you friend. Me you friend. You come my home. I go you home. Maybe. You home is like here, yes?' Jen brushes at her jeans and twists her legs around so that she can push herself up to a kneeling position.

Jen smiles. 'I live in a city called Dublin, not too far from the sea,' she says. 'But it's nothing like here. I've never been to anywhere like here and I don't think I will be again.'

'We write. Letters. Pictures,' I say.

'Yes, I would like that,' Jen says. Then she palms her forehead. 'That reminds me – I forgot to send Francis a postcard.'

'Francis is good friend?'

'He's the only one I have,' she says.

I know how rare it is to have a friend you can trust. Someone who will stand by you through the hardest of times. Too many people have proved to be false friends to me. They mock me behind my back. They call me names and say I bring too much trouble on our little village. Mama would have known the right words to say to me. She would have known how to handle the situation. The five of my friends who share in the visions were all able to run home into the arms of their mothers and tell them what they saw during the first days. For me, I only had Tata. But he does not share the same strong faith as Mama did. Or, if he does, he never puts it on display. So it was only in Veronika and Stela that I could confide at first. I dared not say it to Tata or my brothers at that time. Even now, I sometimes see the scepticism in Tata's eyes. How can God take his wife and then send the Gospa to visit his daughter? It does not make sense to him. It does not make sense to me.

'Have you ever asked her if you can see your mother?' Jen asks.

'Many, many times,' I say.

'What does she say?' Jen asks.

'She smile,' I say. 'She tell me Mama is happy.'

'Maybe someday she'll let you see her,' Jen says. 'If you keep asking her she might say yes.'

'Maybe,' I say as I shrug my shoulders. 'I do not wish to annoy Gospa. Maybe she'll move to the next village!'

This time we laugh for much longer. We laugh until our sides hurt and our tears become different, almost lighter.

'Maybe we shouldn't joke about it,' Jen says, once we have composed ourselves once more.

'Do not worry,' I tell her. 'The Gospa, she laugh too.'

'I wish my da would laugh again,' Jen says as she starts to fiddle with her hands. 'He used to laugh a lot. And he made Ma laugh too. Sometimes she laughed at nothing, and then Da would laugh too. I'd be the only one not getting the joke. It would take them ages to calm down until they were able to speak. Ages. And then they would forget what they were laughing about in the first place.'

'I see you father, maybe?'

'I don't think you'd like him very much,' she says. 'He's different now. He doesn't like to joke so much any more. Not now Ma is gone.'

Behind the mountains, the day has begun to break. The night has passed so quickly.

My shoulders grow cold and I hunch them up so they are close to my ears. Shivers run down my spine and I sense it, like a dog senses thunder before it calls. 'Sshh,' I say and push Jen down so she falls back onto the grass. I lie flat beside her with my left ear as close to the ground as I can get it. 'Sshh,' I say again. 'Listen.'

Jen lies still. She doesn't move a limb and barely takes a breath.

'They coming.'

20

YUGOSLAVIA

CHARLIE

The stomping of feet along the uneven narrow road has ceased. Those who rushed and hurried in the darkness are now out of sight. The milicija too are nowhere to be seen. Maybe they have found something else deserving of their chastisement. There is no house nearby, no inviting light in a small rectangular window, no locals, no pilgrims, no sound. Even the crickets are refusing to chirp. Across the way, Connie is sitting with Louis on a stone wall. I hear his sobs and his ranting through a bubble of tears.

And I've no idea why it is him who is crying when it's my daughter who has gone missing. My wife who is dead. I'm sick of hearing them all talking about Louis and how he has troubles of his own. Like he's the only one in the world who has ever faced hardship. If I never see his face again, it'll be far too soon. Connie sits beside him, rubbing his arm like he's a little child who has just had a fall.

'Things aren't too good at home,' she says to someone who passes by and asks if he is all right.

'When are things ever good with anybody?' I shout over to her. 'Just look at us all. A bunch of hopeless cases waiting for a miracle that's never going to come.'

She pulls back like I have just slapped her in the face.

'You can say what you want about yourself, Charlie Carthy,' she snaps back, 'but I'm no hopeless case. Neither is anyone else here. Just because you'd rather be propping the bar up, leaving your sorrows with the slops at the bottom of a pint glass, doesn't mean the rest of us would.'

I can see she wants to have a proper go, but she holds herself back. I can see the thought in her eyes – it wouldn't be fair for her to berate a man whose daughter is nowhere to be found. So she says no more. She just goes back to poor Louis who looks like he has the problems of the entire world resting on his bony little shoulders.

There's a mad man hammering at the back of my eyes. I don't think I've ever had a headache like it. Not even on the worst of days when an all-dayer turned into an all-nighter. Any second now my legs will buckle and go from under me. I'll crumple onto the stony ground. There will be a little strength left in my eyes, just so I can look up at the stars and search for Sarah's face. She would know what to do. She would know where Jen is and how to find her. One thing's for sure, she wouldn't be in the middle of a darkened dusty road feeling sorry for herself. I'd get a good kick up the backside from her and a telling off too.

'Get your act together, Charlie,' she would roar. 'Our daughter needs us.'

I've taken more beatings than anyone deserves. I don't want any help, I've told them a thousand times. I don't want anyone calling around. I want them all to just leave me alone. For the love of God, just let me be.

'It's only a proud man who says he doesn't need help,' Suzanne roared at me one day, even though I had closed every window and pulled every curtain in the house. 'Put your pride away, Charlie. People are reaching out to you. Let them in.'

I told her what she could do with her help. I told them all what they could do with their help.

'We don't need anyone,' I said to Jen when she crept down the stairs and met me crouched down on the last step. 'You and me will be just fine on our own.'

Except we weren't.

For too long I told myself I could get a handle on things. Truth is, my problems started long before Sarah died. I think now of when I began to hide the naggin of whiskey in the shed – on the back shelf between the cracked pots and used newspapers. Little sips helped me get through the day when all I could do was stare at brushes that were going stiff in their jars. Sarah didn't notice or, if she did, she didn't comment.

We argued more and more. Jen would grab her headphones and go up to her room where she would stay until the next morning. It was always about the same thing. Money. The one thing that we never cared about when we were sweet sixteen and had the world at our feet. All that bothered us back then was when we could catch a stolen kiss or have a cuddle under the plastic shelter of the 27A bus stop.

The interest rate on the mortgage was going up and up each year. The bricks and mortar soon became a noose around my neck. I never bothered Sarah with the bills. If she looked after Jen and the house, then I'd look after everything else. That's the way it should be, my old man always told me. I was the one who had to provide. And so I did. Well, I tried to anyway.

I tried to stay away from those poker sessions for the first while. Just sat on the same stool wondering how long I could nurse the pint that was in front of me, afraid to count the change in my pocket in case the next one might be my last.

Most of the sad cases came out of the room before closing. Those who weren't playing were thrown out after last orders and not invited to stay for the lock-in.

I used to laugh at those that stayed behind. Poor fools should have more sense. I was happy enough to heed that advice and I knew it would have been the last straw for Sarah if I wasted what we had on a game of cards.

I had the cop on to walk on past the bookies next door too, even when they were all huddled around the radio, gabbing about an outsider with great odds who was sure to beat the favourite. More times it turned out to be a three-legged horse with a jumped-up trainer who put the word out that his filly came from the finest bloodline. But there was always a time when the horses came in and I'd curse myself for not having had a harmless flutter on the one with the 10–1 odds. There's nothing harder than seeing a man standing at the bar with a pocket full of crisp green notes when you know it could have been you.

My old man had left me enough to see us through the first few winters after the business dried up. Though I was never good at managing money, I made sure the mortgage got paid every month. I also had supplies coming out of my ears and clogging up the small space that I had in the shed. I was buying stuff that I didn't need just in case I did.

Then I missed my first payment. When the first letter arrived in from the bank, I kept it hidden from Sarah underneath the piles of old books that nobody ever came to collect. Soon I had as many letters as I had books. Most were never opened, as if in some way this would make the words on the printed paper disappear.

Then came the night when everything changed. I'd gone to the toilet in The Beauvalley House just at the same time that the barman was asking everyone had they no homes to go to. When I came back out he was putting his jacket over his shoulders and slamming the door behind him. I could have called to him, told him to hold up, but instead I hid behind the pillar at the end of the bar and waited until the door had caught on the latch behind him.

From underneath the door of the poker room, the light glowed like precious gold. I should have walked straight out of the bar behind the barman and gone home to my wife and daughter, but something pulled me towards that room. Something was niggling at me, whispering in my ear, telling me to go in.

What harm will one night do? What else would you be doing but going home and staring at the badly wallpapered wall.

I rolled my shoulders back, all sure of myself, and pushed the door open like I owned the joint. I didn't flinch when they all held their cards close to their chests and turned to eye me up and down.

'I heard there's a game going on in here,' I said, and more than one of them raised their left eyebrow in disgust.

You could have cut the smoky air with a blunt knife. 'Who's your man?' I heard someone mutter. 'He's some neck barging in here when he hasn't been invited.'

'Didn't your aul one teach you any manners?' some upstart with long greasy hair and blackened eyes piped up from the back of the room.

I was about to turn around and leave the room when the owner, Pat O'Mahony, came out from the shadows, the sleeves of his crisp white shirt rolled up above his elbows and his hair all slicked back like he had just smothered it in a bucket of grease.

'Were you born in a barn, Charlie Carthy?' he said as he reached out and pulled a free chair out from under the makeshift poker table. 'Close that door behind you and sit yourself down. If Sergeant Purcell gets wind of this he'll have me shut down by the morning.'

It was easy as that. No invitation. No pass needed. I sailed in with the wind and bobbed on placid waters for most of the night.

But it was all a tease.

Looking back, part of me thinks they rigged the game that night so they could draw me in and get me hooked. I won that first game and went home with a right few bob in my pocket. Enough to get us through a week's groceries anyway. But the quiet waters soon swelled, growing more turbulent each and every time. The more I went back to that room, the more frenzied they became – fierce and violent until eventually I capsized. No one pulled me up. They just left me there, glad that it was me and not them who had bad luck visited upon them.

I lost my shirt once. And then I just kept on losing it. Every time I went back, I played a worse hand than the time before. At home, I became withdrawn. Sarah and I would spend the weekend rowing, not caring that the windows were open and the whole street could hear us. But I always tried to apologise the next morning. Tried to patch things up. Sarah stopped playing music in the house. Most nights she would turn off the oven and leave my dried-up dinner by the sink for when I decided it was time to come home. Sometimes she took Jen and said she was staying at her mother's for the night. Other times she walked around the house acting like I was invisible. There were times when I wished I was. Times when I felt things would be better if I just disappeared off the face of this sorry earth. Those times come back to haunt me still. Over and over again.

And then there was the morning when I woke up and felt like something might just go my way that day. The sound of vinyl being placed on the record player downstairs, the needle settling gently in the groove, was followed by the sound of Sarah humming the tune of the title track of my David Bowie compilation album. When I went downstairs, she put a cup of hot tea into my hand and kissed my unshaven cheek.

'Let's sit down and talk tonight,' she said as I went towards the back door, trying not to spill the tea on her washed linoleum floor. 'We'll get through this rough patch. I know we will.'

I spent the day tidying the shed, throwing out old things that had gathered cobwebs over time. Any stagnant air that had lingered over my head seemed to disappear. Talking would be a start.

At dinnertime, Jen popped her head into the shed and nodded her approval at the newly cleaned shelves.

'Ma asked if you could pop up to the Littler and fetch her a sliced pan for the morning,' she said. 'I would do it only Francis got a book from the library and there are words in it that he doesn't understand. I told him I'd help him read it.'

'You need to tell young Francis that you won't be able to help him with his work forever, Jen,' I told her as I stood up and tried to remember how much loose change I had left in my jacket pocket. 'You'll be moving on to secondary school soon. What's he going to do then? It's not like we can dress him up in a skirt and sneak him in to sit beside you now is it?'

'I know, Da,' she said.

When I kissed her lightly on the forehead, she smiled and hugged me tight.

'You're a good kid, Jen,' I said. In my head, I added, *you deserve better than me.*

Up at the Littler, I had enough brass in my pocket for a small sliced pan. I had some notes hidden under the mattress of the bed but I wanted to keep them there. I had to start making an effort to save whatever I could. Get the banks off my back, just a little bit. I would just tell Sarah that they were all out of the full pans and this was the best I could do. I was handing the money over through the hatch when I felt a tap on my shoulder. It was Pat O'Mahony, his big arms cradling two bags of bulging coins.

'There you are now, Charlie,' he said. 'Will we be seeing you tonight in the back room?'

The young fella inside the hatch handed the bread over to me but I could tell he was taking in every word Pat O'Mahony was saying.

'I don't think I'll make it up tonight, Pat,' I said. 'I'm having a quiet night in with the missus instead.'

I held my hand out towards the young fella inside the hatch, my palm facing upwards.

'There's no change, mister,' the young fella said. 'In fact, you were five pence short but I'll catch you again.'

Pat O'Mahony stood there and I could have sworn I saw a smirk start at the corner of his mouth.

'It's a big pot tonight,' he whispered, making sure to jangle the bags so that the coins chimed. 'Only a fool would miss out. We're starting early too. No lock-in. Word has it that someone's missus has squealed to Sergeant Purcell, so we're kicking off at seven tonight. If you're not there by then, I'll take it you're not coming.'

I don't know whether it was the fact that he was calling me a fool or the way he looked at me as if I was some poor eejit who didn't know a gift horse when it was kicking him square in the jaw. But even though I had the chance of patching things up with Sarah, and even though I knew the worst thing I could possibly do was go out to The Beauvalley House that night, I could think of absolutely nothing else but that stupid game and the money I had hidden under the mattress as I walked back into our cul-de-sac.

Needless to say, she tore the strips off me before I had the chance to place the bread on the table. Jen put her hands over her ears and marched out of the kitchen and straight up the stairs before slamming her bedroom door behind her.

'What do you mean you have to go out?' Sarah roared. 'You said we were going to talk tonight. There are things that need saying, Charlie. I want to talk to you about stuff. Important stuff.'

I went on the defensive.

'No, *you* said we needed to talk, not me. And besides, I forgot that I promised Pat I would give him a hand behind the bar tonight. He has a lad on holidays and is short-staffed,' I lied.

'Pat O'Mahony? Pat O'Mahony?'

Sarah was no fool.

'Since when have you been friends with that miserable so-and-so? Mrs Baldwin heard he has all sorts of wagers going on up in that pub of his. There's more men falling out of there with sore heads and empty pockets, whatever it is he's putting into the drink. You'll do well to stay away from Pat O'Mahony and his pub.'

'Don't speak to me like I'm a child,' I said. 'I'll be home later and we can talk then if it's so urgent.'

'Urgent! Urgent! You don't know the meaning of the word,' she snapped back as she moved across the kitchen and pulled out the loose top drawer.

I recognised the red ink that was stamped across each letter before she had a chance to take them up in her hands. How had she found them?

'These are *urgent*, Charlie,' she said as she waved the unopened envelopes in my face. 'But of course you'd prefer to bury them beneath the rubbish in that shed of yours.'

'There's no rubbish in there now,' I said. 'Go check if you don't believe me. I spent the day clearing out junk so I could have it looking better.'

'Yeah, and you thought you'd just throw these letters out too so you wouldn't have to show them to me,' Sarah cried as she slammed the envelopes onto the table.

There wasn't much I could say. I was caught.

'How long were you going to keep this a secret from me?' she asked.

Her voice softened and she moved closer, her hand reaching out towards mine. I don't know why but I pulled away.

'Why don't you just go, Charlie,' Sarah sighed. 'Go if that's what you really want.' She turned her back on me and left the room.

Every part of me told me I should follow her into the front room, that I should wrap my arms around her until her shoulders became still and the crying stopped. Instead, I took one last look at the pile of urgent letters that lay scattered on the kitchen table, then ran upstairs, grabbed the money from under the mattress and headed straight out the door.

And there was a glint in Pat O'Mahony's eyes when he saw me charge through the doors of The Beauvalley House. *Here's this poor sucker back again for more battering*, I could hear him saying in his head, *and by God we'll give it to him tonight.*

Except they didn't.

When I stepped out the door of the pub that night, I stood straight and held my head high. I looked up and watched large drops of rain fall from the sky. I stood with my arms stretched wide, feeling the weight of coins and notes in my trousers, yet having never felt lighter.

'This is it!' I called to the night. 'No more. I'm finished. Time to get back on track. Time to make things work. No more hiding. No more secrets.'

When I looked at my watch, I could see it was just gone ten o'clock. Jen would be in bed, I thought, but Sarah would still be up. I would creep quietly in through the front door so she wouldn't even hear me coming. Then I'd take the notes and coins from my pockets and throw them on the floor at her feet. Then I would hold her and kiss her and tell her how things will be different from now on. That I would go down to the job centre in the morning and start looking for something new. There was bound to be work out there for someone with my skills and work ethic. They'd see I was a hardworking man who had plenty of experience working for himself all these years. Everything would be all right from here on in. Everything would work out. I just knew it.

That night, I took the long way home. I walked by the woods where Jen and Francis like to sit, listening to the sound of the trees as they swished in the wind. I took off my jacket and let the rain soak my skin, enjoying the coolness of its touch. I had been lost for too long. My eyes had been closed to the world. But no longer.

As I strolled, I kept my hands tucked deep and let my fingers brush the crisp notes. Tomorrow, after I went to the job centre, I would ask Mr Baldwin if I could borrow his car and I would take Sarah and Jen off to Malahide for the day. Sarah always said she wanted to live there. That dream didn't seem too impossible any more.

By the time I got home, the cul-de-sac had water pumping out of open drains and there was no sign of the rain letting up. As I walked up to our house, I saw that it was dark inside, though the front door was ajar and the doormat soggy with rain. I reached into my pockets to get a grip on the green notes as I stepped inside, ready to throw them at Sarah's feet. But when I stepped inside the front room there was no one there.

Jen appeared behind me.

'Where were you?' she asked. 'Ma's been crying all night. Nothing I said would make her stop.'

'Where is she now?' I asked as Jen looked down at the money in my hand.

'Where did you get all that?' she asked.

'I won it.'

'You won it. Where?'

'Never mind. Where's your ma?'

'I don't know. She went out. All I know is that she was crying and crying and then she ran out of the house.'

'Did she say anything?'

'She said a lot.'

'Like what?'

'Like how her heart was broken and how she never thought her marriage would come to this.'

'Come to what?'

'I asked her the same thing,' Jen said. 'She said she never thought the laughter would go out of her marriage. And that if the laughter was gone then the love would surely follow.'

I put my hands up to my face and rubbed it hard.

'But she said she wasn't going to let that happen,' Jen said. 'She said that Granny always told her never to go to sleep on an argument. Granny said it's not healthy. So Ma said she was going to find you, wherever you were. She said she would try The Beauvalley House first but if she wasn't back in half an hour that I wasn't to worry. She would keep looking until she found you and she wasn't going to give up on you just yet.'

I threw the money over by the fireplace and fell down onto the couch.

'Go back up to bed, Jen,' I croaked. 'Things will be better in the morning.'

I can remember drifting in and out of a fitful sleep, only waking when lightning lit up the street outside. As I lay there, I dreamed of Sarah, young and carefree. She had a brightness in her green eyes that made her look celestial and she mouthed inaudible words to me that slipped through her broad pink smile. Mostly, I tried to reach out to her, to grab hold of her hand. But just as our fingertips touched, she would move away as though caught by a strong breeze. She was there, but not there. Within reach, yet so far away.

I woke to a loud banging on the front door. I pulled myself off the couch and tried to separate my dreams from reality. Still I felt her next to me, walking with me as I opened the front door.

Two members of An Garda Síochána stood in front of me. They asked if I was Charlie Carthy. Husband of Sarah Carthy.

I'd never felt pain like it. Never before. Not ever.

Until now.

21

DUBLIN

SUZANNE

It was hard to take in, what I discovered just a few days after Sarah was left fighting for her life. As if things weren't bad enough. Eventually, his name was all over the newspapers, of course, but we didn't find out that way. I found out first. Then I had the job of telling the rest of the family.

Before this, we had already found out that Sarah had been pregnant at the time of the accident but lost the baby due to the trauma. I knew they had been trying for many years after Jen. When the mood took her, Sarah talked to me about it. How she would love a little sister or brother for Jen. How it might put the spark back into Charlie's eyes. When the doctors told him, Charlie realised that this had been the news she wanted to tell him the night of the accident. They had lost Sarah and a much-wanted baby. I thought surely this was enough devastation. But it turned out there was more to come.

Louis closed up The Humble Jumble after Sarah's accident. He didn't tell me that he was closing shop, but I saw the sign hanging in the window: *Closed Until Further Notice*. I didn't think much of it at first; I didn't have time for the shop, anyway. If I wasn't on my knees in the tiny chapel of the hospital, my time was spent by the bedside of my only sister, who lay motionless beside an intermittently beeping machine.

I sat in that isolated room in the hospital, listening to the soft footsteps that moved along the corridor. Sometimes, I would hear the sound of a child skipping along the glossy floor. When they squealed, the mother would shush them, but I wanted them to squeal some more. The silence was too deafening. Sometimes, I left the door open, hoping that the familiar sounds of life would bring Sarah back to hers.

Ma was so exhausted that her legs went from under her twice when she was standing at Sarah's hospital bed. Da simply walked the corridors, back and forth. Doctors and nurses came to know us by our first names. Even the canteen ladies would top up our tea and put an extra scone on our plates on our brief trips out of the room for food. When Ma went to go for her purse, they would touch her shoulder. 'Don't worry about it, love,' they said, before walking back to where they were stationed behind the counter.

We had a round-the-clock rota so that Sarah was never on her own. After Ma collapsed the second time, the nurse told her she was to go home and rest, otherwise she too would end up in a hospital bed. Da was to take good care of her, the nurse said. She would call if there were any changes. Sarah was in safe hands, she told them, and they were to look after themselves for now.

Charlie held his daughter's hand tight every time they came into the room, only letting it go to bring his hand up to cover his mouth. But he couldn't hold the pain in. His whole body would shake until Jen brought him over to a chair. Then the shaking would stop and the crying would begin. Both of them. Completely broken.

I took over Ma and Da's shifts, which meant I was eating and sleeping in the hospital as if it were my own home. Sarah was so seriously ill, everyone knew she could go at any time. Sometimes, I would take a break and park myself on one of the plastic chairs in the canteen and watch the hordes of people trample through the wide hallways, all eager to see their loved ones.

It was on one of those breaks that I thought I saw Louis' cowboy hat bob among the crowd. He disappeared before I had the chance to stand up from my chair and search him out.

One day the nurse came in to me and insisted that I take a break from the hospital too.

'Go out and get a bit of fresh air for yourself,' she said. 'It's not good to be breathing in this stale air twenty-four seven. We'll call you if there are any changes.'

The last thing in the world I wanted to do was leave Sarah alone, but I knew Charlie was coming up with Jen and that they too needed time with her. Maybe it wouldn't be so bad for me to take a step back, I reasoned, and let the family be together.

I took the bus into town and spent the day rambling around St Stephen's Green, watching youngsters try to catch slithery fish with their miniature nets. I threw bread to the ducks that glided along the calm pond and watched as the water rippled behind them. I found a free patch of grass and lay down on my back and watched the sky turn from blue to grey. And I stayed there as tiny droplets of rain fell down and settled on my lips. During that time, I recognised the beauty in the world. It was a fleeting feeling. But it was definitely there.

On the bus ride home I pressed my nose against the glass and watched the rain fall harder. People who didn't have umbrellas placed coats over their heads or sped up, eager to find shelter. Up ahead, I saw a familiar man fumble with the lock of the door at The Humble Jumble, so I pressed the bell of the bus and got off at the next stop.

'Louis,' I called inside to him as I tapped on the window.

My clothes were saturated and my feet soggy.

'What are you doing here?'

He only turned his head slightly to acknowledge me before twisting the key in the barrel of the lock and inviting me inside.

'Louis,' I said as I pushed the door open. 'What on earth is wrong?'

Still he did not answer. With his back to me, his shoulders began to shake. Then it poured out of him like a rushing stream. Hard cries of pain, not unlike the ones we had all shed over the previous days.

I said nothing, just went into the back room and filled the kettle. When I came back out Louis was sitting on a plastic crate. His eyes were raw, his face haggard. Still he couldn't look me in the eyes when I said his name or when I handed him the cup of hot tea. We sat there in silence, listening to the rain as it pelted the front window.

'Do you want to talk about it?' I asked after I could take the quietness no more.

'I guess I'm going to have to at some point,' Louis said, as he placed the cup of tea on the floor beside his feet.

'A problem shared …' I offered.

'Somehow I don't think this problem will be halved,' Louis said. 'In fact, it can only escalate what has already happened.'

Philip's name came up straight away. With everything that had happened to Sarah, I had forgotten that other people had problems in their lives too. After the accident, it felt like the universe had focused in on us and that we were the only ones in the world who were having our lives ripped apart and torn asunder.

'Remember when we met Father Petar on our first trip?' Louis said.

I remembered it well. It was the day after I had my experience on the mountain. The day after the beads turned gold. Louis and I had been sitting at the rear of the church, just on the outskirts of the fields, when Father Petar approached us. Maybe he had sensed the worries of Louis' mind because he laid his hand on his right shoulder and knelt down beside him.

'Dear friend,' he said, 'how can I help?'

I shook the priest's hand and then left them alone.

'We talked for hours that day even though I knew Father Petar had more important things to do within the parish,' Louis said. 'He never left my side, just listened and nodded as I told him about Philip. I saw him absorb my problems as though they were his own. The man looked like he had too many crosses on his back, and here he was trying to lighten my load. I lost track of how long we sat beneath the boiling sun but eventually my legs felt less heavy and I stood up from where I was sitting. The last thing he said to me before he looked at his watch and shuffled off towards the church was that I should always have a place in my home for Philip. If Philip had proper support and somewhere to stay instead of on the streets, then we could work on his recovery. No one is ever beyond redemption, he told me.

'Philip had been living on the streets for so long,' Louis said. 'After he was moved out of the flats near the shopping centre, he stayed in a heroin den in the north inner city for months. It was a run-down complex with spent needles on the stairwells and meaningless graffiti on the walls. But there were families there too, who tried to get on with their lives as best they could. An up-and-coming dealer who saw himself as untouchable had a flat two doors up from where Philip was staying. His aim was to get the kids hooked young. Kids who were impressed by the confident strut of his walk and dazzled by the gold watch he wore on his wrist. Soon, the flats became so overrun with addicts shooting up that people were afraid to walk by the gates of the complex in case they got mugged. But one day the wind changed and almost overnight the inner city saw people in the community stand up and say, "That's it, we've had enough." Some said they were vigilantes but they called themselves "concerned parents" who wanted to get the dealers out and clean up the streets of heroin once and for all.'

Louis continued, his eyes focused on the floor: 'Philip was too out of it at the time to even notice what was going on. Every week there were marches on the flats where the crowd would move through the gates of the complex and stand outside the dealer's flat. "*Pushers Out! Pushers Out!*" they chanted while one of them sprayed the same words on the door. It went on for weeks and months. It was hard for Philip and his so-called friends to even get outside to get their gear. But somehow, the dealer was able to get it smuggled in to them. Then one day, Philip got out of the flat and went up to Connolly Station where he slept rough for a night. I don't know why he chose to do that but I thank God every day that he did.'

'Why?' I asked. 'What happened?'

'The people had had enough of what was going on right under their noses in the Harley Street flat complex,' Louis said. 'The dealers simply weren't listening. They stood their ground and refused to leave. Truth was, there were people above them who put the fear of God into them. Even though there were addicts being buried every week, a group of parents shouting slogans and making idle threats wasn't going to stop them dealing. But they underestimated the parents. The night that Philip slept close to the tracks of Connolly Station was the night that over fifty people marched to the Harley Street flat complex. Just after midnight, they moved quietly through the streets. They wore dark clothes and some covered their faces with balaclavas. When they reached the door of the dealer, they stood there chanting his name but he refused to come out. Two doors up inside the den, an addict took a lethal overdose. Nobody noticed him as his heart stopped beating and he slipped away. The group stood there for over an hour before a brick was thrown through the dealer's window. That kick-started a frenzy and next thing they were charging into the two flats and pulling out furniture, before setting it alight in the centre of the yard. They dragged the dealer up off his chair and left his gold watch sitting next to the batch of smack he had been chopping up. They went into the heroin den and pulled out the dead addict and two other women who had both lapsed into drugged comas. They set fire to a small wooden stool inside the flat where the used syringes lay, and the flames quickly spread to the torn curtains that were pulled across the window. What they didn't realise, until the fire brigade came to put the blaze out, was that the newborn baby of one of the women addicts had been sleeping in the back room as the flames took hold. I heard that the screams of the mother when she eventually came around were like something from a horror film.'

Louis told me how Philip came home after that. After he heard about the Harley Street fire, Louis wandered the city centre looking for him until he found him in a café run by the Capuchins for the homeless. A priest they called Brother Hubie was sitting down beside Philip when Louis walked in. The three of them shared a pot of tea and talked about trivial things. But Louis noticed a change in Philip, and when they were finished, they bid Brother Hubie goodbye and left the café together.

Philip went home with his father that day. He told Louis and Joanie that he'd had enough of everything and that too many of his friends had died over the past while. He said he could fight this and get through it, with their help. He would clear his debts and he was willing to go back on the methadone programme if they let him stay in the house.

'I thought all my prayers had been answered,' Louis said.

Louis' wife, Joanie, was reluctant but eventually agreed. His daughter, Linda, moved out of the house and went to stay with Joanie's sister. There was no way she was staying in the same house as 'that useless junkie', she told her parents.

'I couldn't refuse him even if I'd wanted to,' Louis said. 'Not when he was standing there asking for my help. All I saw before me was my son as a little child, lost and broken and not knowing what to do. Something about this time made me think things would be different. I saw this little glimmer of hope that I wanted so desperately to cling on to.'

Joanie started to go out again. Just short walks at first. Philip spent most of his time in his room, but never made a fuss, nor was he demanding. He seemed content to be back home, wrapped in the safety net he needed. Most of all he was trying, Louis said, harder than he had ever seen him try before.

'The doctor agreed to start seeing him again. He brought in a new counsellor who Philip liked and could relate to,' Louis said. 'But his headaches worsened and sometimes they were so bad that he would have to lie in pure darkness until they eased. Each week he complained and the doctor prescribed him something stronger. In a way it didn't make sense to me that they were treating an addict with more tablets. It was just another drug to get addicted to.'

One evening, after what had seemed like weeks of him lying quietly in the black of his small room, Louis popped his head around the door and asked him if he was taking his tablets. 'I am, Da,' he replied without lifting his head out from beneath the sheets.

'The following day I had a phone call in the shop,' Louis continued. 'Joanie was worried about him. She could hear weeping through the bedroom door. Thick sobs that poured from his heart like he couldn't stop. Joanie had knocked gently on his door and when she went to twist the handle it had been locked. She didn't know how he had got the key. One of the rules when he moved back in was that he wasn't allowed to lock his bedroom door.

'"I'll have a talk with him when I get home tonight," I said. "Don't worry. Everything will be fine."'

Louis told me how the rain poured hard and heavy that afternoon. Roads in the city centre were waterlogged, flooding the engines of cars, which in turn blocked the way of the double-decker buses. So he stayed late in the shop, tidying things that didn't need tidying. Then he went over to the church across the road and sat on an empty pew for a few hours, praying to a God who didn't seem to be listening. Even though it was night by the time he left, there was still gridlock everywhere with numerous accidents on the road. Joanie had visited her sister for the evening to check in on Linda and, Louis suspected, to get away from the atmosphere with Philip back home. She returned at the same time as him. They stood side-by-side in the driveway and both looked up to see the bedroom light on in Philip's room.

'That's a good sign. See,' Louis tried to reassure her.

'I often wonder if Joanie had a premonition at that moment,' Louis told me, 'because she reached down and grabbed at my hand, and I could feel the coldness in her body transfer into mine. In the darkness, I tried to place the key into the lock on the front door until I realised it was already open and had been left slightly ajar. Inside, the house was too still. Too empty. I left Joanie standing at the bottom of the staircase, her hands clutching at her chest, as I took the steps two at a time. The bedroom door was open, the ceiling light too bright for his eyes. On the top of his crumpled bedsheets was a letter that lay beside numerous torn empty boxes of prescribed tablets. From where I stood, I could see the scrawl of his writing. It resembled that of a child.'

Louis threw his head back and his voice croaked when he spoke next.

'Joanie came up behind me. I felt her hand on my shoulder. She tried to steady it as it shook. I opened the letter and began to read it and then time just seemed to stand still,' Louis cried.

'He said he was sorry. That he loved us both so much. And Linda too. But the pain was too much. Too much to bear. He wanted to fall asleep and never wake up. Only then would the nightmare stop. He could never be helped, he said. There was no hope. We were to tell Linda that he loved her. That he was sorry. Sorry that he wasn't the brother he should have been. Things would be better for us all this way. And he wouldn't hurt no more. Or hurt anyone else no more. Thanks for always being there, he said. Even when he wasn't.'

Louis then told me what transpired that night. After Philip took every pill the doctor had prescribed him for the headaches, he walked up to the nearby flats and robbed a car that had already been stolen from somewhere else that day. Louis suspected Philip needed to get into the city and fast, so he could buy heroin. He drove at high speed up the Beauvalley Road and hit a young woman who was crossing. That young woman was Sarah. And he never stopped. Just kept on driving, right up until the car he was in hit a low wall at the Esso garage, crashed close to the fuel dispenser and knocked Philip unconscious.

Louis told me that Philip was brought into the same emergency room as Sarah and the same qualified doctors and nurses worked on him as he lay motionless on the bed.

They both lay in a comatose state.

One, a young mother with her whole life ahead of her.

Another, a poisoned junkie who didn't want to live any more.

That's what Louis told me that day.

Philip was responsible for Sarah's accident.

Sarah, who had woken up that fateful morning thinking that everything in her life would soon be all right. All she needed to do was sit down with Charlie and tell him her good news. Then they could look forward to the future. They had wished for this for a long time. Years had gone by but now the time was right. She would tell him that night after Jen had gone to bed and they were sitting side by side in the front room.

Except she never got the chance.

After Louis told me about Philip, I felt numb. This man, who I worked with every day, suddenly felt like a stranger to me. The numbness turned to anger. I wondered if he could have anticipated his son's actions. Why wasn't he there to stop Philip getting in the car? Why didn't he call the guards as soon as he saw that Philip was gone from the house? Surely he could've prevented things from getting so bad?

I stood up and walked out of the shop that day feeling nothing but horror and disgust. I watched buses pass me by and didn't move as their wheels splashed dirty puddles into my face and onto my clothes. Twice, I bent over a wall and vomited. When I arrived at Sarah's room in the hospital, Charlie took my coat off and handed me a towel. I was like a drowned rat, he said, and if I wasn't careful I'd end up with pneumonia.

I asked Jen to leave the room and she did so without asking me why.

'What's wrong, Suzanne?' Charlie asked.

I couldn't speak at first. I had to rewind it in my head and make sure what I heard was true. I had to try and put so much into one sentence because one sentence was all I would be able to speak.

'Jesus, what's wrong, Suzanne?' he asked again. 'You're starting to frighten me now. Is it your ma?'

I shook my head and stood up to hold his hands.

'I've something awful to tell you, Charlie,' I cried, 'something really, really awful.'

Later that evening, when Charlie had calmed down, I convinced him to bring his daughter home. They wouldn't get much sleep, but at least they'd be away from the hospital. When they had gone, I moved through the wards on each floor, trying to see if I could find Philip. I needed to know what condition he was in. I wanted him to be worse than Sarah. For him to be dead and her to live. I stopped looking after a while when I realised it was Sarah I needed to be close to. Not him.

It was only after her funeral, after they lowered her into the ground, that I felt that anger leave. I knew it wasn't going to bring Sarah back. I didn't see Louis at the funeral, but two weeks later I called into the shop.

'I thought it best to stay away,' he said.

And I just nodded.

It took time. A few weeks, at least, before I could feel somewhat normal around him. We had had some sort of closure, I suppose, what with burying Sarah. But Philip was still in hospital. Louis said things were not good.

And Charlie?

Well, Charlie pressed the self-destruct button. Aside from the drinking and the vomiting and the no food, no electricity, no coal for the fire,

Charlie also managed to find his way up to The Humble Jumble and smash the windows in. The guards asked Louis if he knew of anyone who held a grudge against him. And though he did, Louis said, 'No.'

There was no easy way to tell Jen that the son of the man her aunt worked with was responsible for her mother's death. So I just told her, straight out. She was quiet for a bit. How could someone so young process something like this?

'Poor Louis,' she said eventually, and then I held her tight as she wept.

They are home tomorrow. Mr Baldwin said he will meet them off the plane. I don't know if it will have been a wasted trip. At least I tried. You get weary from trying sometimes. So very weary.

And though I mightn't say it, I know how Charlie sometimes feels.

Lost.

Broken.

Hopeless.

Scared.

Because I feel it too. I really do.

22

YUGOSLAVIA AND DUBLIN

JEN

Iva and I listen to the sound of heavy boots as they trample the soft earth, making fine dust rise up and sting the eyes. Behind the mountains we see the glow of the rising sun appear on the horizon. The hours have tumbled into one another without us even noticing and a new dawn is about to break.

We close our eyes and hold one another tight. If we are still, maybe the milicija will pass us by. Maybe they will not notice two frightened children whose bodies are wrapped together and entangled in the long grass.

Iva murmurs prayers in her native tongue. She whispers them in my ear. *Sveta Marijo, majka Božija, moli za nas …*

The scent of roses fills the air. Across the way, I see pilgrims who look like small dots as they climb the big mountain. Though it is early morning, there is activity around us once again.

I hear voices as they draw closer.

Thick accents from northern highlands.

Then I see them nearby. Young men with broad shoulders and strong arms who move quickly through the fields.

'There they are!' one calls out.

'Can you see them, Malachy?' someone shouts from behind him. 'Are they hurt?'

One of the men runs towards us. Iva's eyes are still closed when he reaches us and she jumps when he crouches down over us both.

'They're all right!' he shouts back. 'They're safe!'

The Scotsman hands me the bottle of water in his hand and then reaches into his haversack to fetch another for Iva. After we drink it all down, he holds out his hands so he can pull us both up to a standing position.

'There have been a lot of people out looking for you,' he says. 'The entire village has been so worried. They'll be glad to know you're both all right.'

'Where Father Petar?' Iva asks him as she steadies herself. 'Safe? Back in church?'

The Scotsman looks behind to where his friends are now gathered in a semicircle, all of them sipping warm water from plastic bottles. They shrug.

'Let's get you both back to your families,' he says. 'They might be able to tell you more.'

***

A large crowd has gathered at the entrance to St James' church. They huddle together in groups and enjoy the warmth of the morning sun. In their hands, they hold makeshift maps and they pass around a photograph of a rose which someone has taken and who says it has the face of Jesus inside it.

'They've found them!' I hear someone shriek as we come into view.

Da bolts out from the centre of the crowd. He is back wearing the same T-shirt he had on the day we arrived and his hair is messier than ever, even though it is slightly hidden under the rim of Louis' cowboy hat. He races so hard that he stumbles over his own feet and almost goes tumbling to the ground. He gets his balance back and moves towards me with more urgency than I have ever seen him do before.

'Jen,' he cries, his arms stretched wide, before he throws them around me. 'Thank God you are okay. I thought I'd lost you forever.'

I look deep into his eyes. As always, they are dominated by black circles and his lids are pinched and heavy. But there is something different about him and I know straight away what it is. For the first time since Ma died he is sober.

'You've no idea how worried I've been,' he says, as he pulls me closer.

I hold back just a little.

'You never came to the mountain. I wanted you to come.'

'I know,' he says rubbing at his face. 'I'm sorry. I'm a fool. A damn fool. I'm just so relieved to know that you are safe and well.'

'I'm able to take care of myself,' I say. 'Haven't I been doing it for long enough?'

Da looks away. I know I've hurt him. But I don't want to stay mad. I stretch out my fingers and take hold of his hand.

'Let's go home, Jen,' he says, 'home to Dublin.'

I nod.

***

Da tries to arrange for an earlier flight home, but, as the guide tells him, it isn't the Costa de Sol we're in. This is Yugoslavia. Things are different over here.

I tell him I want to visit Iva one last time before we leave. He doesn't seem keen to let me go alone, so I tell him he can come with me to her house.

At the step of her front door sits a man who wears an unwashed vest and work trousers. He picks at the dirt that is lodged in his nails and every so often looks out at the mountain and shakes his head. Iva comes out from the house as we approach.

'My tata,' Iva says as we walk up the path. She puts her arm around the man and kisses him gently on the head before inviting us inside.

Da says he wants to wait outside. He hovers around Iva's father but they don't speak to one another. They don't need to. I think they can read one another's thoughts. Or some of them, anyway. Before I walk into Iva's house, I see her father stretch his hand out to Da.

Iva, Veronika and her brothers are inside. Even Stela has called by to see what all the fuss is about with Iva's new friend. They talk to one another in their own language, and when they laugh, I laugh too. Da is calling me from outside. It's time to go, he is saying; time to go home.

'Write,' Iva says as I leave. 'Pictures too.'

I promise her that I will.

***

Da sits at the back of the coach and presses his nose up against the window. Someone starts a decade of the rosary and I see him roll his eyes. When he sees me looking at him, though, he winks before folding his arms and closing his eyes to sleep.

We speak a little on the plane. Somehow, I feel lighter than I did going over.

Mr Baldwin picks us up from the arrivals hall and takes the suitcase from Da's shaking hand.

'Well,' he asks, 'did you find what you were looking for over there?'

Da says nothing.

'Any miracles to report then?' Mr Baldwin jokes. 'Did you find God?'

I don't know what Da found over there. I don't think it was God.

I'm hoping that he found himself.

At home, he makes me toast with the fresh bread Mrs Baldwin has left for us. He burns the edges and puts too much butter on it but I don't complain.

'Will we hit the sack, Jen?' he asks. 'It's been a long aul day.'

As I lie in the bed, I hear the stairs creak. I hear Da pace around downstairs. I know he wants to go out. I know he can taste the froth on his lips of a freshly pulled pint. The Beauvalley House is up the road, begging him to come. For just the one.

But he doesn't go.

He stays.

At home.

With me.

***

I rise with the sun and pull the curtains back from my bedroom window. I thought I would see Francis sitting on the kerb but he isn't there. I've an ache inside me that makes me groan. I've never wanted to see him so much.

The sound of Da snoring travels up from where he lies on the couch. I dress in silence, placing Ma's purple mohair cardigan over my shoulders. From under the bed, I pull out a plastic bag that I brought home from the village. As I creep downstairs, I'm careful not to slam the front door as I go outside.

At our usual spot in the woods there is a field mouse peeping out from behind a fallen log. His grey tail curls up so it almost touches the thin whiskers on his nose. As he sits up on his hind legs and paws at his tiny ears, splinters of sunlight slip through the tall trees above my head. I sit here among the familiar boughs and limbs and look around to see what has changed in the past week while I was gone. The thick frayed rope still hangs from the strong branch and sways gently in the summer breeze. Close by, I can hear the gush of the stream. The brown fabric couch has been replaced by a single mattress, which is stained and torn in places. An empty bottle of milk rests against a nearby tree and birds fly down to peck at the crumbs that lie beside it.

On top of the mattress there is a sleeping bag that is clean and shiny. The fabric is blue on the outside and mint green on the inside. There are no rips, no tears, and when I touch it I can feel that it is stuffed with down feathers that stretch right into the hood. From my backpack, I take out a pile of ham and cheese sandwiches that are wrapped tightly in tinfoil. I'll leave them in the hollow of the old oak and hope the old man gets to them before the woodland creatures do.

I've been waiting for too long and I don't think Francis will come at all. But then I see him walking through the trees. 'Where were you?' I ask. 'I thought you'd be waiting for me outside the house when I got home.'

He looks different.

'I thought ya might be tired after your flight,' Francis says. 'I didn't want to disturb ya.'

And I know he's lying.

'Are ya here long?' he asks.

'Long enough. Did you get your hair cut or something?' I ask, my two hands resting on my hips.

'Had ye a good time?' Francis asks without answering my question.

'I did,' I reply. 'I brought you back something.' I dig my hands deep into the pockets of my jeans and pull out the small plastic bag. 'Here,' I say as I hand it to him, 'I got this for you.'

'What is it? Is it a stick of rock?' he says with wide eyes.

'Close enough,' I laugh as he takes the small stone out of the bag.

'A stone?' he says. He holds it up to the sunlight and examines it as though it's a rare gem.

'Not just any stone,' I tell him. 'I got it up at the top of the mountain, Francis. It's a special one.'

'*You're special*,' I hear him mutter under his breath and I feel myself blush.

We sit there for the rest of the morning and I tell Francis everything I can remember about the trip. He asks me questions that I'm not able to answer and he makes me repeat things over and over again.

'Did ya really say a prayer for me over there?' he asks. 'And ya told your one about me?'

'Her name is Iva,' I say. 'And yes, we talked about you. She wants me to write to her.'

'Like a pen pal?'

'I suppose.'

We are quiet for a time. Francis looks awkward as he rubs at the stone and throws his eyes around the woodland, so that they fall anywhere except on me.

'Are you all right, Francis?' I ask as I move closer.

He wipes his eyes with the sleeve of his thin wool jumper. I've never seen Francis cry before. No matter how hard Old Man Nelligan beats him and no matter how much the lads from the school mock him, he always manages to hold it in. In front of me, at least.

'What is it?'

I kneel beside him but it only makes him cower more as he turns his back towards the old oak. I stand up and take a few steps back, and I'm wondering if I should just go and leave him there by himself. There are no bruises on his face. No cuts on his arms. Even the clothes he wears are well-fitted and pressed. As I study him, I can see that his hair has been trimmed, and combed through too. And his nails are so clean that the tips of his fingers are red raw from the scrubbing.

'If you don't tell me what's wrong, I can't try to fix it for you,' I say.

When he turns his body, it is in slow motion. He keeps a tight hold on the stone in his hand and breathes in deep before he speaks next.

'I'm going away,' he says as he finally looks me in the eyes.

As I struggle to take in what Francis has just told me, I see the field mouse scurry into a hole in the log. A wind picks up that makes me put my arms around my waist.

'Where to?' I ask.

'Many places.'

'Will you be gone for long?'

'Probably for years.'

My stomach sinks and I feel a knot grow in my throat.

'What's happened, Francis?' I ask.

He moves towards me, puts the stone in his pocket and reaches out both hands. I take them and feel a bolt run through my body. 'They've come for me, Jen,' he says and a broad smile spreads out from his eyes. 'I don't know how it happened but you were only gone a few days and they came around to the house banging at our front door.'

He's talking so fast now that I ask him to slow down.

'Is it the social people?' I ask. 'Are they taking you into care?'

Francis shakes his head.

'Who came for you then? You're not making sense.'

Still holding my hands, Francis stands and begins to move us in a circle, spinning us around. His smile, if anything, gets bigger. But the twirling has me dizzy so I break free from Francis' grip and almost fall as I stumble on the twigs. He laughs now.

'You're acting weird,' I say. 'I'm going home.'

I twist on my heel and start to walk away.

'Wait,' he calls.

I frown at him. 'One minute you're crying. The next you're laughing. And I've no idea what is going on. Who is taking you where?'

Excited, he shouts at the top of his voice: 'It's Ma!'

There is a golden silence in the woodland air as everything around absorbs his words.

'Francis, your ma is gone. Just like my ma. Just like Iva's ma.'

I'm weary, all of a sudden, from a thought that I'm not sure I want to bring to the surface just yet. The peace and closeness I felt to Ma when I was in the village has somehow disappeared since I came home. All the comfort of feeling her close when I sat on top of the small mountain has left me. I close my eyes and try to get it back. But it doesn't come.

'Your ma is dead, Francis,' I shout. 'She's not coming for you. Not now, not ever.'

'It's not Ma that has come for me,' he says. 'It's her family. Her sister. My aunt. And all my uncles too. There's loads of them, Jen. And they've come to take me away from him. I'm going on the road. Going travelling with them all. That's why I'm happy and sad and all over the place. I'm leaving. Later on today.'

Then it hits me. This moment will be the last one we will spend together. And like Francis, I don't know whether I'm happy or sad. Who will sit on the kerb outside my house before the sun is even awake? Who will I sit and talk about nothing with in the middle of the woods? And it's not just about me. What about the old man? Who will wake up early to meet the milkman on his rounds and bring the fresh bottle up to him here? So many questions are tumbling around my head. All he has ever talked about since the day we met was his raven-haired ma and how she sang travelling songs to him when he was still in her womb. On his lowest days, when Old Man Nelligan was chastising him so much that he would run to his room, curl into a ball and hide under the darkness of his bed, Francis would think of his ma.

'She sent them to me,' he whispers. 'I just know she did. I never stopped talking to her. Not once. She was always listening to me. Always.'

'Your da won't want you leaving,' I say.

Francis shrugs his shoulders.

'He hasn't said much about it,' he says. 'They were there the other day when I came home. All of them huddled in a corner of the kitchen. The sink was overflowing and Da's head was dripping wet and he had a large gash on his forehead. They all turned around when they heard me come in and Da was sucking in air with deep breaths. A woman turned around and for a minute I thought it was Ma. It was how I always imagined she would look. Hair so black, like the feathers of a raven, and gold dripping from her ears and her neck. 'Stop it now, boys,' she called to the men who each held Da up by an arm, 'your nephew is home.'

Francis sits down on the log, takes the stone out of his pocket and rubs it. 'Her name's Nan,' he tells me of his aunt, 'and she brought me into the other room while my uncles stayed in the kitchen with Da.'

Francis tells me how they sat there talking about his ma and how the years had gone by too fast. She told him that they never stopped thinking about him when they were on the road. Not once. There had been trouble over Ma's burial but eventually Nan and the family were allowed to take her home. They gave her a traditional funeral and afterwards they put all her possessions in the caravan she was reared in, said prayers and then set it alight. Old Man Nelligan didn't object to them looking after the funeral, Nan told him, once he realised it saved him the bother of forking out for one himself.

Nan asked Francis if he remembered living with them. When he took out the photograph of him with Tipper, she took him in her arms and wept. She told him that after the bulldozers moved in to start clearing ground for the new hospital, Nan and her brothers called up to Old Man Nelligan's house and told him they were moving on. He wanted Francis back, he told them. 'The lad will be starting school soon,' Old Man Nelligan said. 'It's a house he needs to be reared in, not living in a wagon and gallivanting halfway across the country.'

'Nan told me that they tried their best to hold onto me,' Francis says, 'but Da threatened them with the Cruelty Man if they didn't bring me home to him. Nan said she would never forgive herself if I was taken by the Cruelty Man. Already there had been a few children who were taken away when they hadn't been to school. And Nan said it was no use trying to hide me because the Cruelty Man always brought a garda man with him who'd grab me by the ears and throw me into his car. Nan wouldn't know where I was taken to. She would just know that I would never be seen again. No one would know if I was dead or alive. At least if I was with my da, then she would know where I was and that I was alive.

'It wasn't my ma at all who I remember from when I was born,' Francis says. 'It was Nan, her sister, who I spent four years of my life with, who fed me and sang to me and loved me as her own. When she spoke, I closed my eyes and remembered the fields, the wagons, Tipper and the burning fires. I felt like I had woken from a bad dream, Jen, a long bad dream. I'm going home. Back to my real home.'

I know how much I will miss him. At the same time, I know he is right to go.

'Will you look after Joey for me?' he asks.

'Who's Joey?' I say.

Francis smiles. 'The old man. We got talking while you were away.'

'Of course I will,' I say. 'I'll keep an eye on him.'

We stay there for the day, watching the sun's rays filter through the leaves. In the soft wind the large trees groan.

Francis takes out a bunch of letters that are wrapped in a piece of frayed thread. They are letters that Nan sent to him over the years when she was on the road, he explains. Each letter contained few words, but many pictures. Pictures of wagons and campfires and smiling faces. The date and Nan's scrawl of a signature with a loveheart at the end of each page. She found them in a box in Old Man Nelligan's shed. The same shed Francis kept his animals in. They were so close to him all that time, but Old Man Nelligan never passed them on to his son. Even without putting the letters to my nose I can smell the hay and the grain and the rolling fields. The paper has browned and the corners are turned in but still they smell like they should: earthy, musty and wild.

'It's time to go,' Francis says eventually. He wipes the loose twigs from his trousers and stands up tall. 'I'll write to ya,' he tells me and I wonder how many more times I will listen to talk about letters from lost friends.

'Take care, Francis,' I say as I go to him and hold him tight. 'Take good care of yourself.'

1992

23

DUBLIN

CHARLIE

Sometimes I talk, sometimes I listen, but a lot of the time I just tell people stories. Mostly, they start off with a not-so-promising premise, but eventually they turn full circle and bring a smile to the listeners' faces. I think they take comfort in knowing there are others out there who walk the same path.

My favourite one is about a man who made a list and lost it. I told it just yesterday evening, in front of about five families who all looked like they had had the hope ripped out of their lives. I told them about this man called Seanie, who was sitting by a window in a late-night café where many other homeless men spent their evenings until they were thrown out on the street. He knew that he had only about ten minutes before they were going to shut up shop for the night because the dinner lady, Sadie, was taking her apron off and coming around from behind the hotplate to reach for the bell.

'Time, ladies and gents, please,' Seanie heard Sadie, with her dangly earrings and yellow-streaked hair, shout. 'Could you bring your empties up to the kitchen and make your way to the front door so we can close up for the night?' She was only short of throwing in, 'Have you no homes to go to?' except she knew that would be pushing it too far.

So Seanie started to look around the room at the familiar faces, everyone wearing the same pitiful look that they do every night at that hour. He was trying to find 'the hobbit', or Brother Hubie, as he prefers to be known. Brother Hubie, Seanie thought, had a wonderful habit – or terrible knack, depending on how you looked at it – of disappearing when he was looking for him and then appearing when he wanted to be left alone. But he needed to see him now because he knew Brother Hubie would make it all right. Or at least make it *feel* all right. Even if he couldn't put the pieces of the jigsaw back together.

It was the list, you see. The one that Brother Hubie had helped him write two weeks earlier. Even though Seanie hadn't written a word in many years, and even though he told him that he couldn't, that he didn't want to, Brother Hubie persevered.

'It's not an obligation, Seanie boy,' he told him, 'it's a necessity.'

Behind him, Seanie could hear the clanging of plates and the smell of Sadie's cheap toilet water perfume at the back of his neck. Her breath was hot like a dragon's and he knew she was about to spout some sour words, so he tipped the cap down over his face and waited for the onslaught. But then a fight broke out over by the hot plate between two men who each thought the last slice of apple pie had their name written on it. Sadie ran over, waving her hands in the air like a mad woman.

Seanie knew that Brother Hubie was always in the café about this time, floating about and laying his hands on shoulders. He would pat the backs of withered and worn men and whisper a prayer or two to them that no one else could hear. He ran the sleeve of his duffle coat across the frosted window, just enough so he could look outside to see if he could catch a glimpse of him. It must have been a Thursday, he thought, because the usual posh nobs were flocking into McPhelan's pub across the way, all suited and booted, happy that it was payday and they could savour a well-earned pint. If he was lucky, Seanie thought, and he got into the doorway of the vacant Georgian building across from the square before anyone else, then they might throw him a coin or two on the way home.

The café was starting to empty out. Every so often, out of the corner of his eye, he would notice Sadie staring at him.

But Seanie needed his list. And it still wasn't there. Not in the pockets of his trousers or coat. Not tucked into his sock or folded into the toe of his shoe.

He closed his eyes and tried to remember the colour of the ink.

Blue.

Then he tried to remember the names at the top of the page.

Karen and the boys.

Seanie knew that Karen had to be the first person on the list, because it was never her fault. Not one bit of it. She didn't deserve what he did to her.

'You have destroyed our family,' she told him on the day he left their home with two black bin liners holding all his tangible possessions. Their boys had stood behind her, watching their once strong father look so vulnerable, so weak, so scared.

It had been twenty years since he saw her last, right up until a week ago. Twenty years since she threw him out for the final time. Before that, she had always let him back in. He was always promising her that he had changed. That he had sorted himself out. That things would be different now. But she stopped believing him. When he left for the last time, he remembered the image of his wife and his three sons, their faces contorted with pain. But he was putting things right. Brother Hubie had told him what he needed to do.

She hadn't recognised him when he called to the door last week. The years hadn't been kind.

'You've aged, Seanie,' she said as she stood in the doorway, unsure if she should let him in.

'How are the boys?' he asked. He stood there like a timid schoolchild, absorbing the beauty of his wife's face. He wanted to reach out and touch the deep lines etched around her eyes.

'All grown up now, Seanie, with families of their own,' she said with a smile. 'You are a grandfather too, four times over.'

'A grandfather? I never thought I would see the day,' Seanie said.

He wasn't sure he could continue as his voice began to break. Then he heard the voice of Brother Hubie in his head. *Deep breaths, deep breaths. You can do it, Seanie Boy.*

'I'm sorry, Karen. Sorry for everything. For the drinking, the gambling, the lies, the hurt,' he croaked.

Seanie watched the lines of his wife's face soften. Her shoulders lowered and her folded arms fell to the side. She stood back from the doorway and invited him in.

Number two on the list were Eddie and Nora.

Eddie had lived on the same road of terraced houses since the day he wed. Others his age had moved on and, each year, more and more young families came to live on the street. But he didn't mind the high-pitched screams of the youngsters as they played. He didn't mind them kicking the ball into his rose bushes or ringing the doorbell and running off. And he always gave them five pence to go to the shop so they could buy fizzle sticks or coloured eating paper to eat after they had their tea.

Eddie was at home getting ready to visit Nora in the nursing home when Seanie called. He had already brushed back his silver hair before placing his flat cap on his head. And as he struggled to put his coat on – his bones stiff from arthritis – he didn't once ask for help from his only child.

'Come with me, son,' Eddie said after the first half hour of awkward silence. 'She's not herself any more and she might not recognise you, but at least the nurses will believe that she actually has a son. God knows, she does enough talking about you.'

'Is she happy in herself, Da?' Seanie asked as they pulled into the gravelled driveway of the nursing home.

'Happy out, Seanie,' Eddie said. 'The nurses tell me that every time a fancy car pulls up in the driveway of the home, your ma gets out of her bed and goes to the window. "That's my Seanie coming to see me," she says. And the nurses all nod and say, "Of course it is, Nora, now let's get you back into bed, dear."'

Seanie remembered when he used to call and see her in his company car all those years back when he was a young buck with guts and ambition. And he was glad that that was the memory she was clinging onto in her final years.

Nora didn't say much while Seanie and Eddie sat by her bed.

'Sorry, Ma,' Seanie said.

And though her eyes were vacant and body limp, Seanie's heart swelled when he thought he felt her squeeze his hand.

Number three on the list was Vince.

Vince had been like a brother to Seanie. All six foot of him with his shovel-like hands, timid personality and heart so tender it must have been made of soft clouds. When Karen threw him out for the last time, Vince had been the next person Seanie latched on to.

'I need your help, mate,' he pleaded as he stood at Vince's door.

And Vince didn't step back as the stench of stale whiskey blew into his face.

'Come in, buddy,' Vince said in a whispering tone that exuded an unnatural strength. 'Let's get you cleaned up.'

Two days Seanie lasted in Vince's city centre bedsit before he could no longer take the withdrawals. While Vince was away, Seanie cleaned him out of every last cent. He took the watch that Vince's ma had bought him for his birthday, even though the silver was only plated and it wasn't worth much. He took the steel-toed black boots Vince had saved up for when he was promised a few weeks' work down at the docks. He took the small radio, a collection of stamps, a set of keys that even Vince didn't know what doors they opened. He took Vince's post-office book, two knives and a bent gold Claddagh ring that might have only fitted a child. And he took Vince's duffle coat, his only coat. The one Vince used to put over Seanie at night when the shaking took hold. He left nothing behind but his rancid smell and a trashed bedsit.

Seanie didn't know what had happened to Vince after that, how life had turned out for him or where he was living. They had knocked down his old bedsit and turned it into one of those fancy grocery shops. But Brother Hubie helped Seanie write a letter to Vince, one he delivered to Vince's parents' house, which was just a few doors down from where Seanie grew up. The tremors had been particularly bad for him that day, so Brother Hubie accompanied him on this visit.

'It's good to see you,' Vince's da said as he placed his arm around his wife, 'but Vince passed away two years ago. Died suddenly in his sleep. A heart attack, the doctors said.'

Seanie couldn't speak, so Brother Hubie asked if they could go and visit his grave.

'Of course you can,' Vince's da said. 'I know Vince would love a visit from you, Seanie. You were his best friend.'

Number four on the list. Seanie just couldn't remember.

That was why he needed to see Brother Hubie.

Seanie could remember that he wanted to put Brother Hubie on the list, but Brother Hubie said, NO. And when Brother Hubie said NO, he meant NO. 'There is no need to put me on the list, Seanie Boy. I'm around you all the time. I'm here for you whenever you need me,' he had said.

'Time, ladies and gents, please!' Sadie roared again. She was barking orders like she owned the joint.

He scratched at the cut on the back of his head and cursed his mind for how weak it had become. So weak that he couldn't even remember a single name on a short list. And he knew he only had himself to blame; there was only so much abuse his brain could take: the alcohol, the pills, the heroin, the pain, the regret, the thrill, the hit, the want, the need, the numbness, the yearning.

For what?

He didn't know.

One thing he did know was that he didn't want to be where he was three weeks ago, waking up under the glare of the emergency room lights. Although his eyes were shut, he heard them talking to Brother Hubie, saying how he had nearly been gone. How it would have been too late if she had found him even minutes later.

As Seanie buried his head in his hands, knowing the café doors would soon be locked, he remembered being in the recovery room and Brother Hubie standing by his side.

'It's all right, Seanie Boy,' he said. 'You're going to be all right.'

At the door, near the foot of the bed, Seanie remembered seeing a figure but he couldn't speak, so he couldn't ask Brother Hubie who it was. 'If it wasn't for her finding you on her way home from work, then you wouldn't have made it, Seanie Boy,' Brother Hubie told him. 'She brought you here herself. She said she couldn't wait for the paramedics.'

And there it was. He could see her.

Now, back in the café, Seanie felt a hand on his shoulder.

'Seanie Boy,' Brother Hubie said, 'it's time for Sadie and the others to lock up now for the night. They have been working hard all day serving up meals and they need to get on home now. Have you somewhere to go tonight yourself?'

Seanie stood up from the table and buttoned up his duffle before fixing his cap so it was firmly on his head.

'I'll be all right, Brother Hubie,' he said. 'It's mild enough tonight.'

'How are you getting on with the list?' Brother Hubie asks.

'I thought I was doing fine, that was up until now,' Seanie said as he gathered his black bin liner from the floor. 'There's just one more person. Just one more and I'm done.'

Seanie walked slowly over to the hot plate just at the same time as Sadie was taking off her apron and letting down her hair. And he saw Sadie looking at him, the way everyone on the list looked at him when they saw him approach: unsure, nervous, scared.

'Sadie,' Seanie said as he pushed his hands deep into his pockets and tried not to look at the floor, 'I'm sorry for giving you a fright.'

Sadie grabbed her coat and put it over her shoulders. 'It's all right, Seanie,' she said. 'Just don't do it again, ay?'

She reached into her handbag and took out a piece of crumpled paper.

'Here,' she said as she handed it to him, 'I found this on the floor the other night. I think it belongs to you.'

Sadie winked at Seanie, threw the keys over to Brother Hubie and headed out the door. Seanie opened up the crumpled piece of paper and read down to the bottom of the page. A smile stretched across his face.

Number four read: *Sadie.*

***

I have told this story many times over the past few years. I tell it mostly to the families of addicts who I meet through the homeless charity I work for. These families come to us because they have nowhere else to go. I haven't the strength to tell them my own story – I'm still not quite there yet – so I tell them this one instead. And I think they take some comfort out of it, knowing that there are people out there who will help their loved ones, even at their lowest point.

And when you've been in a similar situation then it's a bit easier for them to believe you when you tell them, 'There is hope.'

It was Suzanne who introduced me to Brother Hubie, not long after I went inside to dry out for the last time.

Things were up and down when we came back from Yugoslavia. One day I was putting on a shirt and tie and scouring the streets for a job, and the next I was going on a two-day bender that led to more search parties than I care to admit. Suzanne called up one day with her ma, da and a counsellor in tow. Enough was enough, she said. It was time for an intervention. And it was because she cared about me. Everyone cared about me, apparently. For the love of God, I didn't know why.

I passed by Louis pushing Philip in a wheelchair when I came out of rehab the first time. That sent me straight back in. But I don't care to talk too much about it, except with the lad I meet on a Friday who sits me down on a long couch and lets me talk away for the guts of an hour before standing up, shaking my hand and telling me he will see me next week.

Suzanne moved in with Jen during these stints inside. It meant she wouldn't have to be shipped out to a foster family in some area far away from her school. And when she was allowed to visit me, after the first six weeks, she would always talk about the village and how she still wrote to the girl she met there.

I've been clean now for the past five years. I won't say it's been easy, but I'm doing all right, so far.

I came to realise that there was no avoiding Louis. Suzanne was back working at The Humble Jumble and Jen would go there after school most days to give a dig out. It was never said out loud, but the feeling was that Louis wasn't responsible for his son's actions. I knew it, too. It just took time to accept. And though I never asked directly, Suzanne brought it up in conversation over time.

'Louis' son is coming on well in the rehabilitation centre,' she said to me one day, without mentioning Philip's name. 'They think he will be back walking again with only the aid of a stick in a few months. Louis said he is looking forward to getting him home full-time.'

And I wanted to scream at her, tell her that isn't he lucky to be able to bring him home. That it's not his body or his ashes or his bloodied and torn clothes that they are bringing home. I wanted to say it but I didn't. I didn't because I knew it would only drag me back down into that gutter I had fought so hard to get out of.

'Only he has a long road ahead of him. A lot of things have come out over the past few months,' Suzanne said. 'Turns out Louis' son talked about a lot of things with his counsellor and now the guards are looking to formally interview him when he is up to it. Apparently, it'll be all over the papers in the next few weeks; all about the parish priest, Father Keogh, the one who was here before Father Dennehy. People are saying that he was abusing young altar boys some years back. And it looks like Louis' son was one of them. Louis thinks that's the root of his problems.'

When I got back on my feet, I started looking for work again. Things were certainly picking up, but a man with my trade wasn't as in demand as others. Plumbers, tilers, bricklayers, plasterers, electricians – there was no shortage of work for men with those skills. But that was not quite the case for a bookbinder.

Suzanne told me about Brother Hubie, who had moved out from the city centre to live in the block of flats up beside the shopping centre near the underground passageway. He knew that the heroin epidemic had travelled out from the city. Young men were being left homeless because their families couldn't cope. He convinced the council to give him one of the largest flats and he filled the three rooms with as many beds as he could. When the young men of the area and beyond had nowhere else to go, Brother Hubie put them up in this flat. He took them off the street and got each and every one of them into a programme that let them work to fight their addiction while keeping a roof over their heads.

He didn't always succeed, Brother Hubie; there were always those who fell through the net. But he was there for them if ever they came back. Always willing to help when they asked for it. He says that one day off drugs is better than no day off drugs. People from all parts of Dublin soon got word about what he did and his work became so in demand that he formed a registered charity. Suzanne introduced me to him when we were out shopping for a birthday gift for Jen for her twenty-first birthday.

'I think I'll cook her something nice tonight,' I told Suzanne. 'My spaghetti bolognese is her favourite.'

I couldn't understand why Suzanne laughed so hard.

We met Brother Hubie on the way out of the shopping centre. When we got talking, Suzanne told him I was looking for work.

'Well, I have an opening for a counsellor,' he said. 'Someone who can relate to the people who use our services.'

Seemed all too much of a coincidence to me, and the way he looked at me it was like he already knew my story.

'I only know him through Louis,' Suzanne said when I questioned her after he left. 'He helped his son out when he was living in town. You don't have to take the job if you don't want to, Charlie. But then again, sometimes things like this aren't coincidences, they are God-incidences.'

'Don't start with that bull again,' I said as I nudged her arm.

And she just winked at me.

The next day, I had an interview with Brother Hubie, who offered me the job.

And here I am today, telling stories about people just like me.

***

'Are you ready, Da?' Jen calls up to me. She pounds up the stairs, taking them two by two, and then bursts in through the door without knocking.

'You're lucky I'm decent,' I say as she wolf whistles.

'Well, look at you,' she says as she moves closer and plants a soft kiss on my face.

'Will I do?' I ask.

'Of course you'll do, Da,' Jen says. 'I haven't seen you look this well since … never!'

She reaches down and picks the burgundy silk tie up from where it lies on the bed. With slow movements she pulls up the collar of my white shirt and wraps the tie around my neck. When the knot has been tightened and the tie smoothed, Jen stands back and wipes her eyes.

'Do you think she will mind?' I ask. She knows I am talking about Sarah.

'Not at all,' Jen says. 'I think it will make her happy. Very happy indeed.'

'I'm going to miss you for the next few weeks,' I say.

She moves forward and I pull her close to my chest. She is still my little girl, my baby, my saving grace.

'I'm going to miss you too, Da,' Jen says. 'But it's something I have to do.'

'You'll call every chance you get, right?'

'Every day if I can,' she says, 'I promise.'

'You know I would prefer it if you didn't go,' I say, even though we've had this conversation a thousand times over.

'I've made my mind up, Da,' she says. 'I'm going and that's the end of it. I'll be fine. There will be loads of other foreign aid workers over there. We'll be well-protected.'

I don't want to argue with her before she goes. She is due to catch a flight to Scotland straight after the ceremony.

'Have you enough money?' I ask, even though she earns twice as much as me.

'I have, Da. I told you, I'll be fine,' Jen says. 'I'm going up to the hospital before I go to the airport. The doctors are giving me supplies of antibiotics as well as other medication. Even the dentist has put together boxes of toothbrushes and toothpastes for me to bring. Once I meet up with Malachy and his friends in Scotland, we'll be able to stock up their Land Rover with supplies before we start our journey. I'll be in good company. Don't you worry.'

But I can't help but worry.

The war has been raging across Yugoslavia for over a year now. Images of devastation are shown on the news each evening. Dubrovnik has been destroyed in the shelling and people talk about gunfire coming from the hills. There is no electricity, no water, little means of communication for people. Civilians stay hidden in shelters and cellars as they try to withstand the cold winter. Schools and hospitals are being attacked and many children have already been killed or maimed. They desperately need aid. And Jen, along with some others who she had kept in contact with over the past ten years, have answered their call.

'Maybe I should go with you,' I say, but she just stands back and puts her hands on her hips.

'You … come with me!' she says. 'I thought you said you would never set foot in *that country* again?'

'I did,' I say, 'but this is different. I want to be there for you.'

And it hangs in the air for too long.

'You've always been there for me,' she says, even though I know she could not have forgotten all those years when I wasn't.

Outside, I can hear the rev of Mr Baldwin's car. We move over to the window and look out to see him fiddling with the white ribbon he has Sellotaped to the bonnet.

'Are ya right, Charlie Carthy?' he roars up when he sees us. 'It's the bride who's supposed to be late to the church, not the groom.'

We move back into the room and I take one last look at myself in the mirror. I brush at the sleeves of my suit jacket and shake out the leg of my trousers.

'Time to go, Da,' Jen says as she links my arm and guides me out of the room. 'Connie will be waiting.'

24

YUGOSLAVIA

THE FRANCISCAN

That first winter I spent in prison was the harshest our country had seen in years. The black bars of the cell window turned white and sharp icicles hung like stalactites against the glass-free frame. Even the rats must have found more suitable quarters to invade because we stopped feeling them scurry around our feet at night as we slept.

In those early days, after they pulled me from the church and took me far away from the village, we, the prisoners, never complained about the overcrowding. We knew that if it was just one man in the cell, he would surely die from the bitter cold. We kept one another alive during that winter, even though we could feel the grasp of death close by our side.

Conditions were dire. The toilet was a mere hole in the ground that frequently overflowed and caused people to be sick. There were too few beds for us to share and the blankets were of the lightest polyester, which did not quite reach down over our ankles nor up above our shoulders.

During the night, you could hear grown men cry like children. They called out the names of their loved ones over and over again. In the morning when they woke, they would run up to the bars of the cell and shout at the wardens to let them out.

'I am an innocent man!' they would scream through chattering teeth. 'I do not belong here. Set me free.'

And the wardens, with their winter hats pulled down to cover their ears and their fleece-lined jackets zipped up to the top of their necks, would walk up to these men and look straight into their pleading eyes before saying: 'One more word from you and I will put you in solitary confinement for a month.'

The men knew that not many people came back from solitary confinement. If they did, they returned as ghostly figures with bulging eyes who looked like they had just spent a month with the devil himself. So the men would stand back from the bars and return once more to their crying.

The beatings were frequent. We were all enemies. Enemies of the state. Of the regime.

During interrogations, they deprived me of food and sleep. They pushed for me to confess to things with which I had nothing to do. I was accused of being a spy for various political parties or of being the leader of a new revolution against the regime. I found it best to say nothing. That way, they could not twist and turn my words. But they threw me into a crowded cell nevertheless and I stayed there for many months, thinking about my family. Thinking about the children.

There were some who were intrigued.

'Ah, I have heard about your little village,' one man said. He had been interned for speaking up for political prisoners. 'My mother travelled there not too long ago. I don't think I ever saw her speak about a place and its beauty so vehemently in all my life. She urged me to go there one day. Maybe I will visit this place that is so close to heaven. That is, if I ever get out of this hell hole.'

'What is your name?' I asked the man.

'Jakob, Father,' he said.

'I will pray that you get there one day, Jakob.'

A week after we had this conversation, the man became ill with stomach cramps that left him writhing in pain, day and night. He burned with a fever, even on the coldest of nights, and though we called and called for the wardens to come and help, no one ever did.

Jakob grew so weak that he could not rise from the bed. He was unable to eat the little bit of food that was offered, and within weeks his body became so frail and hollow that he could barely speak one word.

'You must help this man,' I pleaded with the warden one morning. 'If he does not see a doctor, he will surely die.'

'We have called for the doctor,' he said. 'He will come.'

'That's what you said yesterday. And the day before. And the day before that,' I protested. 'So many weeks have passed and still no doctor in sight. Surely you can see how much pain he is in.'

The warden, a balding man with a swollen belly, just laughed through his nose and began to walk away. 'Ask that God of yours to send a doctor, priest,' he mocked, 'and if he can't send a doctor, tell him to send a miracle instead.'

I could do nothing but sit by Jakob at night, wipe the sweat from his brow and tell him that a doctor would surely be here by morn.

'I know he will not come,' Jakob whispered one night. 'He will not come because they did not and will not tell him to come. Already the authorities have created so much false evidence to use against me in court. But I have the support of many on the outside who promise they will put up a good defence. I have good lawyers. This is what they are afraid of. They would rather see me dead than in the courtroom where I can publicly defend myself. No, Father, they would much rather sentence me after I have gone.'

'Hush, Jakob,' I urged. 'Do not talk like this. Do not give up hope. Think of your wife and your children who need you and who are waiting for you.'

'I do, Father. Believe me I do,' Jakob said. 'It is only thoughts of them which have kept me alive this long.'

For many nights, Jakob cried out in agony as the rest of the men in the cell covered their ears or buried their heads in their hands. Still no doctor came. Every one of us watched him slowly die from the pain, and none of us could do anything to help him.

Then one morning, just as the sun flooded the cell floor with a brilliant light, Jakob raised his head towards the window before taking his last breath. I prayed over him during his passing and closed his eyes before placing a sheet over his face. Only when I told the warden that Jakob had died did a doctor arrive.

'We were expecting you weeks ago,' I told him, but he just looked at me with a confused stare.

'No one called for me,' he said as he examined Jakob's still body. 'I was not aware any prisoner was ill.'

I did not have too much time to grieve for the man who had become my friend. They moved me out of the cramped cell and into one of my own, where I stayed for many months. A lawyer worked on my case from the outside but the hearings were always adjourned for months and months at a time.

When the time came, I was convicted of sedition and sentenced to two years in prison. They moved me even further away from my home.

Though it was far away, my family came to visit when they could. My father, Josip, held my mother, Vesna, up by her arm as they walked into the visiting room of the prison. He patted at her frail knees when she started to cry and shushed her like you would quieten a child. From a paper bag, she would take out letters that my brother Tomislav had written. I was able to read just two lines before the guard snatched them away. But Tata told me not to worry. The letters did not say much. Tomislav was clever. He knew not to make my situation more difficult by writing of things that were still happening in the village. 'He keeps a journal at home,' Tata whispered. 'Your brother speaks to many people who have visited the village. They tell him their stories and what they have witnessed. Tomislav keeps everything documented and safe beneath his bed.'

On the day of my release, although I was hundreds of kilometres away, I made arrangements to go back immediately to the village they had pulled me from almost three years earlier. I have remained here ever since.

***

The years since my release have been busy. There is too little time in each day for all the work that has to be done. Parishioners come to hear me celebrate Holy Mass; they come to me to help them find food or work. They come to me so I can hear their confession and to ask me for my prayers. Recently, they ask me when the war will be over; when the shelling will stop; when they will see their loved ones who have gone off to fight in this horrible war. Most of their questions I am unable to answer. I tell them to pray. To put their trust in God. And then I ask God that they may have the strength to do so.

As I stand in the grounds of St James' church, I watch people come and go along the streets of this small village. In my mind's eye, I see a village that will rise once the war has fallen and open its doors once again to those who seek this place. I see millions of pilgrims fly over seas, travel through mountains, cross over lands and be witnesses to the happenings in this village. For it is here where the Gospa has her arms outstretched, ready to hold those who hear her call. It is here they will feel close to God. Right here, in the moment, before their very eyes.

My thoughts are interrupted by the sound of a familiar voice.

'Father Petar! Father Petar!' Iva calls, almost tripping over her frayed and undone laces.

'Why are you always running?' I say. 'Slow down! You will do yourself or someone else some damage!'

'I'm sorry, Father,' Iva says as she tries to catch her breath. 'Look, she is coming!'

In her hands she waves a letter that is crinkled and torn at the edges. I wonder how many hands it has passed through, how many roads it has travelled on, even what great oceans it has crossed before it reached Iva.

'She is coming, Father Petar. And others too. They will bring aid for those who camp on the outskirts of the village. Food and medicine. Clothes and shoes. Look! She tells me so herself.'

Iva holds the letter out and waves it in my face. She jumps up and down like a schoolchild and her smile stretches wide across her face.

When I talk about the visionaries I still refer to them as children, even though they are children no more. There have been so many challenges these past years. The milicija do not frequent the village so much any more. They gave up trying to stop the droves of pilgrims who were not put off by their presence and who continued to come to the mountains, to the church, to our homes. I counselled the children as best I could, despite the constant protests from the bishop. I tried to teach them not to fear for the future but rather live in the present. They worried about how their lives would turn out. The visions continue every day. There is no sign that they will stop. I encouraged them to do as any normal teenager or young adult would do. To go to school, to university if they could. To date. To make other friends. Not to isolate themselves from society. They must experience life, I told them. Some of them felt a calling and so I encouraged them to take this sometimes challenging path. Iva was one of them.

'Is this why you did not last in the novitiate, Iva?' I joke. 'Because you spent all day hopping around like a rabbit and waving things in the sisters' faces?'

'Well, if I stayed there, then I would never have met Ante and fallen in love,' she says and so I tease her no more.

'Come, walk with me,' I say, as we move past the open church doors. 'You can tell me more of what is in this letter of yours.'

Old men and women shuffle inside the church and then are forced to hunch down as we hear the sound of a bomb falling in the distance.

'Please God it hit only a vacant field,' Iva says as she blesses herself.

Our village has remained untouched so far in this war. A few weeks ago a fighter plane circled overhead and I feared it had instructions to drop a bomb on the village. But no bomb fell. I watched a large grey cloud form in the sky and it did not dissipate, no matter how many times the plane flew around.

Yet all around, there is destruction. Too many men have already lost their lives in the fighting. They hide in the mountains that catch fire in the summer and freeze over in the harsh winter. Men have lost limbs from frostbite and have watched their friends and comrades die beside them. The shelling is relentless in Sarajevo. Schools, hospitals, workplaces. Children have lost one parent or both. They cry about the war they do not understand and want no part in. But still there is fighting. Still there is hurt. Still there is death.

'She is coming here, back to the village,' Iva says. 'It has taken three months for this letter to arrive, and yet it arrives on the day she is due to be here!'

She is pointing at the date written at the top right-hand corner of the page. I know of whom Iva is talking. It is the Irish girl who arrived here in the village almost ten years ago. Of the many pilgrims who have come here over the years – I think some have said it is over one million – it is this girl I remember the most. On the day the milicija took me away to prison, the guards taunted me about the trouble they said I'd brought to my people. Later that night they visited me in my cell to tell me about the foreign girl who had gone missing in our village. It was all my fault, the guards chastised, for filling tourists' heads with nonsense. That night I prayed for her safe return and, sure enough, my prayers were answered. Though the milicija did not tell me so for many days. When I got out of prison, Iva spoke to me much about the girl and told me how the entire village came out that night to search. They have written to one another over the years, Iva and Jen, and they share stories about their lives; how they differ, yet how they are ultimately the same. Both have struggles. Both have joy. Both realise their friendship is deep-rooted and will bind them forever. It helps them on their journey through this life.

I have done my best to protect the children over the years. How they have grown since those early days. Soon, they will start families of their own, God willing.

It was both a surprise and a joy to see how, over the years, the pilgrims just kept coming. The planes got bigger. Some were so big that they could not land on the small runway of Mostar airport. But the pilgrims did not mind the three-hour journey from Split or Dubrovnik. It gave them a chance to witness first-hand the natural beauty of our country and also time to think of the reason why they found themselves on this journey. Most of them, at the end of their stay, travelled back along the same route. However, the road was very different to the one they came in on.

It is not easy for the children. The bishop has not changed his opinion. And he is not the only one who has tried to discredit them. But the children do not lie. I believe them when they tell me that she still appears to them. Every day at the same time. No matter where they are.

'Why are these apparitions still happening, Father?' pilgrims ask me.

I don't have to think about the answer for too long.

'When she first came, what is it the Gospa said?' I always ask.

And they look at me with blank faces.

'Peace, peace, peace and only peace,' I tell them. 'Peace must reign between mankind. This is the message she brought with her in those early days. This is the message she *still* brings. And look at us. Look at the world. We are simply not listening. This is why she still comes. This is why she *must* come.'

'Look!' Iva shouts, and I turn to see her point towards the road.

Beneath the glare of the broiling sun, I see a group of people climb out of a dust-covered jeep. They wipe the sweat from their brows and take long gulps from plastic bottles. Although they are now older, I recognise their faces, for most have been here many times before. People seldom visit this little village only once.

'Jen,' Iva calls, and she is running again, this time so fast that she trips over her laces and falls flat to the ground.

Jen peels the backpack from her shoulders and throws it out of her way. When she reaches Iva, she too dives down so she is lying by her friend's side.

'Why is it that every time we meet, you fall?' Jen jokes.

She rises up to her knees and scoops her hand under Iva's arm as she helps her to her feet. They do not speak for a moment but study one another.

'I can't believe you are really here,' Iva says.

'Hey, your English is almost as good as mine now,' Jen replies.

They wrap their arms around one another and remain in a tight embrace until I cough gently.

'Father Petar is a good teacher,' Iva says. 'The best!'

'Hello, Father Petar,' Jen says. 'It's good to see you. We've brought aid for the camps. Food, medicine, clothing. As much as our jeep would take. And there is more to come. People are donating stuff every day. This is only the beginning.'

I am almost lost for words. 'You have no idea how much this means,' I manage to say.

They are still holding hands. Like two long-lost sisters who have been reunited after years apart.

'I have so much to tell you,' Iva says to Jen. 'Things that I could not possibly convey in a letter. Things about Mama.'

Jen's eyes light up and her mouth opens. 'You've seen her?'

Iva looks to me but I do not say a word. Then she nods to Jen who takes a deep breath. 'Oh my …' she says.

I glance down at my watch. 'Iva,' I say, 'look at the time. We must go.'

She grabs Jen by the wrist and swings her around so that she is facing the church. With her free hand she blesses herself, just as the bells toll from St James'.

'Come,' she says to Jen with great urgency in her voice, 'I will tell you everything later. For now we must hurry.'

Jen looks down at her own watch and realises the time. She allows Iva to pull her and, as they run through the people who have gathered near the steps, Iva says, 'Hurry.'

Overhead, there is the most beautiful smell of red roses wafting in the air.

'Hurry,' Iva says again. 'The Gospa. She is coming.'

AUTHOR'S NOTE

This book is a work of fiction. It is loosely based on the story of Medjugorje, a small village which is located in present-day Bosnia and Herzegovina (part of the former Yugoslavia). My history with Medjugorje began way back in the early 1980s, when I visited the village as a ten-year-old child. I went back several times during my teens. I remember the rolling hills, the lush vineyards and the tobacco fields, and how the church of St James with its two steeples stood solidly in the centre.

It was obvious that the local farming people had little, but what they did have they gave to the many pilgrims who descended on their small village in droves. We were welcomed into their homes; some even took to sleeping on the floor so a visitor could have their bed. Each evening they filled the table with food and wine from the earth, and though they spoke little English, they got by with kind expressions and sincere eyes.

Why were so many people visiting this little-known village with the unpronounceable name in communist Yugoslavia? They were there because six local children claimed to have seen the Blessed Virgin, the mother of Jesus, on a small mountain called Podbrdo. People were instantly curious. Could it be possible that the Mother of God had appeared and was still allegedly appearing to them? Over the years, there have been many Marian apparitions around the world, including Fatima and Lourdes to name just two. And so the news about these claims coming from Medjugorje spread very quickly, attracting people not just from within Yugoslavia but from all across the world. It is said that over forty million people have visited Medjugorje since 1981.

In 2011 I returned to the village for the thirtieth anniversary of the alleged apparitions. I had not visited in over twenty years. As the coach pulled into the dusty narrow street, I could see that commercialism had inevitably arrived. However, the authenticity still remained intact. The mountains, the church, the vineyards and the fields were still there – the essence of the village I remembered as a child. While I was on this trip, I spoke to many people who shared stories with me about what the village meant to them. I went home and subsequently compiled two books of testimonies from people from all walks of life, titled *Medjugorje: What it Means to Me* and *Medjugorje and Me: A Collection of Stories from Across the World*, which were later published by Columba Press in 2012 and 2014. The second book was translated into Italian by Edizioni Piemme in 2016. My own reason for travelling there, as well as my family connection with the place, is detailed in these books.

I can remember doing a radio interview with Ireland's national broadcaster, RTÉ Radio. I had just published my second book of testimonies and the host asked me if I would be writing any more on Medjugorje in the future. My response was quite simple. I told him I felt I had written enough on the subject, but who knew what the future held? In all honesty, I thought I was finished with all things religious and was looking forward to concentrating on writing fiction once again.

And so I did. I worked on two fiction manuscripts in between the non-fiction ones – both of which were historical fiction, a genre I love to read. Most writers know about the arduous wait that occurs when manuscripts are out on submission with publishers, and I found that the best way to cope with this, for me anyway, was usually by writing something new.

Around this time, my sister visited from New York. We talked about my writing and the frustrations of trying to get fiction work published in a heavily competitive and sometimes saturated market. She made an obvious suggestion: 'Why not write about what you know best? Why not write a work of fiction based on Medjugorje?'

That is how the journey began and the result is *Pilgrim*.

For readers of this book and for those who may not know anything about the story of Medjugorje, it is important for me to outline what is 'fact' and what is 'fiction'.

The prologue is fact. On the 24 June 1981 six young children claimed to have seen a vision of the Blessed Virgin on a small hill called Podbrdo. The children ranged in age from ten to sixteen. They said that a beautiful woman appeared to them, holding the baby Jesus in her arms. They ran away frightened, but returned to the mountain at the same time the following day and saw the same vision, who this time spoke to them.

The characters in this book are fictitious. When writing the character of Iva, I tried to imagine what it might have been like for the six children back in the early days. I learned that one of the visionaries, Ivanka, had lost her mother the year before the apparitions began. I used this one piece of information as a basis for Iva's predicament in the novel. The rest of the details about her family, home life, siblings, conversations and situations were entirely made up from my imagination. I am very grateful to Danijela Susac, who is from the former Yugoslavia and who works in Medjugorje, for recounting to me what life was like as a child growing up in a farming village in a country under communist rule. Also to Eleana Canny who advised me on the local dialect.

Likewise, when it came to the character of Father Petar, I gained inspiration from the three main priests I knew of in Medjugorje: Father Jozo (who spent time in prison during the early years), Father Slavko (now deceased and who was a close aide to the visionaries for many years before his death on Mount Križevac in 2002) and Father Svet, who was stationed in the US when he heard about the apparitions. Father Svet came home to visit his family and the communist police took away his passport, so he remained in Medjugorje. I have met Father Svet many times. Over the years, he has worked with the Mother's Village (an orphanage set up after the war to help those children who had lost their families) and with the Merciful Fathers (a rehabilitation drug treatment centre in Medjugorje). These three Franciscan priests gave me much inspiration when writing the character of Father Petar.

Over the years, I have heard many stories from people who have visited Medjugorje. What I found out is that nobody is exempt from troubles and life is not always a smooth and easy road to travel. This is where I gained inspiration for the characters of Charlie, Jen, Suzanne, Louis, Philip and Connie – through everyday people from different walks of life. When telling Philip's story I needed to gain insight into the heroin epidemic that gripped Dublin in the 1980s. During my research I came across a book called *Pushers Out: The Inside Story of Dublin's Anti-Drugs Movement* by André Lyder. I gained inspiration for some of the scenarios relating to Philip from the factual information contained in this book, e.g. the marches on the drug pushers who lived in the flats complex in the inner city and the burning out of the flats. I had also interviewed a recovering heroin addict for one of my non-fiction books, and although the future is bleak for many people who are caught up in this horrific addiction, he, at least, managed to break free from the grip of heroin.

Sometimes there are people who help us through our journey. And sometimes, there is Providence.

And so the story of Medjugorje continues to this day. As I write this, the Vatican has not yet sanctioned the apparitions. Although a commission was formed and their findings have been submitted to His Holiness, the world still awaits the decision of Pope Francis. And there is much speculation. Some say that the apparitions cannot be sanctioned as long as they continue, and they are allegedly still continuing today. However, there is talk that the village will be recognised as a Marian Shrine. Either way, opinion remains divided and no one knows exactly what the decision of Pope Francis will be. Many feel it has gone on long enough and all sides are anxious to know the findings of the commission.

There is talk that it will be soon.

Until then, the world awaits.

ACKNOWLEDGEMENTS

There are some people who deserve much thanks for bringing this book to fruition. Special thanks to my agent and good friend, Tracy Brennan, who took a chance on me when I was just starting out on my writing journey and who never gave up trying to find the right home for my work, for which I am eternally grateful.

To the team at Mercier Press. I am so honoured to be published by Ireland's oldest publishing house and would like to thank everyone involved in the production of this book. To Patrick O'Donoghue, commissioning editor, and Deirdre Roberts, marketing and general manager, for choosing *Pilgrim* for Mercier's fiction list. To my editor, Noel O'Regan, for guiding me gently through the editorial process. Noel's keen eye for detail and his expertise carefully shaped and moulded the early draft of this book into the finished novel it is now. Huge thanks to Wendy Logue in editing and production, and Alice Coleman for the most beautiful book cover design. I'd also like to thank Emma Dunne for her proofreading.

I have made some good friends in the writing community and I never cease to be amazed at the support fellow writers show one another. In particular, I feel a lot of gratitude and love towards Carmel Harrington who has been a good friend and immensely supportive to me over the years. And to Margaret Madden who is always great company at the many writing events we attend. I am deeply humbled and forever grateful to Donal Ryan for his beautiful words which feature on the cover of this book. Thanks also to Danijela Susac and Eleana Canny for helping answer my research questions.

Of course, huge thanks to my family. You are my world. My husband, Darragh, and our children, Lauren, Kirsten and Darragh – the greatest gifts in my life.

To Darragh, Esther and all the family, thanks for the never-ending kindness and love throughout the years. And to my oldest and closest friends, for the laughs and the tears – you all know who you are.

To my sister Suzanne, for having faith in me as a writer and for encouraging me to write this book in the first place. To my mom, Maureen, for her boundless enthusiasm, faith, strength, good humour, support and love. To my sister Joanne, who held the fort in work as I took time off to concentrate on the editing process. And to my brother Kieran, who himself has much creativity beneath his skin.

To our darling Nicky, who brought so much joy into our lives, and to all our loved ones who have passed on.

To pilgrims all over the world.

And to my dad, Kieran, who is always by my side.

This one is for you.